Sly Darkness

Sly Darkness

A Novel

By

Kya Aliana

Sly Darkness by Kya Aliana

This book is a work of fiction. All characters, Riverwolf Pass, and events in this book are purely figments of the author's wild and rampant imagination. Any similarities to people, places, or events you may know of are absolutely coincidental.

Cover Art by rc

Cover Design by rc

Interior text design by Kya Aliana

All rights reserved. Publishing a book takes a lot of work and effort! Kya Aliana goes through a lot of work to write, edit, revise, publish, and promote her books. No part of this book may be copied or reprinted in any way without the author's permission. Freely copying copyrighted materials isn't cool. In fact, it sucks big. You're dissing the author out of money that he/she deserves. Writing a book is not easy, and making money off it isn't any easier. Don't be a downer, share the book but don't copy it. Your friends and family can buy their own copy of this book if they really want to. Thank you!

11 10 9 8 7 6 5 4 3 2
Copyright 2012 by Kya Aliana

First proof printing: December 2011

Publication date: July 31st 2012

ISBN: 9781468043822

PRINTED IN THE UNITED STATES OF AMERICA

Sly Darkness by Kya Aliana

Author's Note

Hello everybody, and thank you for picking up this copy of Sly Darkness. This book takes place in the town of Riverwolf Pass, which I wrote about in my last novel, Impending Doom. This is not exactly a sequel to Impending Doom, though you will get a couple extra references if you have read Impending Doom, including the "six months ago" reference talked about in this book.

While I published "Impending Doom" before this book, I feel it flows better when "Sly Darkness" is read first... then the mystery of "Impending Doom" is accented with the reference of "six months ago" mentioned in this book. I guess I was just one step ahead of myself, as par usual.

Thank you so much and I hope you enjoy the book! Thank you all!
- Kya Aliana

Sly Darkness by Kya Aliana

Sly Darkness by Kya Aliana

Chapter One

They followed me. Wherever I went, they always followed me. They circled overhead, waiting for me to die. It sounded as if someone was scraping a machete across the tops of the oak trees. The sound used to send chills down my spine, but then I got used to it. When they first started to follow me, seeing them made my stomach do flip-flops, somersaults, cartwheels, and any other type of gymnastic tossing, turning exercise you could possibly imagine. But, after a while, I found the sight of them soothing to my soul. Seeing them let me know that everything was okay, normal, natural... if you could call my life those things...

I walked down the long straight stretch of street they called King Street. They followed me. My heart no longer picked up when I saw them. I no longer felt panicked. I no longer felt anything for them other than the awareness that they were there. The town looked interesting from the main street. Although I'd never been there before, I felt a peculiar sense of home... how could I not? After all, I'd heard about this place my entire life.

It was as if I could stay there and never be thought of as different... but I knew that wasn't true. I would always be thought of as different, especially with those... *things* following me. They only made me more different than I already was, which trust me, I didn't exactly need going for me, if ya catch my drift.

They called the town Riverwolf Pass. I didn't know why they called it that or what the hell a riverwolf was, or if it even was an actual thing. I intended to find out. No, I wasn't planning on asking anyone. I don't talk to people very often and I wouldn't talk to them at all if it wasn't - at least at some times – necessary. I planned to find out what a riverwolf was on my own, just like I did everything else... on my own.

I walked through the town slowly, my eyes darting around

Sly Darkness by Kya Aliana

trying to soak it all in. It was just how I pictured it would be... it had barely changed at all since... *No,* I told myself, *I'm not going to go take a stroll down Memory Lane... not again... not now... not today.* My mother and her stories were gone, and I needed to accept that.

Kids talked, laughing and teasing each other. School must be letting out for the day. Most of the children didn't notice me... That changed when I walked 'round the corner and faced the high school students. Some gawked at me, others quietly whispered to each other about me, others crossed the street to avoid me, and the others – the outcasts like me – didn't seem to mind at all.

The people whispering assumed that I couldn't hear them. They were wrong. I could hear every single word they said. *Careless teenagers*, I thought to myself as I hunched over, pulling my hoodie up and then scrunching my hands in my pockets.

My greasy black hair hung in my eyes and I slung my head to the side to knock it away. My heavy feet thudded against the sidewalk, my enormous size 16 black boots smacking the ground every stride. My worn out jeans almost had too many holes in them. It'd been months since I changed them. Sure, I washed them every week or so, took a shower, and brushed my teeth. But, it'd been months since I'd actually bought a new pair of jeans. I didn't need them anyways.

I was sorta heavy set, not fat, it was pure muscle. I wasn't one of those guys who said it was all muscle when it wasn't; I worked out for at least half my day. I had nothing better to do. It was a well-known fact that I looked like a thug... a twenty-something-year-old-thug. That was why most people left me alone. I liked being left alone; it gave me time to do everything I wanted to do. Most of the stuff I did wasn't the least bit impressive. I wrote sometimes, but only in a journal. Writing made me feel like I had somewhere to inscribe my feelings and thoughts so that, like the city dwellers who shunned me, I might leave something after I am gone. I think I got that from my mother... she never kept a journal, but she was constantly writing letters to... *No, I won't think of her.*

Sly Darkness by Kya Aliana

I sketched part-time, but I wasn't very good at it. I only sketched when I needed to remember how something looked. One might think that being a loner and all, I would love a book for company, but that was not so. I'd never read a book with a plot good enough to entice me.

Other than all that, I roamed. I went from town to town whilst they followed me. I wasn't looking for a place to stay; I could never have settled down in a place for a life time or longer than a meager week. I left and forgot about the town, and the town forgot about me... if, that is, they ever even noticed me.

The high school and its students had a preppy cliché feel to it. The cheerleaders were going over cheers and stretching on the front lawn while fifty feet away there were the jocks tossing around a football. The geeks were having a heated debate about how easy it would be to make – and get away with making – crystal meth in the chemistry lab. The clique that consisted of the anti-cheerleader girls (who ironically acted just like the cheerleaders) were talking about taking a trip into Boone and hooking up with some college guys from App State.

The others – the nobodies – slowly drifted away from the school campus, leaving only the preps, jocks, geeks, and cliques in the school vicinity.

As I rounded the corner, I felt a sharp pain in the back of my head. I turned to see a football lying on the sidewalk. I rubbed my head, thinking that it hurt more than it should have... after all, it was only a football. The jocks were all laughing as one of them jogged toward me, sideways, looking at all his jock buddies.

"Yeahyeah, I'll catch up with you guys later." I heard him say as he got closer to me. He turned around to face me, and continued to jog up to me. He bent down and picked up the football.

"Sorry about that... some of those guys can kind of be ass-holes sometimes."

"Yeah, it's nothing new. Don't worry about, kid." I said, turning around to walk away... to find where they kept the town records. It almost felt weird to call him "kid." I was only

Sly Darkness by Kya Aliana

eighteen, although I looked and acted as if I was older. No one questioned my age... ever. They assumed I was twenty-something and on my own, leaving only the second part to be true.

"I'm Chad, just in case you were wondering," he stated, sounding rather cocky and almost offended that I hadn't asked his name. I jumped... I hadn't expected him to follow me. I paused and looked at him. I wanted him to leave me alone. Me and guys like him clashed big time. I hadn't gotten along with a jock since... well, since before shit hit the fan when I was fourteen.

"Nice name," I commented in a monotone, not actually meaning it. I wished I was somewhere else. Why was he even talking to me?

"You're new around here," he said. It wasn't a question, it was a statement. I guess I shouldn't have been surprised. I knew this was a small town when I came into it... I should have known that it would easy enough for any residence to deduct I was new to this town. I mean, it wasn't as if Riverwolf Pass was New York City. Nope, Riverwolf Pass was one small town, a town where everybody knew everybody and that was that.

"Yeah, just came here today," I said. I was horrible at keeping a conversation going, not that I ever tried very hard or anything... especially with a meat-head jock.

"So what's your purpose here, uhh... sorry, I didn't catch your name."

"It's Zander, with a Z not an X and no, it's not short for Alexander either." I had to explain that to people, otherwise they thought I was an Alexander and I wasn't. Alexander was the name of a goodie-goodie-two-shoes kid... not me. I was your normal, everyday, ordinary thug. I was the kind of guy that when I happened to be walking behind a teenage girl – not on purpose mind you, I tried my hardest to stay away from teenage girls – she began to clutch her purse tighter and walked a little bit faster. When that happened, I normally just crossed the street before she started screaming "pedophile!" or "rapist!" I learned that when that happens, those "good guys" respond and wind up beating the fuck out of you. I hate that, especially because I'm never trying to

Sly Darkness by Kya Aliana

do any harm to the girl. Not to mention, I wasn't even old enough to be a real pedophile, not that I ever would be. Stupid stereotyping by association; I hated it.

"Nice name," Chad commented, mocking the same monotone I'd used to comment on his. "Now remind me again why you're here?" he asked with a slight sneer.

"You don't really care, so why don't you just get lost?" I started to walk away faster, wondering why I hadn't done that sooner.

"Hey wait!" Chad's voice came from behind me. I turned to see him chasing after me.

"Boy! you walk fast," Chad said, taking two steps for my one.

"I'm big," I replied, and kept walking at the pace I was going at. I wasn't about to slow down for some jock... wasn't he supposed to be athletic and shit?

"Don't you have any friends you hang out with?" I asked.

"No, not really. I haven't fit in with anyone since…" his voice trailed off and he shook his head. I wasn't about to ask him to finish his sentence. If he didn't want to finish it, I wouldn't push him to. Besides, I really didn't care what those last few words were... especially because he looked like he was fitting in just fine a few minutes ago when he was playing football with his buddies. Why people ever made up self-dramas was beyond me. The way I saw it, life had a lot of its own dramas to keep you busy; there was absolutely no need to make some up... unless, of course, you were a stupid jock-strap-attention-monger with nothing better to do.

"I'm a loner," he said after another six or seven strides.

"Yeah? Well, I'm a *real* loner and a drifter, and I'd rather like it if you'd stay out of my life," I said gruff and tough, feeling a tad bit annoyed.

"Hey, you're the one who paused to watch me play football... I thought you *wanted* someone to hang out with." I guess he had a point, but I didn't care any. I didn't even know why I paused to watch him in the first place. Not to mention I was

Sly Darkness by Kya Aliana

getting tired of talking to him. Did I mention I didn't like talking to people? Well, I didn't. I really didn't like talking to anybody.

"So are you just passin' through, or you here to stay?" Chad asked.

"Why are you talking to me?" I asked, wheeling around to face the dude.

"Uh, because I don't have anything better to do... kinda sad, isn't it?" I didn't say anything, just turned and kept walking. "I'm sorry, that was insensitive of me," Chad said and continued to follow alongside my steps.

"Look, I'm not the sensitive kind. I don't care how insensitive you are to me, just leave me alone."

"If you wanted to be left alone, you wouldn't have come to this small town in the first place." I was silent. Some weird part of that was true, but I wasn't going to admit it. To tell the truth, Chad reminded me of myself, back before I became a loner... kind of sad, isn't it? I heard my old chuckle inside my head and shook it away. The past was gone, blown into smithereens of nothing-that-mattered-now pieces. I was here for one reason and one reason only. I was *not* about to get distracted.

We walked in silence until we reached the end of the street. I saw the sign that signified I was leaving the town of Riverwolf Pass. It was beyond a small town. I thought it could probably be considered a teeny-tiny-tot-sized town.

"Where are we going now?" Chad asked when I stopped walking. He stood there, hands on his knees, panting. I guess I walked faster than I thought I did.

"First off, there is no 'we' there is no 'us' there isn't even 'me and you' or 'you and I' or any other dumb combo that you can think of. There is merely 'me' and 'only me'. The subject of 'you' is your own business and I want absolutely nothing to do with that. Do I make myself clear?" I asked. Chad nodded and motioned for me to give him a minute.

"For Christ's sake, man! Don't you take P.E.? I don't walk *that* fast," I said, rolling my eyes. I didn't expect everybody to be as enduring as I was – I'd been on my own since I was fourteen, I

Sly Darkness by Kya Aliana

couldn't expect the whole world to be the same – but we only went so far... the town was only so big. The boy should have been able to handle walking to the edge of this tiny town!

"It's just, I've been outta it for about the past six months. I haven't done much, including exercise," Chad replied standing up, finally breathing steadily. I rolled my eyes and wondered why I didn't just leave this Godforsaken town.

"So, I take it conversation isn't your thing?" Chad asked after we stood there in silence for a good, long five minutes. I shrugged.

"Got any place to go tonight?" Chad asked.

"You're a chatty sort of fellow, ain't cha?" I asked, turning to face him. He backed down after the look I gave him. Nobody loved my eyes, nobody even liked them. Kids used to tease me about my mother first looking into my eyes when I was born and screaming at the sight of them. That was back when I had friends... if you could call them that. My eyes were constantly changing colors; however, it was always a dark color. Today it felt like they were black, a deep coal black. Yesterday they were a royal purple. I've never come across anyone with purple eyes before or black for that matter, unless we're talking about beady black eyes that belong to a small animal such as a rat.

Chad didn't want to upset me. That much was obvious, so he took a step forward and tried to not show that he was taken aback from the sight of my eyes.

"Well, back when I used to have friends we talked a lot. Ever since... well, I just haven't talked in a while. Feels good to talk, you know. 'Sides, you seem like a cool guy. If you're here to stay maybe we could hang out some," Chad said with a forced smile. *Didn't have friends... what did he call those good-for-nothing jocks he was playing ball with?* Was the first thought to come to mind... then, I could find myself able to relate. Those types of people didn't make the best friends.

"I'm not staying," I said quickly. I wasn't sure how much longer I wanted to stay. I was considering pulling outta town later that night, perhaps sooner if I could get this kid off my ass so I

Sly Darkness by Kya Aliana

could find out the information I needed without him being a busy body and asking why.

"Oh, where ya headed? College?" Chad asked with a disappointed look upon his face.

"Not 'no' but 'hell no'! I dropped out of high school when I was fourteen and I sure as hell ain't goin' to a college. I got all the education I need."

"That's why you're roaming the streets freely at twenty and don't know what you're doing."

"I'm eighteen," I said.

"That's cool. I'm seventeen, but I'm real mature for my age," Chad said excitedly.

"That's just dandy! I can clearly see we have so much in common... I mean, we're practically like twins. You understand me so well." I let my sarcastic side free. It felt good to joke around, even if I was slightly annoyed while doing it. It'd been months since I had the chance to be sarcastic. I remembered when I was thirteen and the friend-proclaimed sarcasm king. Every single chance I could be sarcastic, I was. That was a looooooong time ago. When I was thirteen I never thought for one moment I'd be out roaming the streets at eighteen, talking to some werid-o who wouldn't leave me alone for some unfathomable reason.

"Hey, look, if I'm just bothering you just let me know," Chad said, putting his arms up in defense.

"It's called sarcasm buddy, you should get used to it if you're gonna be hangin' 'round me," I said with a snort. I spoke before I thought and then I wondered why I hadn't just simply said "Hey you know what, you are bothering me and I would like it if you would leave me alone now. Please go." It was unlike me to say please... there was something weird about this kid. Something I connected to... some odd part of him called to my inner-self.

"So that means we can hang out? Cool! Where are we headed?... ops, sorry, where are *you* headed? I have to learn to remember there is no 'we' or 'us.' Don't worry though, I'll figure it out soon enough." Was this kid for real? Did some alien mother-

Sly Darkness by Kya Aliana

ship come and drop him off? Because, it wouldn't have surprised me in the least if that had happened.

"Okay, you can follow me, but don't expect me to talk back," I said truthfully. I knew it would take me some time to get used to having company again. And it would take a helluva long time before my communication skills came back into play. Maybe I'd get lucky and the kid would give up talking to me. But there was something in the way he followed me around like a little, sick, lost puppy that put some weird bout of doubt in my mind.

"Okay, I can talk. I love to talk… it doesn't bother you when I talk does it? Because, if it does, I can totally not talk."

"Chad, listen, talk if you want, if you don't want to, then don't," I said, turning and walking back into town. My stomach lurched and gave a loud growl.

"Whoa, was that your stomach? God, you must be hungry," Chad said. The look on his face was pure astonishment. It was as if he'd never seen a hungry teen before!

"Uh, yeah, it's been a while since my last meal," I said with a shrug. I guessed it wasn't that long, a measly six hours, but for me, that was long.

"Well, you got money? 'Cause if you don't I could totally loan you some. I mean, there is this killer restaurant that, like, makes totally shweet pizza." Killer? Like? Shweet? Were we in the 1980s? Was Molly Ringwald on a movie poster? No. So why was this kid talking like he was from the '80s?

"I got money, kid."

"Don't call me kid, okay? We're close enough to the same age, even if you do look a lot older," Chad said. I decided I wouldn't call him a kid anymore. If he had the balls to stand up to me and tell me not to call him a kid and not seem timid, he didn't deserve to be called a kid.

We walked in silence to the pizza place. I took in the rest of the town. There really wasn't much there, a general store, two gas stations, not so many restaurants, a library and a town hall that joined with the police station. It was a quaint little town. I looked up at the sky and saw that it was a perfect day out, no

Sly Darkness by Kya Aliana

clouds, a blue sky, and the sun beating down. I noticed a mansion high on the mountaintop.

"Who lives there?" I asked, nodding up towards the mansion.

"No one right now. A family moved in not too long ago… about six months back. It didn't work out though. No one is there now. You wouldn't believe how much this town has changed in the past six months… how much panic's happened in the past week," Chad said, opening the door to the pizza parlor.

"Well, what's the cause?" I asked, sitting down at a booth, Chad sitting down across from me.

"It's a long story," Chad said, brushing it off. Before I could say another word, the waitress walked up to us. She was a pretty little thing, with blond hair and blue eyes. Her uniform dress was low cut and short.

"Hello," I said, pausing to look at her name tag. "Petunia," I continued, offering up a warm smile. She smiled back politely and then turned to face Chad.

"What can I get you?" she asked.

"Uh…" Chad stammered looking at me.

"A medium size pizza with pepperoni, mushrooms, banana peppers, and black olives and I also want the biggest soda you can get here, Coke **not** Pepsi. And then whatever you want to drink," I said to Chad.

"Sprite." The waitress nodded and walked away. I felt my teeth grit as Chad watched her ass move while she walked all the way back to the kitchen. Women were not sex objects… when would stupid guys learn that?

Sly Darkness by Kya Aliana

Chapter Two

"So where are you headed?" Chad asked me after we got the waitress to box the leftover pizza.

"I dunno, my friend, I dunno," I said honestly. It was weird how easily the conversation was going. I hadn't talked freely like that in two weeks and then there I was, talking to Chad like we'd known each other for years on end. I wanted Chad to trust me... I needed him to trust me if my future plans were to work out. *No, stop thinking like that.* I thought to myself. *You're here on a mission... you're here to get one thing... don't get sidetracked.*

"Well if you're interested in staying here a few days, there's a room the general store owner rents out to visitors," Chad said.

"Oh, I don't know if I have money for a room. I've been short on cash recently. I'll probably just sleep in the park or something... if I sleep at all that is. Some nights, I just stay up and watch the stars slowly move across the sky and then fade out after the sun rises," I said as I walked down the sidewalk, kicking a pebble along.

"You really are a loner aren't you?" Chad asked, a sympathetic look crossing his face.

"Yeah, but I'm used to it by now," I said with a shrug.

"How long have you been, you know…" Chad asked and then looked worried I would take it offensively. I didn't. It was a fair question.

"On my own? Since I was a little older than fourteen," I answered, walking along down the sidewalk, wondering where we were wandering.

I noted they were still following me. They always followed me. Chad hadn't noticed them yet and I wondered when he would.

"I've only been a loner for the past six months," Chad said

Sly Darkness by Kya Aliana

with a sigh.

"You keep bringing that up. What happened six months ago?" As soon as I asked that, I wished I hadn't. I didn't need to know his problems; I had enough of my own without bringing Chad's into the equation.

"You wouldn't believe me if I told you." Chad said with a distant look in his eye. I could tell he wanted to tell me, but was worried for some reason. I couldn't help but wonder why, and then wonder why I wondered in the first place. What was with this kid? Why was I continuing to talk to him? What did I see in him? These were all questions that had no answers for the time being. I would find answers... I always found my own answers. Even when there wasn't a way to find the answers, I made a way to find them.

"Try me," I said with a sneer, I knew more about what I would and wouldn't believe than he did.

"Maybe later... anyways... hey check out that girl!" Chad said, turning his head to watch her walk down the street. I looked but merely shrugged. I didn't see anything special.

"That's Cutie! Boy! is she a fox!" Chad said and grabbed his heart as if it would beat out of his chest if he didn't hold it in. I wanted to scream at Chad that women weren't sex objects, but that would cause a scene, and I didn't feel like dealing with that. Besides, guys like him never change.

I looked back at her again, but saw nothing asides from a normal average girl. She was walking alone down the street; I could see her lips moving and her feet shuffling. One more glance and I saw she was enjoying listening to her iPod. She wore tight camouflage pants decked out with rhinestones on them. She was a petite build... then I noticed it, correction: them. The reason Chad liked her. She had the chest of what one might consider "goddess like qualities." She pulled her jacket tighter around her as the April wind whipped around the corner, revealing her long dark-brown hair. She had a single streak of red on the right side of her head. She brushed it back and continued walking down the street in the opposite direction of us.

Sly Darkness by Kya Aliana

"Her name's Cutie?" I asked.

"Nah, that's just what I call her. Her real name is Sarah Peterson. She just moved here about three months ago, a transfer student."

"You like her?"

"Yeah, hands off! She's totally mine!" Chad said, glaring at me.

"Geesh, back off." I said. I had no intention of getting with that girl. I didn't get involved and I wasn't planning to either. I wouldn't be in town long enough to even start to form a relationship with a girl.

"Don't even think about laying a hand on her gorgeous body," Chad said; he was rambling on in the background. I didn't pay a lot of attention to him. Of course, I knew the gist of what he was saying. Oh, Sarah's so cute. Oh, she's so wonderful… I think it's love. Blah, blah, blah. I had heard it all before and didn't want to hear it again.

"Catch stick?" I asked, offering up my pack of cigarettes.

"I don't smoke, thanks though," Chad replied with a half-smile, as if he was scared of what I would think of him. Truth be told, I didn't care in the least. *All the more cigarettes for me,* that's what I thought about it.

I didn't smoke to be cool, I smoked to calm my nerves, and you know to take the edge off. It wasn't easy being on your own, although I would never admit that to anyone. I wanted people to think I was tough as nails, whether that's the truth or not. I made it on my own, it was just difficult sometimes. But, I didn't need people worrying about me all the time. It was better that way.

I lit my smoke and started listening to what Chad was rambling on about. He wasn't talking about Sarah Peterson anymore. Instead, he was talking about tonight. He said he and a few friends were headed out to the train tracks for some fun.

"Thought you were a loner?" I speculated, raising both my eyebrows.

"I am… was... Well, truth is, I like today. It's been a good

Sly Darkness by Kya Aliana

day. I'm feeling like doing something fun tonight and 'round here, that's what we do," Chad explained and then told me where the train tracks were. I said maybe I'd show. I planned on showing up, but I didn't want to seem overly excited. Truth be told, it sounded like fun. Drinking, a night train, yep, both those things amounted to a fun time. I didn't have anywhere else to be… or crash. I assumed that I could crash at the train tracks and nobody would think anything of it.

"Well, this is my stop," Chad said, stopping at the bottom of his driveway, nodding up to a two story house. Chad stood there awkwardly looking at me, shifting on his feet from side to side. I got the hint.

"Well, I better go. I still gotta scope out the town some more, you know," I said, tossing up my hoodie. I knew Chad didn't want me coming into his home. After all, what would his perfect parents think of me?

"I guess I'll see you later… tonight at the train tracks?" Chad asked, slowly walking towards his house. I shrugged and mumbled a maybe. He called goodbye to me and jogged the rest of the way up to his house.

I walked down the road, peering into the shops and stores along the street side. I found myself face to face with the enormous library. All the other shops closed at five. It was five-fifteen. The library stayed open until seven. The illuminated purple and pink sky told me that sunset neared and soon it would be dark out… as well as cold.

As of right now, the library was the only place for warm sanctuary. I faced two choices, one: freeze outside until I headed over to the train tracks and two: go against all my rules and knowing what's right and go into a, yes, a real library with musty old books and good old fashioned literature that I'd never even heard of, in order to seek refuge. Yes, dramatically phrased, but incredibly true.

I walked past the doors and immediately saw a girl to my left reading on a bench. I looked at the cover of the book, it was completely black, in silver print there were the words "Call of

Sly Darkness by Kya Aliana

The Wild" on the worn spine. She was a cute girl, blond hair, green eyes, and a slender face with a sharp pointed nose. Her cheeks were red, presumably from the cold, and she wore black eyeliner that made her eyes look slanted, like a cat's.

"Call of the Wild, eh?" I asked, sitting down next to her. I wondered what was with me today. Talking to a random guy was one thing... talking to a girl was another. Not to mention talking to a girl about a book I hadn't ever read, or heard of, or know who it was by. What had come over me?

"I bet a guy like you has never even heard of this book," she said and pushed her snobby little nose right in the air and turned back to her book.

"Oh yeah? Well, maybe I have. Maybe I'm a big fan of the author. Maybe I even met the guy who wrote this book."

"I doubt it," the girl said with a quick sneer.

"No, I did. Really... what was his name again?" I asked, pretending to think hard.

"Jack London," the girl said with a smile and suddenly seemed interested in what I was saying.

"Oh yeah, good ol' Jack... met him at a book signing in New York not but three months ago," I said with a smile.

"Oh, how interesting," she said, sounding sincerely entranced.

"What's your name?" I asked, not wanting to give away the fact that I'd never known the guy existed before she said his name.

"Victoria," she replied with a smile. Her teeth were straight, there was no doubt that she had braces before.

"I'm Zander, with a Z."

"Nice to meet you, Zander with a Z," she said with a smile and shut her book. Score one for me; I got her to put down her book to talk to me.

"So what else do you read?" I asked with a smile, not exactly knowing why I was talking to this girl.

"I really like Gone with the Wind," Victoria said, an odd grin on her face.

Sly Darkness by Kya Aliana

"Oh yeah, I met the guy who wrote that too," I said, boasting now.

"Girl," she corrected.

"Huh?"

"It was a girl who wrote that," she explained with a slight giggle.

"Oh, okay, so I never met her. But I am serious about meeting Jack London," I said, trying to wear a sophisticated look upon my face.

"Ahuh," she said in a tone of voice that hinted she didn't believe me, nodding her head slowly. "So you're new around here? I don't recall seeing you before."

"Yeah, just got here today."

"Oh really? Where do you live?" she asked, standing up now.

"Where do I live?.... uhh… in the mansion, on top of the hill, you know," I said, making something up. I recalled Chad saying no one lived in the mansion, so fact being fact and I being me meant that I would probably seek haven there anyways. In which case, it wasn't a lie.

"Oh, it's too soon," Victoria said with her head tilted sideways.

"What do you mean too soon?" I asked.

"A family just moved out of there," she said with a puzzled look upon her face, as if she was remembering something.

"Oh yeah, I bought it from them. You know, I thought it'd be good for a first home for me. I'm just moving away from my family," I said. Where were all these lies coming from? Why was I even talking to this girl? Why was I acting like I would even stay here for longer than a week? I never stayed anywhere for longer than a week.

"You're a terrible liar," she said with a giggle.

"No shit," I said, shrugging. "But I really am living there, even if I didn't buy it from the last people personally."

"Yeah, the Dyebukos were odd people. There was a fire

Sly Darkness by Kya Aliana

that started in the basement and they died. A bunch of people did actually, they were having a party," Victoria explained.

"Whoa!" I said. "Remind me not to go in the basement ever," If there was one thing that creeped me out it was ghosts. I didn't like ghosts. When people asked me why, I replied by saying that I'd seen too many. It's no joke, though most people think it is.

"Well I better get going, my mother will be wondering where I've gotten off to," Victoria said and started to walk out the door.

"Hey wait, could uh, could I just have your number?" I asked. I wanted to curl up inside of myself when I heard the words that escaped my lips. I didn't even have a phone to call her on. Not to mention that I didn't even talk to her long enough for her to think to give me her number. I didn't even like her that much. She wasn't that pretty. She was just another face.

"I-I don't know…" she stuttered, backing up slowly. "I don't even know you."

"Oh, come on!" I pleaded. "I could tell you more about that Jack London character," I said with a smile. I'd have to do some serious research on him, but at least it would give me something to do.

"Jack London… he died in 1916," Victoria said with a laugh.

"Oh…" I said, pride shot down like a stupid duck in open season.

"It was nice talking to you," she said and walked out the sliding doors.

I continued into the library... ready to meet my fate. This was it. The reason I'd come to Riverwolf Pass. The library... the only one I'd ever been in.

"Excuse me?" I asked the first librarian I saw.

"Can I help you?" she asked, peering down at me from above the reading glasses on her nose.

"Yes. Can you please direct me to the children's desk?"

Sly Darkness by Kya Aliana

Chapter Three

The wind whipped around me. One would think that it would be warmer in April than in January, but the temperatures seemed to stay the same. Oh well, summer was on its way. I thought about how I would love this town in the summertime. It was then I realized that I didn't want to leave Riverwolf Pass. I'd never wanted to stay anywhere before... and when I thought about why I wanted to stay here of all places, I honestly couldn't think of any reasons.

There was that girl, Victoria or something, but she didn't exactly seem like my kind of girl. After all, I didn't even have her phone number. I didn't know why I talked to her in the first place. After great debate, I decided it was because I was bored, feeling outgoing due to my talk with Chad. Yeah, that must have been it. Because I knew that even if I did have her phone number, I wouldn't have called her... or maybe I would have. She looked nice, wholesome, and well-read.

I saw the railroad tracks. No, scratch that: I heard the incomprehensible voices of drunken teenagers talking. That was how I knew I was headed in the right direction.

The moon was full and gave off enough light to let me know that they were still following in my tracks. I wondered how long it would be before Chad noticed them. They'd been following me ever since I was four years old. They watched me grow up and watched me move out on my own. I'd love to say that they protect me, but they don't. They're just... there, waiting for me to die. They won't kill me. They aren't there to kill me. I don't know why they follow me. I don't mind it that much. I've gotten used to it. I used to think they followed everybody. But, I slowly learned that they only follow me. I was special... very special.

"Zander?" a voice came from behind me. It could only be

Sly Darkness by Kya Aliana

one person. Only two people knew my name, Victoria and Chad. It was a guy's voice, so that meant it was Chad. I spun on my feet and turned to face him.

"You showed," he said with a look of excitement on his face. He was alone. I wondered why he wasn't hangin' with his friends.

"Yeah, I figured what the hell. 'Sides, I didn't have anything better to do," I said with a shrug, wanting to pass this whole ordeal off like it was no big deal... but it was. It was a huge deal, actually. The last time I socialized was before I took off on my own.

"Well, I'm glad you made it," Chad said, and we started to walk towards the swarm of drunken teens that gathered around the railroad tracks. I could barely hear the music over the kids' voices. I didn't know the song, but what else was new? I'd stopped listening to music when I had to leave my home. Sure, I'd heard some music here and there, but I never paid attention to what the title was or the artist for that matter. It was somebody's iPod that was playing. No doubt it was a current pop song, the beat and lyrics gave that much away.

"So you want me to introduce you to some people I know?" I noticed that Chad didn't use the word 'friend.' I wondered what that meant. I shook my head no. I'd met enough people today.

"Okay..." Chad stammered, not knowing what to do. I pulled a cigarette out of my pocket and then changed my mind. I knew I shouldn't smoke, and I really was trying to quit... I'd been trying to quit ever since I started running low on money about two weeks ago. Sure I'd managed to pick some up here and there, but I barely had enough money to eat, which ruled out cigarettes. I was on my last pack, and I didn't think I'd get another one any time soon, so I decided to stop smoking... or at least saver my last pack.

"You know, they say the graveyard up there is haunted," Chad started with a smile.

"They say most graveyards are," I said wearing a smirk.

Sly Darkness by Kya Aliana

My heart pounded and I didn't want to think about the graveyard anymore.

"No, seriously, about six months ago there was this girl, Alice, she went up there to get with a guy and they both disappeared. They say her ghost still haunts the place," Chad said, shining his flashlight in his face. Panic lurched in my chest. What was up with the 'six months ago' routine I kept hearing about? What exactly happened six months ago?

"What exactly happened six months ago?" I asked, almost scared to.

"I'll tell you later," Chad brushed it off yet again, pretending to look around for someone.

"Have you ever even talked to that girl... uh, Sarah?" I asked.

"No, but boy is she a looker or what?" he asked.

"So you don't know the girl and yet you wanna get with her?" I asked.

"You got it," Chad replied.

"Is she here?" I asked. Chad shook his head sadly, as if this was some dreadful thing.

"Maybe she'll show," I offered hopefully. Chad shook his head.

"Nah, she never does. She's too good to come out to the train tracks," he explained.

We reached the throng of drunken teens shortly after those words were spoken. I looked around for Victoria, but I didn't see her. I mingled around, looking for a cooler of beer or a keg or something. I didn't find anything open to everybody, so I figured it was a B.Y.O.B. thing. Couldn't blame 'em either, I sure as hell wouldn't want anybody snagging my beer from me.

Walking along the side of the tracks, my hoodie wasn't heavy enough to keep me warm, and my backpack was too heavy and pulled on my shoulders. I didn't like having to carry that horrid thing around. First off, it smelled bad and second off, it was too heavy. I didn't keep much in it, a tooth brush, hairbrush, a heavy blanket, a sleeping bag, nothing special, just the

Sly Darkness by Kya Aliana

essentials... the bare minimum.

I found a group of gothic teens that kept to themselves; I decided to listen in on their conversation. They said nothing of interest; just talking about the mansion on top of the mountain they called Utopia Point. They were saying it was haunted and debating whether they wanted to go check it out or not. How much stuff around here was allegedly haunted? The graveyard and the mansion on top of the hill both were... but why? I came to the conclusion that it was mere folklore. People in that town must get so bored with their life that they have to make up stories to keep themselves entertained. That's why I always planned to go to New York City, which was before I was on my own. Yep, good ol' New York City, you never hear of people getting bored with their lives there or making up silly nonsense stories to amuse themselves... at least not about haunted mansions and graveyards.

I made my way back to Chad. I stood next to him but said nothing. We were both in a haze. No, we weren't drunk, or buzzed, we were just silent and felt like keeping to ourselves.

"What was that?" Chad asked with a jump. I wondered why he was so jumpy. Ever since we'd been here he was looking around over his shoulder every five seconds, and jumping at every break of a stick in the woods.

"Probably some teenagers in the woods getting it on," I said with a shrug, stuffing my hands in my pockets, wondering what to do next. I was bored and needed adventure. I was actually reconsidering my decision to stay in Riverwolf Pass for longer than tonight. If this was what they did for fun... well, it just wasn't my idea of fun. Besides, I'd gotten what I came for.

"No seriously, I hear voices," Chad said with a start. "Angry voices." We both listened hard and sure enough we could hear the incoherent voices of a teenage girl and guy fighting.

"I think we should make sure we're not dealing with something serious," Chad said and started off into the woods.

"Hey, man, we should leave it alone. They probably just got in a fight about whether the guy should pay for her movie ticket or something," I said. Never the less, I chased after Chad.

Sly Darkness by Kya Aliana

Yet again, not exactly knowing why. The closer I got to the scene, the more I became clear that this wasn't a silly couple's fight.

"I said no farther, Benny!" a girl's voice strongly echoed in the woods. I heard a guy arguing with her, and that made me mad. My hearing was heightened. I obtained the remarkable ability to do that, zone in on places to make it louder and track the voices. I never knew why I could do that, and whenever I tried to tell anyone about it they all called me crazy. But it worked for me, so I stopped telling people about it and just started doing it.

"This way," I said and Chad followed me. I was surprised he could see me in the darkness of the woods. I could hardly make out the trees that surrounded me; some were surely no more than two feet ahead. My hands flailed in front of me until I saw a dimly lit section of the woods. As I approached it I discovered that the light was coming from a battery run flashlight/lantern. I could make out the silhouettes of two teenage kids, one boy and one girl. The boy was trying to take off the girl's jean skirt, which was already unbuttoned. He wouldn't give her back her shirt and she was crying. I hated it when girls cried. I didn't find it annoying; I found it heart-wrenching. When a girl cried in front of me, she could get just about anything she wanted.

"Leave her alone!" I demanded, bustling myself into the scene. I crossed my arms, making fists with my hands to push my biceps up in hopes to scare the guy away.

"Stay outta this, buster," the guy demanded with vigor. I backed down a couple steps and tried to decide what my next move would be. Which would be the smarter decision, to stay out of this or to get mixed up in it? I sized the guy up, wondering if I could take him. It would be close if it came down to a physical fight. He looked like he could be on the football team's defensive line. But – and I didn't mean to sound vain – my muscles were nothing to scoff at either. After careful consideration, I concluded that Chad and I could probably take him together if worse came to worst.

"Fine, I don't care if you give me back my shirt or not. I'm leaving! I never want to see you again," the girl said, tears

Sly Darkness by Kya Aliana

streaming down her face. If she wasn't crying I would've laughed at the dramatic and soap-opera quality of her voice. She started to walk away, but the guy grabbed her arm.

"Ouch! That hurts," she exclaimed. My heart leaped at those words. How dare he hurt her! Even if I didn't know who she was, or what exactly started all this, or whether she led the guy on or not, he shouldn't hurt her... She was a quarter of his size... and a girl!

"I don't care if it hurts, Vikki, just give me what I want," the guy demanded. She exclaimed a loud "NO!" and he thrust her to the ground.

"You can't just go around dressed like that! You can't just lead guys on like you do and then not give them what they want and ***need!***" the guy said, kicking her side so she rolled over on her back.

"This has gone far enough," I said. Without thinking, I let my fist free. It connected with the guy's face. He fell to the ground and cupped his nose. I looked at my hand, and although I couldn't see the blood, I felt it.

"You broke my nose!" he exclaimed and stood up, fists ready to connect with *my* face.

"Uh, Chad…" I said, realizing what I'd done.

"I can't see anything, Zander, much less fight," Chad said, sounding sincerely apologetic. There was no time to complain or argue with him. I dodged down, missing his right-hand fist and shot back up, punching him with my left hand. I allowed all my anger for this guy to flow out of me and into my hands.

In the end, he only hit me once, right on my cheek. I was sure there would be a bruise. But, at least I'd prevented an uglier scene from taking place.

"You haven't seen the last of me!" the guy exclaimed before pushing me down and running out of the woods. I landed on top of the girl who remained shirtless.

"I-I, uh, I'm sorry," I said, quickly standing up and turning the other way. She stood up. After she put on her shirt, she asked if I would turn around. I turned only to see Victoria standing

Sly Darkness by Kya Aliana

there.

"You're the guy from the library?" she asked. I nodded. We were both blushing, cheeks as red as a summers rose.

"Thank you," she said after a minute. I'd seen the look that she wore on her face before. It was like she had expected me to be a 'bad boy' and then here I was, saving her from a terrible situation... I'd surprised more people than I'd like to admit. Just by doing stupid common stuff too, like handing back a wallet that someone dropped, or making sure a blind person isn't short-changed. I mean, geesh, don't other people do that sorta thing too?

Chad came out from the darkness and eased the terrible awkwardness that hung in the air. She shivered from the cold. I looked around, wondering if her jacket was lying on the ground somewhere. I didn't see a jacket. By the time I was ready to offer her my own hoodie, I saw that Chad had already given her his. She said thank you, and then we stood there in a solid minute of silence. None of us knew what to do or say.

"Well, I'm terribly embarrassed," Victoria finally said, breaking the silence. "I'm not normally a damsel in distress... I should have never followed Benny out into these woods, I probably deserved what was coming to me."

"No!" I exclaimed, heartfelt and all. "No girl deserves what he was about to do to you," I said, lowering my head.

"Thanks for saving me," she said after a minute, and I felt a hand on my shoulder. "You still want my number?" she offered. I shook my head no.

"Hmm, well, it's very cold out here... do you know which way to get back to the train tracks?" Victoria asked. We all felt awkward around each other. We weren't exactly the group that got along and would hang out together. Chad was the shy one with a dark side and a traumatic incident that he wasn't willing to share but talked about frequently without giving away any information. Victoria was the goodie-goodie-two-shoes girl that all the guys wanted by day, and a vixen by night... and part time damsel in distress. Although she said she wasn't normally the damsel in distress, her aura said differently... not to mention the way she acted. Her words echoed in my ears. *Still want my number?* Like hell I did. I wasn't looking for a sloppy second that always needs rescuing as a girlfriend... come to think of it, I wasn't even looking for a girlfriend.

And then, there was me. How to describe myself... I did not know. All I can say is that I didn't fit in Chad's category or Victoria's... I was my own person... sometimes I felt like I was my own species. Sometimes, I felt like there was no one out there who was like me, or who could even understand me in the slightest.

"Uh," I said while looking around, trying to recognize anything. Truth was... we were lost. I'd been so carried away with finding the girl that I didn't take notice of my surroundings or which direction I went. All I was focused on was saving that girl from a terrible fate.

"Well you're the one who came out here and wasn't in a rush!" Chad snapped. I could sense that he was incredibly aggravated.

"Now, now, there is no need to feel perturbed," I said, looking around, trying for my own sanity not to freak out. Victoria and Chad both looked at me with a shocked expression on their face.

"What?" I asked, turning around, wondering if there was a ten foot snake on my shoulder or something. With the way they were staring at me, I wouldn't be surprised.

"Perturbed? Where did a guy like *you* learn a word like *that?*" Victoria asked, raising her eyebrows. I sighed.

"Just 'cause I live on the streets and am on my own doesn't mean I'm not smart. I mighta dropped out of high school, but I did obtain a G.E.D." I said with a snarky look on my face. I hated it when people categorized me as a stupid drop out teenager with nothing to do.

"Sorry, I just didn't know," Victoria said, turning her nose up.

"Whatever, just forget about it and let's work on finding a way outta here," I said, shivering. I wasn't used to the cold... not

Sly Darkness by Kya Aliana

in April anyways. Sure, I expected it in January and such months, but April? That was ridiculous.

I listened for the voices of the teenagers who were currently partying near the train tracks, but heard nothing. I didn't even know where I was...

"Hey, what if we just listen for the train and then head in that direction."

"Hey smarty, the train goes all through these woods. It's a circle. We'll never be able to track our way home like that," Victoria said, turning to Chad, as if waiting for his suggestion.

"Well what's your suggestion?" I asked, trying not to let my tone sound too annoyed.

"I, well, I'm the girl," she insisted.

"And your point is?" I asked, crossing my arms, happy that I didn't give her my hoodie after all. Then, I felt sorry for Chad because he did.

"I shouldn't have to come up with things… you two are the men, figure out something," she said.

"You have the right to vote now don't you? And you can get a job. I figure that if you can do those things, you can at least try to come up with a plan," I said, picking up the lantern, turning to look for our footprints. As much as I hated to admit it, Victoria was right, that train idea would never work.

Sly Darkness by Kya Aliana

Chapter Four

After stumbling around in the woods playing follow the leader – me being the leader – and pretending that I had the slightest hint of what I was doing, we found our way back to the train tracks. Lucky for us, we weren't very deep into the woods. I played it off like I knew what I was doing the entire time. I didn't want them to think I was stupid, mainly because I wasn't. I was good at getting myself out of situations I didn't necessarily want to be in. I learned at a young age that I wasn't going to get free help from people, so I might as well start doing things for myself if I ever wanted to be in a good place at a good time.

Victoria went off and started flirting with other guys. Chad and I stayed away from the gaggle of teenagers, having too much experience with them already.

"That Victoria sure is a vixen," Chad said, leaning back as if he was trying to look up her skirt as she bent over to pick up the bracelet that she dropped. No, scratch that. It wasn't *as if* he was trying to, he *was* trying to.

"Yeah, well, some girls are like that," I said with a sneer. Girls like that always bothered me. Meaning, the girls who could be respectable girls but, they didn't believe that so they decided to be sloppy seconds. Why would any girl in her right mind choose that?

"So, you sure had a chance with her… she offered you her number and you turned it down. Why?" Chad asked, looking at me as if I was part-way crazy, half-way stupid.

"I'm not one for sloppy seconds," I said with a shrug.

"Yeah, well when was the last time you even had a girl?" Chad asked. The words stung more than they were meant to. Maybe I hadn't exactly "had" a lot of girls in my day but, I was a good guy. I didn't want to hurt girls, and I didn't want them to hurt me. I wasn't the heart breaker type of guy and I wasn't the

Sly Darkness by Kya Aliana

kind of guy who got into a relationship unless it meant something… to both me and the girl that is. Besides, I wouldn't ever phrase it as I "had" a girl… "made sweet love" to a girl maybe. "Was intimate with a girl," possibly… but not "had" a girl, that just sounded wrong! Girls were people too… girls had feelings… girls shouldn't be treated half as bad as they were.

    I walked off, up the dirt road, without saying a word. Chad chased after me.

    "Hey man, where ya goin'? I didn't mean it in a bad way… it was just a question. Listen, I haven't ever had a girlfriend really. Not a good one anyways. Hey, wait up." I slowed my pace, not exactly knowing why. This guy just really pissed me off and for some unfathomable reason; here I was, waiting up for him. I left my hands stuffed in my pockets, and hunched over a little bit more. I didn't want to give away the fact that I was slowing my pace.

    "Okay, you're heading into a haunted graveyard," Chad said, panting. I stopped and he finally caught up with me. I knew he wasn't going to give up, so I just decided it would be better for the both of us if I stopped and let him catch his breath.

    "I gotta get up to the mansion," I said with a strong voice. The words came out harsher than I meant them to. "I don't have time for ghost stories."

    Chad frowned.

    "It's not just a story, it's the truth," Chad said, shivering a little bit. He still held his coat in his hands from when Victoria gave it back to him. She winked, but wouldn't give him her number. Chad seemed genuinely disappointed.

    "Oh, and what makes you so sure?" I asked. Chad frowned for a second time.

    "I don't know." It was clear he did know he just wasn't going to tell me.

    "I'm freezin' out here," I exclaimed and started to walk faster again. Chad slipped on his coat and followed. "I'm going to that mansion on top of the hill whether it's haunted or not. There has to at least be a fireplace and matches and even if there isn't,

Sly Darkness by Kya Aliana

well, it has walls to keep out the wind, right?" I asked. Chad nodded.

When we hiked up the trail to the mansion, Chad was more jumpy than before. Do not ask me how he was more jumpy, because it was near impossible, but somehow, someway, Chad managed it. I pretended not to notice so I wouldn't have to ask, and he wouldn't have to tell the story that he so wanted to tell someone, but wanted people to think he didn't want to tell. I was smart like that, knowing people's feelings. Some said it was because I had no feelings of my own, but that's not true. It's weird how when you're different, people alienate you and make up nonsensical things about you to make themselves feel better and more normal. I've decided that people do this because they're insecure about themselves.

"They're some freaky stories about that old mansion, you know," Chad said when we came up to the mansion's front doors. "I'm sure some of it isn't exactly true, but, like, a lot of it has to be."

I rolled my eyes and pushed the door open. I wished I had a lantern or flashlight. It was so dark that I could barely make out the stairwell that loomed before me. I pulled out my lighter and I could see a tiny bit better.

"Sure, this place will keep you warm for tonight," Chad rambled on in the background. "But don't go expectin' me to stick around this place all night. This place sure does give me the creeps; then again, it gives everybody the creeps. At least you know no one will find you up here. Nope, no one in their right mind comes up here ever, much less in the middle of the night." Chad's motor-mouth showed no signs of slowing, so gradually I let it fade out in small increments so as I knew he wasn't going to ask me something, or say anything of importance.

I walked over to the fireplace and after a good ten minutes of hard work, I had a blazing fire going in the house.

"You think anyone will notice the smoke?" I asked, raising my eyebrows.

"Nah, not at nighttime anyways. I wouldn't have one lit in

Sly Darkness by Kya Aliana

the morning though," Chad warned. He finally settled down a tad and took the seat next to me.

"So you're gonna stay here all night?" Chad asked, rocking back and forth in front of the fire. His knees were pulled up to his chest and his eyes seemed distant, as if they were in some other dimension.

"Yeah, why not?" I asked with a slight chuckle.

"Okay, but it's your death wish. Whatever you do, don't go into the basement," Chad warned.

"Why not?" I asked, my heart leaped and then thudded hard. Maybe he'd tell me some story about it, something that happened in it. I didn't know if I really wanted to know why or not.

"Just don't okay?" my heart slowed. It was probably just some more folklore.

"Look, it's getting late," I said, oddly enough shunning Chad for not telling me the story. I didn't know why I was doing such a thing. All I knew was that I wanted to hear a story and Chad wasn't going to willingly tell me one.

"You're right, I better be gettin' home. Wouldn't want my parents to find out I was gone. They would freak," Chad said as he stood up. I didn't bother to get up. I was comfortable lying on my side, watching the fire roar with its natural fascinating blaze.

"I guess I'll see you tomorrow?" Chad half way asked half way said. I nodded.

"I can come by in the morning and bring you some breakfast," Chad offered. I almost snapped at him, saying I didn't need his damn charity, but my stomach had other words.

"Yeah, that would be great," I said with a half-smile.

The minute Chad left - and was safely out of sight - I shot up from my comfy position on the ground. I wanted to feel the cool air against my skin again, look around the outside of the mansion. I've learned that it was always good to psych out where I was staying before I fell asleep.

I caught a chill the moment I stepped outside. I'd forgotten how cold it was when I was lying next to the fire, loving the

Sly Darkness by Kya Aliana

emanating heat. I shivered, but only for a moment. I told myself I'd be back inside in no time. I just wanted to check out the basement, that was all. I didn't exactly know why Chad had called it a basement; it was more of a root cellar. After all, it didn't even connect to the house.

I opened the door and it creaked so loudly I thought that one could most likely hear it all the way in the town of Riverwolf Pass. For a moment I was worried that the noise would blow my cover... but then I decided I was being childish. I didn't like to act childish; I wasn't a child any more.

I didn't even like to remember being a child. I never thought back to anything before the age of thirteen, and I certainly didn't want to try. I blocked stuff out intentionally, and the other stuff I wished I could block out. I'd kept a journal ever since I went out on my own. I was positive there were memories in there that I'd written down that I never wanted to see or remember in my life. I never re-read my entries. Once I wrote it all down, the page remained there, unsurpassed by human eyes... or any eyes for that matter.

To my vast disappointment there was nothing much in the basement. Ashes from a fire... I remembered Victoria saying something about a fire happened up here. I turned to go up to the house and that's when I saw it... a flash of what used to be there. I saw a girl, a beautiful girl, waltzing by with some guy. They were holding hands. The wind swooped her white dress up in such a manner that it put Marilyn Monroe's most famous picture to shame.

She stopped in front of me, releasing the hand of the boy who was with her. She tilted her head and then smiled at me. I reached out to touch her; no vision had ever been like this before. My hand fell right through her as she laughed and shook her head. She turned back to the boy, kissed him, and looked back at me. They were somebody important... I would come across them, I just knew it. They were linked to my destiny... what other reason would I have seen her so vividly like that?

The vision was etched into my mind with the clarity of

Sly Darkness by Kya Aliana

something lazered into crystal.

That happened to me every now and then. I didn't know why it happened. Nobody else I ever knew had the ability that I did. It's happened to me ever since I was five. I don't remember the first time it happened. I just remember that when it first happened, I thought nothing of it. I figured it happened to other people too. I thought that other people saw what I was seeing. It took me a couple years to figure out they didn't. I never mentioned it to anyone. Besides, who *wouldn't* call me crazy if I said I could see small glimpses of past events that happened where I was?

I made my way back inside. I found some throw pillows and a blanket on the couch and made myself a comfortable bed in front of the warm fire. I laid there thinking for a while. I thought about lots of things, my old friends, my old girl, my old life, and then going off on my own. I thought about Chad, and this town, wondering if this was my ultimate destination. Was I destined to stay in Riverwolf Pass? I didn't know why I was so attached to the town, even after learning what I came here for was no longer here. But, I didn't want to leave, and I didn't think I ever would. This felt like home... I guess it would have been my home if my mother-- *No, quit thinking about her. Please don't think about her. You'll cry if you think about her. Please don't cry.*

I shook my mother as far away from my mind as I possibly could. My eyes slowly began to close and I allowed my brain to surrender to the sleep and world of dreams that awaited me.

*   *   *

My eyes slowly started to lift, seeing the morning sunbeams lying atop my blankets. As I looked around the room I began to notice things I hadn't last night, such as the stairwell railing being made of a gold-like substance, the eloquent wood carvings and decorations upon the walls, and the old-timey feel to the furniture. The mansion was alive around me. I lied in it,

Sly Darkness by Kya Aliana

trespassing. I didn't belong there. I was street scum; this was a millionaire's - maybe billionaire's – home.

I was hungry; I must have been because I imagined the smell of bacon and eggs coming from the kitchen. My stomach was doing front flips with joy. I wished my brain would tell it the smell wasn't real. My stomach started roaring loudly. I half consciously walked into the kitchen, wondering when Chad would be there with breakfast. I opened the door into the kitchen and there stood a girl cooking bacon and eggs. I didn't believe my eyes. I almost made myself believe that I was dreaming. After all, why would a girl be standing in an abandoned mansion - where I happened to camp out the night before - cooking bacon and eggs?

"Hi, did you sleep well?" she asked, raising an eyebrow. I nearly jumped at her words. I didn't know why I wasn't expecting her to speak. Somehow, she caught me off guard with that one.

"Uh, I, uh, yeah, I guess I did," I said, rubbing my eyes. I wondered if I was hallucinating. I didn't know why I would be, but that seemed more realistic than having a girl in the kitchen talking to me.

"You kept the place rather warm with that fire. For that, you have my thanks. I don't suppose you would like some bacon and eggs? Do you like your eggs scrambled?"

I couldn't talk. I was speechless. Who was she? She looked so familiar, and yet I couldn't place where I had seen her before. My mind trailed to my followers… did they send her?… I didn't know how exactly they could, but…

"Hello? Are you awake or are you one of those people who sleepwalk?" she asked with a slight laugh.

"N-no, I'm awake," I said, the stutter unintentional.

"Good, because I have some questions for you," she said with a smile as she sat down at the table and placed two plates, slap full of food, on it, one in front of her and one next to her. She had questions for me? *She* had questions for *me*?

"How are you cooking?" I asked, my groggy mind wondering if this place had electricity. There was no way… Chad said this place had been abandoned… then again, if that was true,

Sly Darkness by Kya Aliana

what was this girl doing in the kitchen cooking?

"Oh, there's this old cook stove," she said, pointing back to where she'd cooked. "You just have to start a fire and that heats the top so you can cook."

"Oh, Th-thanks," I said, sitting down and stuffing the food in my face.

"Slow down, Cowboy, your food isn't gonna run off on ya." There was something in the way she called me "cowboy" that made my cheeks go red. I hadn't ever been called cowboy before. I wondered why she called me that.

"I-I-I'm sorry," I said, hanging my head.

"Don't be," she said with a smile, trying to catch my eye. "What's your name?"

"Zander, with a Z, and it's not short for Alexander so don't call me Alex or Alexa or anything like that."

"You got it, Cowboy." Why did she call me cowboy?

"So, uh, w-what's your name?" I asked, still half way trying to figure out if this was a dream or not.

"Sarah," she said. I thought to myself that Sarah was an awfully mundane name for a girl such as her.

"I wish I had a nickname I could tell you to call me by, but I don't. I'm new here."

"Oh," I said, not exactly sure what to say. I was sure I'd seen this girl before, I just couldn't remember where.

"So, Zander, do you always talk like that?" she asked. My eyebrows scrunched together in confusion. Talk like what?

"Uh," I said, not knowing how to answer that, mainly because I didn't know exactly what she was referring to.

"Your stutter," she said, jutting her head forward toward me as she scooped up another fork full of eggs.

"Oh, uh, no, I-I don't. It's probably because it's early or something," I said. I hadn't even realized I'd been stuttering. This girl did crazy things to my head and I didn't even know her.

"Sorry, I didn't mean to bring it up. Sometimes that happens to me to, you know. I stutter when I don't mean to. Anyways…" her voice drained in my ears. I wanted to listen to

Sly Darkness by Kya Aliana

her, it wasn't that I didn't. I just couldn't focus on her. It was too much of a shock to find her in the kitchen cooking me breakfast. What girl in their right mind would see me sleeping in an abandoned mansion and then decide to make my breakfast for me? Apparently this one... Sarah. God, she was gorgeous. She was way beyond hot... she was pretty... beautiful even! She was breath taking, need a respirator, kick start my heart, brilliantly heart stopping, drop-dead-gorgeous. Her dark brown hair shimmered naturally in the light of the kitchen. I looked closer and saw that she had a single red streak in her hair. Looking at her hair made me self-conscious of mine. I suddenly felt like I needed to wash the grease out of my hair. It wasn't hair grease, gel, or mouse, it was grease that one collects when they don't take a shower for a week. My hand absentmindedly went up to my hair and brushed it back out of my eyes.

Her bangs hung just over one of her eyes, her amazing sea-green eyes. One look into them and I was paralyzed. I couldn't even breathe. They seemed to peer right past me; right by my image, searching for who I really was. I could feel her energy pulling me toward her... her personality so different than mine screaming at me to keep talking to her.

I shook my head and started to breathe again, resuming checking this mysterious girl out. My eyes paused, no scratch that, they stopped at her chest. Her goddess like chest... what had come over me? I never checked out a girl like this? I never freaked because of boobs... I worked so hard to not see girls as sex objects... but... but... but her boobs looked so perfect that I thought I might not ever be able to pull my eyes away from them. And I most likely wouldn't have if she hadn't cleared her throat and made my eyes jump back up to hers.

"Enjoying what you see?" she asked with a smirk.

"I-I-I was uh, just you know, uh, drifting back to sleep," I said, stuttering, cussing myself out silently in my mind for sounding like an idiot and looking at her chest... not getting caught looking at her chest, just looking at her chest in general.

"Oh don't worry, I wasn't mad or anything. You're rather

Sly Darkness by Kya Aliana

jumpy, you know that, Cowboy? You should relax. By the looks of it, I'd say you haven't relaxed once in your entire life. Where are you from anyways?"

"Uh, Oklahoma." I said, biting off some bacon. "Norman, Oklahoma."

"You're a long ways from home, aren't cha, Cowboy?" she asked. Why did she keep calling me cowboy? It made no sense to me. I didn't mind it that much. I actually sorta liked it. But what bugged me was that I didn't know what it meant? I'd never had a nickname before. I was always just "Zander."

"I guess," I said with a shrug, wondering why she was still talking to me. I didn't mean to, but I guess I let her voice drift back out again, because next thing I know, I'm looking at her chest again. This time, I caught it before she did. I looked just below them and saw that her T-shirt was riding up a little. I could see her flat, yummy looking abs, just a little mind you. I realized that she was talking and I started to listen again.

She didn't say anything important over breakfast. She just talked about the town mostly, and asked a few questions to me. Then, she cleared both our plates and did the dishes while I studied her features a little more. I planned to sketch her later that afternoon. It was really too bad I wouldn't be able to get her to pose for me, and then maybe the drawing would be everything I wanted it to be.

Sly Darkness by Kya Aliana

Chapter Five

"Hey Cowboy!" she called up the stairs. I wondered what she wanted. Was it too much to ask for a little privacy? All I wanted was a shower. I knew there had to be an Artisan well around here somewhere; there always were in old mansions like this in these parts. I knew the water would be a bitch, near freezing. But, a shower was necessary and beggars can't be choosers. I could deal... I'd taken many cold showers... secret showers... showers where I wasn't supposed to be taking showers.

"Yes?" I shouted, peering down the stairwell. I saw her standing there, looking up at me with those eyes... those soul-piercing eyes.

"What are you looking for?" she asked.

I hesitated on my answer, "Just lookin' around," I said as she started to climb up the stairs. She waited until she was right next to me and then stood up on her tippy-toes so she was closer to my face. I was a greater deal taller than her. If I stood six-foot five-inches then she must be… about five-foot six-inches.

"You want me to show you my room?" she asked, quickly bobbing up and down as if she was bursting with excitement.

"Uh, well, I don't know… wait you live here?" I asked, wondering exactly what she meant.

"No, but I come here often enough to have my own room," she said as she walked past me. I watched her butt as she walked ahead of me. She glanced back over her shoulder after taking a few steps.

"You coming?" she asked politely. I nodded and started to walk, following her.

"I come here to write. Writing's my escape from the world I'm forced to live in. Don't take that the wrong way, I love this world, and it's not like my family's all that bad either. We get along okay, but sometimes life is just hard. I need an outlet, and

Sly Darkness by Kya Aliana

writing is that outlet. My home life is way too busy and loud for me to write there, so I come here. My parents don't worry about me. I sneak out once they're asleep. They think I get up early to go running, then I head to school and they see me in the afternoon, easy as pie," she said with a smile. She seemed like a genuinely happy person to me. I wondered what could be so bad about her life that made her come to an old abandoned mansion to write… why not the library or something? There was something she wasn't telling me. But of course, I didn't press the issue.

"So what do you write about?" I asked, silently congratulating myself on saying something without stuttering.

"Oh lots of things. I write short stories, poems, a couple songs, I'm currently working on my 6th novel."

"Your 6th *novel?* Jesus, how old are you?" I asked. She didn't really say "novel" did she?

"Sixteen, I'll be seventeen in about a week," she said with a smile. I couldn't get over the fact she'd written a novel… five of them… and was working on her sixth. How the hell was that possible? How often did she come up here to write anyways?

"What are your novels about?" I asked with a growing curiosity.

"Well, the first one I wrote when I was thirteen, it's really, really bad. Like, the writing style is anyways…" She chattered on about topics that varied from gangs to vampires and one about pirates.

She said she had no idea what the novel she was currently working on was about, but that the character sculpting and foreshadowing was excellent. I wondered how someone could foreshadow something without having a vague idea about what the story would entail. But, I didn't dare argue with her. Instead, I said how much I would love to read her work sometime. When I said that, she started to blush up a storm and stammered over her words. I felt grateful that at least I wasn't the only one stuttering that morning.

The door to the mansion opened with a creak and I heard footsteps. Sarah frowned at me.

Sly Darkness by Kya Aliana

"Are you expecting company?" she asked. I nodded and she looked less worried. As we went down the stairs, I quickly explained to her that my new bud, Chad, was coming to meet up with me. When we reached Chad, I thought his eyes were going to pop out of his head.

"S-S-S-Sarah?" he asked, stuttering as I had done earlier. So that was where I knew Sarah from, she was "Cutie." She was Chad's crush. My heart started to panic, had I been flirting with her? What if she interpreted something wrong? What if we ended up kissing? *No, calm down, Zander, you didn't do anything wrong, besides, you didn't know it was Chad's Sarah you were talking to.* My heart started to calm down... as much as it could in the presence of Sarah Peterson.

"Hi, do I know you?" she asked, flopping down on the couch, stretching her arms up above her head. My eyes inadvertently gazed at her chest which she so carelessly pushed forward. I shook my head and forced my eyes away from them as soon as I realized what I was doing.

"You okay, Zander? You seem more jumpy than you were yesterday," Chad said with a slight chuckle. "Then again, I suppose a night in this mansion would make anyone a little more jumpy." I faked a laugh and kept up with some small talk until the grandfather clock struck eight.

"Shit!" Chad exclaimed louder than ever.

"What is it?" I asked as he and Sarah both jumped up and started gathering their things.

"School," Sarah explained. "School is starting."

"Hey guys, relax, we were having such a great time. Can't you skip one day of school? I promise it'll be fun," I said, not exactly knowing why I was saying such things. Perhaps it was a fear of being left alone... but more likely it was because they were the closest people I'd had to friends in a very long time. When Sarah turned around to say something - I never found out what - we all stopped and our blood ran cold. We heard the door creek open. We were all thinking the same thing... ghosts... or worse.

Sly Darkness by Kya Aliana

We heard laughter and began to relax, but only for a minute. We all three walked towards the room where the two adjoining doors were. It seemed to take forever to get there. We then saw Victoria with the guy she had been arguing with the night before.

"What the hell?" I said. "You told me no one ever came here, Chad. So far I wake up to a girl cooking me breakfast, you show up, and now two more people are here."

"Well, I didn't know that was gonna happen. Normally no one is ever here," Chad said. Sarah nodded her head in agreement.

"We agree," Victoria said with a slight laugh. "This is just a place where I come to skip school and make out with my boyfriend." I thought she should put an 's' on the end of the last word she said, but I was polite enough to not say such things.

"Well as long as we're all here, and I assume none of us are going to school today, we might as well hang out," Chad purposed. I looked at Sarah, not exactly knowing why, and I saw a moment's hesitation in her eyes, as if she wanted to go to school. But the words to escape her lips were words of agreement. She must have changed her mind. I looked at her with wide eyes, probably from disbelief and she shrugged. We all headed into the kitchen, Sarah brushed by me and whispered in my ear.

"Sometimes, you just gotta say what the ———" Fill in the blank. I almost didn't believe it myself. That sort of lingo coming from a girl like her… now, Vikki would've been a different story, but Sarah, she took me by surprise. She winked and then walked into the kitchen with the others.

I wasn't good at keeping up small talk, so I flipped though the local paper that Chad brought. I listened to the others babble on about school and other such things.

Victoria's boyfriend was getting testy and aggravated, so he left after a few minutes of talk. I could easily tell that he and Victoria weren't close. I felt badly for Victoria. If only I knew the exact reason she acted like a slut. Was it because of home issues? Friends? Her own insecurities perhaps?

The newspaper didn't say much of anything that I found

Sly Darkness by Kya Aliana

interesting... that is until the last page. There was an ad on the back. No, it wasn't an ad. I looked closer and read the details. There was a picture of a kid, no older than sixteen, who went camping in the woods on a solo trip and didn't come back. He looked like a real smart nature-boy, so I figured that there was a strong possibility that he could still be alive out there. He had been missing for six days. His father was offering a 20,000 dollar reward, dead or alive, whichever way they found him - hopefully alive. *20,000 dollars,* I thought to myself, that's a lot of dough... boy could I use a hunk of that.

    That was the moment, the precise moment that the brilliant idea occurred in my mind. I could go find the kid and collect the money. Why not? What did I have to lose... of course I would need the proper supplies to be out in the woods. But the escapade surely wouldn't take longer than two days, maybe three. I could find him, I knew I would be able to... but where would I come up with the cash to buy all the supplies and what...

    "ZANDER!" The sharp voice made me jump.

    "Huh?" I asked, looking around, trying to figure out who said my name. Sarah giggled and brought her hand up to her lips and touched them gingerly. The sight almost made me blank out again. I didn't know why I found it so cute.

    "What were you thinking about so hard? I've never seen an eighteen-year-old boy be so entranced by a free local newspaper before," she said. I was sure my cheeks were red as a crimson sunset.

    "There was this poster in there... about this guy... you know, the one who got lost in the woods," I said, wondering if they already knew about it. Riverwolf Pass seemed like a small town, so I was sure the word was out by now.

    "Yeah, the one who's daddy is offering twenty-thou for," Victoria said, applying her lipstick generously.

    "Yeah, it's had the whole town in a tizzy, this kid going missing... ever since six months ago..." Chad trailed off.

    "Okay, will someone please tell me what happened six months ago?" I asked, frustrated.

Sly Darkness by Kya Aliana

"Alright, listen, six months ago this new family moved into the mansion. A couple kids went missing or were found dead and then half the residence in the town burned to death in the root cellar of this old place," Chad said grimly. "The police tried to cover it up, but how do you cover something like that up? Kids were left as orphans, family suddenly disappeared. My friend, Ivan, skipped town with his little sister before all the aftermath hit. It was fucked up, man, for real. Now the whole town is worried about this kid going missing because they think some messed up shit's gonna happen again. You hear about it, from person to person and then they stop as soon as a kid can hear them. The past week's been panicked, I tell you what... so they're offering a reward for the boy just to set their minds at ease," Chad explained.

"I could really use that kind of money," Sarah said. Chad, Vikki, and I all agreed.

"Hey!" Sarah said, excitedly, she looked as if she'd had an epiphany. "We could all go searching for him, together. And no matter who actually finds him, we split the money. What do you guys think?"

"I don't know..." I started, having already thought something of similar idea through, which would be *me* going out on *my own* searching for him.

"Why not, Cowboy? Ain't you got the balls?"

"Oh I have the balls!" I said strongly, feeling a little bit offended. I was gonna prove it to them that I had the balls to do this. "I just mean we would need supplies for two or three days. It shouldn't take longer than three days to find him, so if we get supplies for four days then we'll have everything covered."

"And what's wrong with getting supplies?" Chad asked, leaning on his elbow which rested on the kitchen counter. I could tell it wasn't one of his normal natural poses; he was merely trying to get a better view down Vikki's shirt.

"Supplies cost money," I stated, looking around the room.

"Well, I have some money in the bank, I know I could access it," Sarah said and then paused for a second. "It's for

Sly Darkness by Kya Aliana

college, but I mean, I'll be able to put back what we take out with the money we'll earn for returning the boy... or body," she said mysteriously. I could tell she was ready for adventure. *Who knew, maybe a novel could come of this,* I thought to myself.

"Sounds good to me," Chad said. Vikki agreed, smacking the gum in her mouth. Chad, getting annoyed with Vikki, hopped up on the counter, using it as a makeshift chair.

"Well, we'll need to make a list of supplies," I said, thinking things through a bit farther. We agreed that since I was new in town and nobody knew me, I would be the one to collect the supplies.

"What do we do about all our parents?" Sarah asked innocently.

"We're gonna be gone for two or three days, Sarah," I said seriously, raising my eyebrows. "If your parents aren't going to be okay with you going out looking for a body... or boy, I think it's best not to tell them."

"After all, I bet they'll forgive you when we are the heroes of this shit-hole town," Chad added in, jumping off the counter and walking over toward Sarah. She turned her head abruptly back to me.

"Okay, I'm in."

"I'm right with you," I said with a smile, wondering how much I would get to know Sarah over the next couple days.

"In," Chad said.

"What the hell," Vikki said, not looking up from filing her nails. So I guess that meant all four of us were in this together. We made a list of supplies as well as some things to bring from our own houses. Like, we each had our own sleeping bags along with blankets and pillows. Chad had a tent we could use. Sarah was going to bring a shovel. And we were all going to bring water and I was going to buy one extra gallon to bring with us, just in case. I also had a whole list of supplies to obtain from the local store. Sarah and I were going to run by the bank and get the money. Then, I was gonna buy the stuff and head back up to the mansion, taking the long way of course, so nobody saw me heading up

Sly Darkness by Kya Aliana

there. We were all going to meet as soon as could later that night. We estimated it to be around mid-night to one thirty. We were going to spend the night in the mansion together, eat breakfast in the morning and then head out on our search.

The hike into town wasn't that bad... for me. Apparently Sarah wasn't used to walking places... or maybe I walked too fast, I didn't know which. I slowed my pace significantly so she could keep up. Chad and Vikki were staying at the mansion until I got back. Neither of them wanted to go into town. I was surprised that Chad didn't jump at the chance to go with Sarah. But I'd figured out that he and Vikki used to have a thing. So, that being a fact, I figured maybe it would be best if they worked everything out and put it behind them before we embarked on a two or three day journey into the woods.

"So," I started, not exactly knowing what would come after it... turns out, it was nothing. For the first time in my life, I felt stupid. Well, I'd felt stupid before, but never as stupid as I'd felt then.

They continued to follow me, watching me and my every move. I didn't know how it was possible, but they seemed to mock me and my stupidity. As if they could do a better job at starting a conversation with Sarah Peterson, hah! The mere thought of it made me laugh. At least I was doing better than they could. I was grateful to Sarah for not making a big deal about them following us. She didn't even seem to notice, which I figured was a good thing. I didn't want to wig her out or anything.

"So you think we'll survive?"

"Pardon?" I asked, not quite catching what she asked.

"With Vikki, do you think we'll survive for three days in the presence of Vikki?" she repeated herself. I wondered if she was being sarcastic.

"Do you know her very well?" I asked, wondering just exactly what she meant.

"Well enough to know that's she's a snob, stuck up, and sleeps around a whole lot... oh and did I mention she's always mean to me and doesn't like me at all?"

Sly Darkness by Kya Aliana

"I thought you were new here," I said, watching my feet carry me along, hoping I wasn't walking too fast. I didn't want Sarah to have to try hard to keep up with me.

"I am. This makes me fresh meat. Ever since the first day at school, Vikki's been on my case," Sarah said, kicking a rock down the paved road. I could now see the bank, where Sarah would be stopping to get some cash.

"I hate girls like that," I said, looking at Sarah. When I peered into her eyes, I suddenly found myself wondering what color my own eyes were, hoping they weren't some creepy color again.

"What kills me is I used to be like that," Sarah said under her breath. She said it so quietly that I wasn't sure I heard her correctly.

"Come again?" I asked.

"Nothing," she said. "The bank's here, you better wait outside. Don't want anyone to get suspicious." I nodded and waited outside for her to come back, thinking about what I would do and say when she returned. I wondered if she was going to wait outside while I got the supplies, or if she would make the trek up to the mansion by herself.

Sly Darkness by Kya Aliana

Chapter Six

Sarah came out of the bank with a smile on her face. That was when I knew everything was going to be okay. She handed me the money and followed me to the general store. She said she thought it would be best if she waited outside. I agreed. I knew it wasn't usual to see a girl like her hanging around with a boy like me. I was just glad she wasn't going to walk back up to the mansion all alone. I was happy and scared to keep her company all at the same time. Happy because she was a pretty girl who didn't seem to look down upon me and scared because she was a pretty girl who didn't seem to look down upon me. It was funny how I could be happy and scared of the same thing. That had never happened to me before.

I walked along the isles of the store, reading and mentally checking off the items on the list as I collected them.

1. A camp stove - I thought that was a good idea… that is, if anybody knew how to cook anything more than eggs. I shrugged and put it in the cart anyways, maybe someone would surprise me.

2. Canned goods - So *this* was what we needed the camp stove for. We didn't need it because somebody was actually going to cook something; we needed it to heat things up on. At least it made sense now. We weren't bringing eggs.

3. Beef jerky - Mmm, now that was one I could go with. If there was one thing I really loved to eat, it was beef jerky.

4. Trail mix - No doubt this was Vikki's item. Who in their right mind liked trail mix anyways? Lord knows Vikki wasn't in her right mind. I chuckled to myself as I crossed the trail mix off the list.

5. T.P. - No comment.

6. Marshmallows, graham crackers, and chocolate - why didn't they just write s'more supplies? Seriously, did they really think I was so stupid I didn't know what a s'more was?

Sly Darkness by Kya Aliana

7. Lighters and matches - I figured I'd better get a lot of those, no telling when they could come in handy. Besides, I'd learned that things got left out when a bunch of people go camping, so therefore a lot of things got ruined.

8. Newspapers - for reading? Oh, for starting fires. At least it made sense now. I decided just to pick up some issues of the free town newspaper on my way back up to the mansion.

9. Peanut butter - better get two jars of that. I loved peanut butter... almost as much as I loved beef jerky.

10. Tortillas - better than bread I supposed. I remembered Vikki wanting bread, but I protested, knowing that if we brought it, it would only get squashed and nobody would be happy.

11. Oatmeal - Blech, who liked oatmeal? Oh wait, don't tell me, Vikki.

12. Water - I thought everybody was going to bring their own water? Besides, nobody would want to carry all that water if I got more. I decided to get one gallon, no more, no less. After all, it didn't say how much water was needed; all it said was "water."

13. Hot Dogs – yummy, a bunch of crushed up random parts of random animals – a necessity to any camping trip.

I brought all the items up to the checkout counter, which looked like the checkout counter one would expect to see in the late 1800s. After the total, I had ten dollars left within my budget. I looked around for something to spend it on that I would enjoy, seeing as pretty much the only thing that I would enjoy on that list was the peanut butter and beef jerky. I saw a case of beer sitting behind the counter and a smile tore at the corners of my mouth.

"Oh and a case of beer," I said, trying not to smile too much. The man didn't even ask for my I.D., he just turned around, grabbed the beer, and rung everything up.

"You going on a camping trip?" the man behind the counter asked. He had a narrow looking face, black beady eyes and stubble. If asked to estimate his age, I would say around forty. He walked awkwardly, almost with a limp. He was slender. Everything about him was slender. His fingers were long; his fingernails were longer than they should have been. He didn't

Sly Darkness by Kya Aliana

look natural; he didn't look natural at all.

"I'm going to look for that boy, the one who disappeared and whose father is putting out a twenty-thousand dollar reward for."

"Yeah, yeah, I knows about 'im... the boy that is. He was in here just the other day," the old man said with fire in his eyes. "I told him not to go out there. I *told* him to stay here in town where it was safe. Them woods ain't safe. They ain't safe for 'im and they ain't safe for you neither." The old man's eyes seemed to dance. There was something he knew that I didn't, something... but what?

"Well I plan to be very safe. I've been camping before," I said, reassuring the old maniac.

"In these woods? Young man, I think not. No one survives these woods, no one, you hear me?" the man screamed, grabbing me by the shoulders.

"What's out there?" I asked with a curiosity so strong that I was hardly thinking for myself anymore. I wondered what those horrors were... or at least what the town people thought they were.

"Horrors that are way beyond your level of thinking, boy." The man shook me back and forth, as if trying to shake some sense into me. "Natural horrors, natural beauty, naturally creepy is what they are. Them woods is naturally creepy. They hold sly darkness I tell you. There's no tellin' what lies beyond those trees. Your deepest secrets will be revealed. Your deepest fears will shatter in the face of the new ones. You go out there boy, I can guarantee that you won't come back as the same person you are now. Your trust will be broken. Your honesty tested. Don't go out there boy, darkness awaits you. The sly darkness awaits you and slowly approaches when you finally think your heart is safe. The sly darkness, boy, do you understand that? Do you know what sly darkness is?" he asked, his eyes wide, nearly popping but of his head. He was scaring me now; I didn't know what to say. All I wanted was to take my things and leave, go back to the mansion, walk with Sarah, talk to her even. I just wanted out.

The man released his grip on my shoulders, it was then I

Sly Darkness by Kya Aliana

realized how tightly he'd been squeezing me. I absentmindedly rubbed my arms, I was sure they were red from where his hands were. I didn't say anything... I couldn't think of anything to say.

"That'll be one hundred and fifty dollars even." I handed him two hundred-dollar bills and got back fifty, just like Sarah wanted. I picked up the brown paper bags and walked outside.

"You okay, Zander?" Sarah asked. That was the first time she'd called me Zander and not Cowboy. For some reason, it struck me as odd and out of place. I wondered how I'd gotten used to her nickname for me so fast.

"Yeah, why?" I asked, walking away from the store quickly. It didn't register that I was walking fast until I noticed that Sarah's feet were trying hard not to trip over themselves in order to keep up with me.

"I saw that guy grab you in the store. I thought maybe he figured out you were underage and trying to buy that beer or something. But then you came out with it, so I guess that wasn't the reason," Sarah inquired.

Her voice simmered slowly in my mind. My ears rang and I could barely hear anything. The words of the old man repeated themselves in my head. *Your trust will be broken. Your honesty tested. Don't go out there boy, sly darkness awaits you.*

"Zander?" Sarah said, and I felt an arm on my shoulder. It was then I realized I'd stopped walking. I shook my head and came back down to earth.

"Are you okay?" she asked, looking into my eyes. I quickly dropped my gaze and muttered a "Yeah.... yeah." I began to walk again, slower this time, making sure that Sarah didn't have to hurry along just to keep up with me. My shoes pattered against the sidewalk and my head started to hurt. I hadn't had a headache in God knows how long.

"Seriously, what happened in there?" Sarah asked after a minute or two.

"Nothing," I said, shrugging. I found myself clutching the paper bag tighter.

"You looked tweaked out, Cowboy, like something or

Sly Darkness by Kya Aliana

someone scared you real bad in there. What happened? What did that old man say to you?" I was silent. After I didn't answer, Sarah went on talking.

"Whatever he said... whatever threatened, don't you pay any mind to it. Everyone says he's crazy. He's been that way for a long time, Zander. No one knows what happened to him but something did happen to him when he was a little kid." There was a short pause in her speech. I couldn't tell if it was because she expected me to say something, or she was trying to decide whether or not to go on talking. She decided to keep talking.

"His name is Wes Determan Jr., his father was recently killed. He'd always been crazy they say, but now he's even crazier! They say he's even crazier than Mr. White." I stopped and thought for a minute.

"Mr. White?" I asked. Though, I knew the name well, I wanted to know what Sarah knew about him.

"Yeah, this guy who went crazy a few months ago. Blabbering about werewolves or some shit."

"Vampires," I corrected.

"Right, those," Sarah said with a giggle. "So, if you're new here, then how come you know about Mr. White?" she asked with a cocky smile, raising one eyebrow in a curious manner.

"Town rumor," I replied quickly... too quickly.

"Uh, well, you know how it is in a small town... word gets around fast and furious, especially if it has to do with someone being crazy," I said, stuttering, trying to save myself. She nodded and we continued the walk back to the mansion in silence.

I thought about Wes Determan Jr., Mr. White, Sarah, the boy lost in the woods, and the darkness. Just what did he mean by darkness? I wasn't sure I wanted to find out. I didn't like the dark... the real fear was of the unknown. What was waiting for me out there? What would be watching me? Darkness... dark... the hidden. I couldn't take it... I suddenly didn't want to go out there, not even for my share of twenty-thousand-dollars.

There was a hidden mystery to the dark... it surrounded you in your most venerable hour – when you were asleep. It

Sly Darkness by Kya Aliana

waited patiently to attack to you... studying your every move. Darkness... the dark side... the dark... none of it was good, and none of it put my mind at ease about going out into some unfamiliar woods, with unfamiliar people.

*   *   *

"Hey, Zander, you sure you're okay?" Chad asked once we were back at the mansion. "You've hardly said a word since you've been back."

"Yeah, I'm fine," I replied, packing my backpack. The truth was: I wasn't fine. I was scared... scared to go out in those woods. I wasn't scared of Jason coming to get me, or Freddy killing me in my sleep. I wasn't scared of something rising from an old forgotten about cemetery, or a ghost popping out and summoning me deeper into the woods. I wasn't scared of vampires coming to suck my blood in the night. I wasn't even scared of zombies or werewolves tearing me to shreds and eating my brains. I was scared of the dark; something much more real than any of those things.

"It's just... well, even Sarah said something weird happened in town, Zander," Chad continued.

I shrugged, zipped up my backpack and started on packing Sarah's pack. Sarah and Vikki were at their houses, and Chad would be leaving shortly. They would all go have dinner with their families, wait until their parents were asleep, write notes to leave on their beds, grab the supplies that were needed, come here and meet back up with me.

We'd spend the night in the mansion together and then leave into the woods first thing in the morning. I needed Chad to leave so I could gather some firewood. I didn't want the girls freezing to death. Let me re-phrase that, I didn't want *Sarah* to freeze to death. I didn't give a rat's ass whether Vikki froze to death or was uncomfortable all night long.

"Well..." Chad said, slowly walking toward the door. "I guess if every thing's okay, I should be getting home now." He

Sly Darkness by Kya Aliana

left without saying another word.

I finished packing the girls' backpacks and then my stomach found its way into the kitchen to find dinner. I supposed I should have thought about dinner when I was in town getting supplies. I was pretty hungry and there was not a lot to eat in this hell hole. I chewed a piece of beef jerky and told myself I'd be able to survive until morning when Sarah would make us all some breakfast before we left.

There was a knock at the door. I thought about ignoring it, I didn't really feel like leaving my comfy position on the couch. Besides, the door was open; whoever wanted to come inside could and probably would. But something inside of me made me get up, something inside of me wanted to be a good host... if you could call me that. I guess I didn't own the place, but it was close enough to any home I'd ever had.

I opened the door expecting to see Sarah. I didn't know why, but I did. I didn't see Sarah, and I suddenly felt annoyed that I got up to answer the door for Vikki.

"Hi, Zander," Vikki said, bringing a finger up to her lip and gingerly touching it. I thought maybe she was trying to flirt with me, but I wasn't sure. I didn't really care either. She wasn't my type, and I didn't like her anymore.

"Can I come in?" she asked timidly.

"Nope, you get to sleep outside tonight, Victoria. Everyone else gets to sleep inside, but *you* sleep outside." I was only joking. I wasn't *actually* going to make her sleep outside... Chad would have gotten mad if I'd done that. She looked offended, but I didn't stick around long enough to find out what she was going to say in response to that. "I'm joking, come in," I offered, walking away from the door. I heard her footsteps following me, her heels clacking away as we walked into the kitchen.

"So, did you get everything packed?" she asked, running her slender fingers with red nails along my shoulder. I pulled my shoulder up to my ear and took a step away from her.

"Yeah," I said, looking any which way but her direction. I

didn't want to be alone with her. I wished Sarah would show up. That's when I looked down at the ground and saw what she was wearing on her feet. "Jesus, Vikki! You wore *high heels* to go out in the woods? Are you stupid or something? Do you have a condition we need to know about? You know, a mental one? Are you 'peshal, Vikki? I bet you're 'bery 'peshal!"

"Gawd, chill out! You're being a jerk, you know that, Zander?" I didn't mean to be a jerk, but how stupid and spoiled was she to wear *heels* out into the woods?

"Sorry," I muttered, but didn't mean it.

"Besides, they're boots. It's not like I wore open toed shoes or something," she justified her actions. I rolled my eyes and wanted to tell her that she was spoiled and wouldn't last one day on this excursion. Not that she would know what excursion means anyways.

I sighed and walked back into the living room to pack some more. Vikki followed me and laid, belly side down, on the couch, pushing her breasts up as much as possible and texting on her cell phone. I felt her eyes piercing me. I wanted to squirm out of my skin.

"Would you stop doing that?" I snapped.

"Doing what?" she asked, sounding more innocent than she really was. I sighed.

"Nothing, Victoria," I said, rolling my eyes. "Nothing that you already don't know you're doing, that is."

"I have no idea what you are referring to," she said, sitting up and placing her hands on her hips.

"I guess you are stupid after all," I stated. I knew it was rude, but I really didn't care. Why couldn't she realize that she didn't have to act like this?

I stood up and walked toward the kitchen. Vikki followed me.

"So, Zander, I was thinking..." she started. *Uh-oh*, I thought, *it can only go downhill from here.*

"Don't hurt yourself," I teased. She scowled at me.

"Well fine, if you don't want to hear my plan, I guess I just

Sly Darkness by Kya Aliana

won't tell you."

"Suits me," I said with a shrug. I didn't know why I was being so mean. I didn't understand why I hated her so much.

"Zander you are such a jerk-off! You're mean, you know that? And one more thing too, your eyes, they're creepy. You're just creepy in general! I hope you seriously get an attitude check because if you don't, you're gonna find yourself alone for the rest of your life!" Vikki said and stormed off. I turned back around and started to mindlessly thumb through the newspaper on the table.

"Don't take any of that personally." I jumped at the voice. It wasn't Victoria's. It was Sarah's.

"Geesh! I didn't hear you come in," I stated, leaning my head back against the chair.

"Sorry," she muttered. She stared at her feet.

"Hey, it's okay. You don't have to apologize. Look, sit down will ya?" I asked. She nodded and sat next to me.

"I'm worried about you, Zander," she said without making eye contact.

"Will you stop calling me that?" I asked. I didn't know why I said that.

"It's your name," she retorted softly.

"Yeah, I know, but everybody calls me that. I liked it when you called me Cowboy," I said, my face turning five various shades of red. Sarah giggled.

"I only called you that because you're always wandering around. That's what cowboys did, they roamed all over the Wild West," Sarah explained.

"Well I still like it," I said, smiling slightly. Sarah looked me in the eye and I quickly looked away.

"I don't know what Vikki's talking about," Sarah said after a second.

"Huh?" I asked.

"Your eyes, I don't think they're creepy." For the first time I could remember, I felt accepted. Finally I knew what it felt like to be accepted by someone. I never knew how lonely I really was

Sly Darkness by Kya Aliana

until then.

Sly Darkness by Kya Aliana

Chapter Seven

Morning came, long, slow and groggy. I sat outside, watching the sunrise as the other teenagers slept soundly inside the mansion. I sat there in silence, wondering what it would be like in those woods. Wes Determan Jr.'s words rang in my ears, stinging them with the bitter cold. What did he mean? Why did he say it? Why was I the one he said it to? Questions nipped at me like a puppy nips at his owner, sharp and short.

I'd never hung out with a crew as long as I'd hung out with Chad, Vikki and Sarah, since I'd been on my own that is. I wondered what it would be like to be with them all day and night long. I wondered if I could handle it.

I watched my followers fly around in the sky, circling overhead. They hadn't a care in the world. Their purpose was to follow me, to watch me, to... protect me? I never understood why they were there. I wondered how I would explain it to Chad, Vikki and Sarah when they finally noticed. If we were going to be out in the woods for a couple days, surely they would notice.

I thought about my mother... I always thought about my mother as I watched the sunrise. It was special. I remembered when I was little... my mom would always wake me up early.

"Come on, sweetie, get out of bed! It's the most beautiful time of the day!" she would sing, dancing into my room. I would always moan and groan, but she would eventually get me out of bed.

We would sit on the porch, her in the rocking chair and I sitting in her lap... the colors would fill the sky. Sometimes we would talk... she would tell me about-- *No, stop it.* I choked back the rock in my throat and squeezed the tears from my eyes, wiping them off my cheeks with my sleeve.

A letter my mother wrote shook in my hands. I tried like hell to steady them, but it did no good. I looked at the letter... I'd found eight years' worth of letters in my mother's desk. I read

Sly Darkness by Kya Aliana

them all... but this one stood out the most.

Westin,
    Do you remember the last day we were together... picking flowers out behind the church on Sunday after the service? You were only eight... but I bet you remember. Of all the horrors I have gone through, I'll never forget you. I wish there was some way for us to keep in touch... though we were only kids, you were always my very best friend. I know they say siblings can't be best friends, but we were the exception.
    I hope someday you get to read these letters I write to you. I hope someday my son will find you and you will care for him as your own. He's a good boy, Westie, and he will grow to be a very powerful man. You remember the book I kept hidden in my room in that very special hiding place? Well, you must give it to him. He's the One.
    I miss you, Westie, and I think of you every day... I have since the last day we saw each other. I fear my days are now numbered... I've seen it coming for a long time and am surprised that I lasted this long. It hasn't been the best situation, but I want you to know that it's been a lot better for me than most girls that this happens to.
    I hope you make the best of your life, fulfilling your dreams, and being the born leader and caregiver I know you were born to be.
    Pay attention to the myths, prophecies, and legends, they will come in handy one day, Westie.
All my love,
Abbey

"Geesh, Cowboy, it's freezing out here!" The voice startled

Sly Darkness by Kya Aliana

me, but I restrained myself from jumping.

"Really? I guess I was too busy thinking to notice," I said, concealing the letter as I turned to face Sarah, who was wrapped up in a blanket. She walked toward me and then sat down next to me. She laid her head on my shoulder.

"It is a beautiful sunrise," she stated. "Do you do this every morning?" I chuckled to myself.

"I haven't missed one on a good-weathered morning since I was two."

"Don't you ever sleep in, you know, like a normal teenager?" she asked.

"No, I can't put my mind at ease enough. I'm always worried about what's goin' on, what I'm missing. I'm just too curious to sleep in, doesn't feel right to even try," I explained. After that, we sat there together. I loved listening to her breathe. Without even noticing it for the longest time, I realized our breathing was in sync.

"What's it gonna be like?" Her words startled me again. I guessed I hadn't realized how entranced in the moment I really was.

"What?" I asked.

"Being out in the woods. I've never gone camping with friends before," she said, she bit her lip gingerly.

"It'll be fun, I promise," I reassured. Sarah nodded and was quiet for a moment. I looked over at her and saw a tear trickling down her face.

"What's wrong?" I asked, brushing her hair out of her face.

"It's just..." she started.

"Damn, what are you guys doing out here?" a voice from behind us asked. We both jumped. I watched Sarah's hand rush up to her face and wipe the tear from her cheek.

"We couldn't sleep. Too anxious about today, I suppose," I said, standing up and walking toward Chad. "Is Vikki up?"

"Nah, but I think we should start making breakfast," he said, eying Sarah. "I'm starving!"

Sly Darkness by Kya Aliana

"Sure thing, Chad," Sarah said as she brushed by him and hurried into the house.

"Whoa, did you hear that?" Chad asked me.

"What?"

"She said my name! My name!" he exclaimed excitedly.

"Yeah, Chad, that's great," I said with less enthusiasm than I probably should have.

"Well, excuse me!" Chad said, throwing his arms out in the air. "Excuse me for being excited about the girl I like."

"Look, it's not that. It's just, well, maybe you should talk to her sometime. She's a different kind of girl," I tried to explain.

"What are you saying?" Chad asked, his eyebrows scrunched together in frustration. "You aren't thinking of getting with her, are you? Remember, I called dibs."

"Hey, Chad, chill out, nothing happened, okay?"

"Yeah... okay... I'm sorry, Zander. Look, I just overreact sometimes." He chuckled to himself. "Guess I really shouldn't be worried 'bout you, though. I mean, Christ, man, if you even believe in love." I smiled a half-smile and followed Chad back into the house.

I wondered if I did believe in love. I wondered if Chad was right to be worried. I'd never met a girl like Sarah before, but I wasn't sure if I liked her... well, liked her enough to actually have a relationship with her. She would always be a friend, I knew that much. Chad was right, he had called dibs. But, did that really matter? She was a person, a girl, a human being, not a game, or the front seat of a car. It seemed wrong to call dibs on a girl.

Getting Victoria out of bed was the biggest hassle ever. Nevertheless, we did it and managed to head off into the woods well before noon.

"Where are we going?" Victoria asked after about thirty minutes of trekking into the woods. The wind whirled around me and the fog was so thick I could barely see anything. I kept catching glimpses of images, though I couldn't make them out. I

Sly Darkness by Kya Aliana

knew we were on the right path. The feeling kept getting stronger and the images were coming more rapidly.

"Into the woods to find the lost boy," I explained for the third time that day.

"But how do we even know where he is?" she whined.

"We don't, Vikki," Sarah said. "We have to look around for clues, camp sites, and other such things like that. Haven't you noticed that's what we've been doing?"

"Yeah, well my feet are tired, can't we rest a moment and have a look around. We must have walked for hours now!"

"We haven't, it's only eleven o'clock, that means we've been walking for thirty minutes... and we already took a five minute break," Chad said, not slowing his pace one bit.

"But my feet hurt!" Vikki snapped, sitting down on a nearby log.

"Well, maybe you shouldn't have worn *high heels* into the *woods*!" I said bitterly, standing in front of her with my arms crossed across my chest.

"They're *boots*."

"Yeah, boots with a *high heel*," I said. I was already sick of dealing with her, and I wondered why she'd come along in the first place.

"You know what? I don't have to take this abuse from you, you know that? I could go down to the police station right now and get you arrested," she threatened.

"For what? You willingly came out into these woods... you willingly wore high heels... you willingly decided to do this... you're gonna get me arrested for not wanting to take a break for your stupid ass to rest your feet?"

"Uh!" Victoria crossed her arms and pouted for a moment.

"Well, I'm moving on. Anyone who wants to follow me can," I said after a second. Victoria rolled her eyes, but followed along with everybody else.

The walk was silent for a long time after that. The fog was getting on my nerves. It was stopping me from seeing what I needed to see. Not only did I keep hitting rocks and tree stumps with my feet and tripping all over the place, I couldn't see the glimpses of the past I caught. I could only assume we were on the right path.

The sun was getting covered by clouds, and I could tell it was going to rain soon. We needed to set up a shelter.

"We could just go back to the mansion and head out tomorrow," Victoria suggested, eying the sky suspiciously.

"It doesn't work like that, Vikki," I said. "We made a commitment to come out here, I'm gonna stay."

"Okay," she gave in with a heavy sigh.

We didn't have time to set up a tent. It was all we could do to tie a tarp to a couple trees. I made a fire with barely enough time to spare. The snow came down fast, covering the ground within ten minutes. It was only a light dusting. But if it kept falling at this rate, tomorrow morning we would be dealing with inches.

We all huddled around the fire as we ate peanut butter smeared on tortillas. It wasn't the best home cooked meal, but with the snow coming down, there wasn't much we could cook over the fire.

Night came quickly and as the snow slowed, the cold became worse.

"I can't believe it's snowing in April," I exclaimed.

"It's fairly normal for these parts," Chad said with a slight chuckle.

"Yeah, haven't you been all over?" Sarah asked, raising her eye brows and the cuddling inside her blanket a little deeper.

"I guess I have. Shoot, I've seen snow in May... it's just, well, on my way up it was warmer."

"On your way up, isn't here," Chad explained. I nodded my head and sniffled a little bit. The cold was making my nose run. The fire only did so much for warmth.

"Gawd, it's so cold!" Vikki said, pulling inside of herself. She looked from me to Chad and then back to me. I sure as hell wasn't about to offer her my coat. She should have thought to bring a heavier one.

Sly Darkness by Kya Aliana

"We're all cold, Vikki," Chad replied stiffly.

"It's so miserable out here! Who would actually do this for fun?" she asked. Her shrill voice was getting on my nerves.

"I'm gonna go grab some more firewood," I said, standing up.

"Good!" Vikki snapped. "Maybe that will make it warmer in here."

"Want some help?" Chad offered.

"Nah, you can stay." He didn't offer twice.

"Thanks, Cowboy," Sarah said with a grateful smile. I smiled back, and then turned to walk into the woods.

It was good to have some time to myself. I loved the solemn feeling the woods emitted. I let a huge breath out into the air and watched it slowly disappear. The fog was lifting and the moon shown slightly from behind a cloud. I rustled over old leaves and newly grown and frozen flowers for sticks and logs. The snow brushed off them easily. I was happy it didn't ice before the snow came down. I knew tomorrow would be a long, wet, muddy journey deeper into the woods.

An image caught the corner of my eye. I turned to see a teenage boy standing at the foot of a tree, looking up. He shook the tree and a nut fell from it on his head. His hand shot up to his head and he rubbed it gently. He then bent down to pick up the nut, stood up and examined it for a moment. I stood perfectly still, knowing exactly what was happening. He took a pocket knife out of his pocket, marked the tree and walked on, whittling the nut. He walked on and slowly disappeared.

The vision of the past made me break into a cold sweat, like the long ones always did. I dropped the firewood in my hands and walked over to the tree the boy had been near. Sure enough, there was a mark there. He'd marked his path. That was great! All we had to do was follow it and soon enough we'd find the boy. I couldn't wait to tell the others. Hopefully, it would improve the current mood.

I picked up the firewood and walked back to the camp.

"Well, it took you long enough," Vikki snapped at me the

Sly Darkness by Kya Aliana

moment I was in sight. I looked at her, and then went to put more wood on the dying fire.

"I was starting to get a little worried," Sarah admitted, her eyes staring at her feet.

"Oh come on, I wasn't that long," I said with a shrug.

"Yeah you were, it was like forty-five minutes," Chad said, raising his eyebrows up. It wasn't unusual for this to happen. Whenever I had long visions like that, they seemed to take me out of it. I never knew how long it took... I never knew how long I stood there... I didn't even know if I was really conscious of what else was going on around me. It was like I was in a different realm, a different dimension... one that already happened... something in the past. I thought about it more and found myself wondering why it happened to me. Why me and not someone else? This obviously didn't happen to everyone. If it did, people would be zoning out all the time. We'd be like mindless zombies for half our life... was that what I was? A zombie?

I went over and sat down in between Chad and Sarah.

"Chad, it's just so cold out!" Vikki complained as she snuggled into his side. Chad put his arm around her and she smiled. Her head rested on Chad's shoulder and pretty soon she was fast asleep.

"I'm kinda tired too," Chad explained as he gently laid Vikki down on the sleeping bag pad. He laid down next to her and pulled a sleeping bag over the two of them as they snuggled up. His eyes closed and soon his breathing was soft and I knew he was asleep.

Sarah and I didn't say anything for a long time, and then the words started flowing suddenly.

"I'm sorry I started crying this morning. God, you probably think I'm just a stupid teenage girl who is scared of everything and spoiled too."

"I do not!" I said too fast. I sighed. "I really don't. Everybody has those moments."

"You don't," she said, biting her lip.

"I do, I just don't show it. Trust me, I won't judge you on

Sly Darkness by Kya Aliana

how you cried before you came out. I see for myself that you're not the winy kind, it was just a fluke," I reassured, scooting closer to her. I could feel her body warmth against my leg and arm.

"I just don't want you to think I have it so good and I'm the lucky one with all the breaks. Because, I've been through a lot more than I look like I have. You know, it may come as a surprise to you, but we're not that far off from being the same." I smiled, not quite knowing what to say. What had she been through? What did she think I'd been through?

"Everybody has their secrets, I guess," I said after a minute.

"I'll share if you will," she offered. I wasn't quite ready to share any of my secrets.

"Maybe tomorrow," I said. My eyes were drooping and I could feel myself relaxing in her presence. "I don't know about you, but I'm pretty tired."

"Yeah, same here," she said. She bit her lip, like she didn't know what to do next. I glanced over at Chad and Vikki. If I didn't know any better, I'd say they were a couple by the way they were snugged up together.

"Listen, I know it's cold out here and the fire only puts off so much heat..."

"Ahuh," Sarah said, nodding her head. I could tell we were thinking the same thing, so that made it easier to say.

"So how about we share a sleeping bag tonight?"

"That sounds great, Cowboy," she said, then paused for a second. I held my sleeping bag open, so she could crawl in with me.

"Well?"

"It's just..." she bit her lip again.

"What, Sarah? Just say it, okay?" I said, wondering what the big deal was.

"Look, I trust you, Cowboy. I don't want you to think that I don't... I just, I don't want anything to happen, okay? I'm not ready. I kinda just got out of a bad-"

"Hey, hey, hey, I understand. I wasn't planning on doing

Sly Darkness by Kya Aliana

anything. It's just cold, that's all." Sarah smiled and crawled inside the sleeping bag with me. I was happy to hear she didn't want anything to happen. It was good she said such things. When I'd asked her to sleep next to me, I hadn't been planning anything... but now that she was next to me and I could feel her breathe, feel her heartbeat, feel her warmth, it surprised me how much I did want to do stuff. I hoped she wouldn't notice.

"Goodnight, Cowboy," she softly whispered.

"Goodnight," I muttered, trying to focus on sleep. She rolled over to face me; I could feel her breath on my face.

"And thank you," she added, smiling at me.

"For what?" I asked.

"Giving me reasons to trust you," she replied and rolled back over. She took my arms and wrapped them around her. I laid there a while, feeling her breathe, watching as the dim fire lit up her face while she slept. She was warm enough for the both of us. Soon, I laid my head down next to her, and slowly drifted off to sleep.

Sly Darkness by Kya Aliana

Chapter Eight

Chad rustled the leaves, kicked the wood in the fire pit, exclaimed a loud "ouch!" and dropped a log. Finally I sighed and sat up.

"Dude, what the hell are you doing? You're going to wake everyone up," I said strongly. I'd been up for a couple hours already. I'd watched the sunrise while cuddled up to Sarah. She slept so soundly. I knew we had a long day ahead of us. Why was Chad in such a rush to wake everybody? He gave me an exasperated look.

"What's wrong?" I whispered, throwing my arms out. I didn't want to be the one who woke everyone up and caused a scene.

"Oh, nothing," Chad said as he kicked the ground beneath him. Dirt and leaves flew onto Sarah's face. She sat up quickly, brushing the leaves off her and onto my sleeping bag.

"Hey!" she exclaimed, glaring at Chad.

"Sorry, I tripped," he said with a shrug. Like hell he did. I wanted to call him out, but I didn't see any good that would do.

"Mmm, it's cold! Where did my snuggle-bug go?" Vikki asked, rolling over to face Chad.

"Come on, Vic, it's time to get up," Chad said, brushing off his pants. Vikki groaned and Sarah laid back down with me.

"What's up with him?" she whispered in my ear. She did it so subtly that Chad didn't even notice. I shrugged and stood up.

"You girls get ready and start making breakfast... Zander and I will be back in a bit," Chad said, glaring at me.

"Where are you guys going?" Sarah asked, rubbing the sleep and dirt from her eyes.

"For a walk," Chad said bitterly and started to go off in the woods. I looked back at Sarah and we exchanged a puzzled look.

Once Chad and I were far enough in the woods that the girls couldn't hear us, Chad wheeled around to face me.

Sly Darkness by Kya Aliana

"Okay, what's your problem?" Chad asked me.

"What's *my* problem?" I asked. "No, what's *your* problem?" I snapped, raising my voice.

"That's *my* girl who slept with you last night," Chad said, stomping his foot on the ground.

"Oh really?" I asked. "Okay, if she was your girl, why didn't she sleep with *you* last night?" I asked, getting angrier by the second.

"Hey, I don't know what you're getting at here, but my bottom line is hands off, dick!"

"Listen, nothing happened! It was just cold last night... and by the way you were snuggle-bugged up to Vikki, I'd say you two were back together. For all I know, you coulda made out this morning!" That was a lie. I'd been up before them and I knew the instant Chad woke up and saw Sarah and I in the same sleeping bag, he was up and furious. Chad sighed.

"If I so much as see you lay one finger, *one finger,* on her, Zander, you're dead meat!"

"Whatever. If you really care about her, maybe you should try and talk to her, Chad. She's actually quite different than she appears," I said, storming back off toward camp.

"Just how much have *you* talked to her?" Chad asked. I turned around.

"Enough," I said. Chad gritted his teeth and his hands formed into fists. His knuckles popped and he made a short grunting noise.

"Look, if you wanna fight, I'll fight, but I don't think you're going to want to explain what happened to your face when we get back to camp," I said, not bothering to turn around to face him.

"Just stay away from her, okay? Just stay away," he demanded, and brushed past me and back to camp.

I stood there on my own for a moment, trying to relax myself. Something caught my peripheral vision, but when I turned to look, it was gone. All I could remember was it was a face... a different face. But what was different about it? I couldn't

Sly Darkness by Kya Aliana

remember.

I walked back to camp to find everybody eating breakfast.

"Sorry, Zander, I ate the last of the food we made... but that's okay, right?" I took a deep breath and used my best self-control method to restrain myself from causing a scene.

"Yeah, that's fine, Chad," I said. Sarah looked at me and I knew she was fully aware that something was wrong.

"I'm not going to finish mine, Cowboy, you should eat it," she offered.

"Nah, you need it more than I do," I said.

"I never eat breakfast anyways," she said, standing it up and forcing her plate into my hands.

"Thanks," I said. She smiled at me and sat down next to me. I knew this couldn't look good to Chad. I had to do something. For the sake of the entire trip, I knew I had to chill out with the contact between Sarah and I.

I ate quickly and stood up as soon as I was done. I went over and started rolling up sleeping bags, shaking the dirt from my own.

"Oh, I should be helping you. Sorry I got dirt on your sleeping bag," Sarah said.

"Are you kidding? It was all over your face, what were you supposto do?" I asked, laughing.

"Yeah, well, still, I should at least help you shake it out. Thanks for letting me sleep with you last night," she said. "And thanks for not making anything happen," she whispered in my ear. I glanced over at Chad. He was glaring at me while Vikki was trying desperately to capture his attention.

"Yeah, no problem," I said, trying to say as minimal as possible.

"I love being able to trust you, Cowboy, I've never met a trust-worthy guy before," she said smiling at me. I loved her smile. Not only did she smile with her mouth, but with her eyes as well. I returned a smile and then walked back over to the fire pit, where my backpack was sitting.

We packed everything up and threw some water on the fire

Sly Darkness by Kya Aliana

to put it out. The snow had melted and the sun was shining. Everything was wet. Leaves from last fall covered the ground, making it slick and easy to slip. I told everyone about the mark I found on the tree. With a little help and luck, we found the trail. We followed it for a while in silence. No one was sure of what to say, what to do. Most of all, everyone was scared of what we would find when the trail ended.

Why hadn't the boy come back? He'd been an experienced camper; he even marked his trail so he wouldn't get lost. What could have kept him away for so long? Maybe a bear had eaten him... when did bears come out from hibernation anyways? No one wanted to say it, but everyone knew that we would eventually find a body.

"I don't understand why I keep falling. My hip has to be bruised to all hell by now," Vikki said. I turned to find her sitting, rubbing her leg. She'd tripped about twenty times in the last four hours. I drew the machete from my belt and walked toward her.

"Zander!" she screamed. "What are you doing?" her voice was shrill and sharp. It made me want to cover my ears, but I just kept walking toward her. "Zander, stop!" she demanded as I stood in front of her. I ignored her plead and grabbed her foot. She tried to scoot backwards; her hands grabbed the wet leaves and grass. I chuckled and swung the machete back above my head. It came down with a hard thud and all was silent. The heel of her boot lay there on the ground. I lifted up the other boot and removed the heel.

"Now, walk thoughtfully," I said, returning the machete to the side of my belt.

"My boots!" she exclaimed. Her face was getting red. She stood up and stomped her way over to me. "Do you have any idea how much those cost me?" she asked.

"Do I look like I care?" I retorted.

Sarah tried to stifle a giggle. Chad glared at me as Vikki's eyes filled with tears. I rolled my eyes, I knew they weren't real. Chad walked over to Vikki and put his arm around. I could hear the murmur of their voices hanging low in the forest. I knew they

Sly Darkness by Kya Aliana

were talking about me. I could hear every bad thing they said about me, but they didn't know that.

I trudged on through the woods, paying no attention to the bad things Chad and Vikki were saying about me. I paid no attention to Sarah, who was walking steadily behind me, cheeks blushing as she pulled into herself. I looked back at her and she forced a smile and looked down at the ground with a slight shrug. Her eyes shifted around and soon I turned my head back around. I caught another glimpse of the boy from behind a tree. Sure enough, when I walked over there, it was marked.

We followed the long path of marked trees for hours on end. I watched as the sun moved slowly across the sky.

"Why would someone mark the trees? It just doesn't make any sense for an experienced hiker to mark them; shouldn't he have like a GPS or something?" Vikki asked.

"Or at least a map... it's not like Hector to mark his path... I went camping with him once before," Chad said, kicking a rock beneath his feet. I shrugged. His guess was better than mine, seeing as he knew Hector before he went missing in the woods.

"That was his name, Hector?" Sarah asked. Chad nodded.

"We buddied around about six months ago... then I just kinda became a loner." I still wondered what happened six months ago. I knew it was weird, but it seemed like they weren't telling me everything. Too much happened six months ago for just a fire to have occurred.

"So I guess it's pretty hard for you now that he's missing," Sarah stated in a solemn tone.

"Not really, we only hung out for a couple weeks. I didn't know him all that well," Chad explained. Sarah nodded and we went on walking for another hour before Sarah suggested we set up a camp. We all agreed, seeing as it was near dusk.

It was considerably warmer than the night before, and that was a relief. The sky was clear, and we could see the sun setting beneath the mountains. I knew it would get colder, but I hoped it wouldn't snow like it had the night before. We managed to set up a tent and started a fire just before the sun disappeared behind the

Sly Darkness by Kya Aliana

mountainside and the darkness really set in.

We had a dinner of warm beans and beef jerky, and for the first time in my life I found beans near edible. I wondered what the woods were doing to me. It was only day two and I liked eating beans out of the can... I figured it was only because they were warm.

We were running out of food and fast. Between meals and snack breaks, the peanut butter and tortillas were completely gone. The beef jerky was well on its way out and we only had three cans of beans left. We had lots of trail mix and one eight pack of hotdogs, though. After a long talk, we decided to skip breakfast and snacks tomorrow. I knew I was hot on Hector's trail and that we would probably find him – or more likely his body – by tomorrow. Then, we would just have to move extra fast and we'd be back within two days. So all in all, if we stretched the food, we could make it home before running out.

"Can I have some of that beer in your pack, Cowboy?" Sarah whispered in my ear. Chad glared at me, but because Vikki had her hand on his thigh, I didn't pay it that much mind.

I'd forgotten that we had beer. Only Sarah and I knew, and with good reason too. If Chad and Vikki knew, we probably would've wasted it during day one. I nodded and smiled as I reached for my backpack.

"Hey, either of you wanna have some fun tonight?" I asked, as I cracked a beer and handed it to Sarah, doing the same for myself.

"Jump back!" Chad exclaimed excitedly. It was the first time all day he hadn't seemed one-hundred percent pissed off at me.

"I'm game," Vikki said, winking at Chad. I wondered what would become of that situation.

I tossed Chad and Vikki and beer and took a huge swig of my own. I glanced over at Sarah, who politely sipped hers.

"That," I said sternly, "is not how you drink a beer." She looked at me from under her eyelashes. Her chin tucked into chest and her cheeks turned flush.

Sly Darkness by Kya Aliana

"I-I've never drank before," she said with a slightly nervous giggle.

"Really?" I asked, raising my eyebrows.

"Really," she replied in a quiet tone.

"God, you're such a tight-ass," Vikki muttered and Chad chuckled. I rolled my eyes at them and looked back at Sarah.

"Look, it's okay. Just take a swig of it instead of sips... it'll be fun," I promised.

"A swig?" she asked. Her four front teeth grazed her lip as she looked at me with hesitating eyes.

"Yeah, you know, like this," I said, demonstrating.

"Oh," she said, looking at the beer can out of the corner of her eye.

"Go ahead, try it," I said. It felt weird to encourage such a 'good girl' to drink, but after all, she was the one who asked for the beer first.

"Like this?" she asked, taking a classic first swig. She spat it out on the ground, coughing and gagging.

"A little smoother next time," I said, trying not to laugh. Vikki and Chad didn't even bother to try and stifle their laughter.

"Give it up, you'll never be cool," Vikki laughed, chugging her whole can, crushing it and throwing it in the fire.

Sarah looked at me and I saw the fire in her eyes. Vikki went to grab another beer, but before she could grab it, Sarah snatched it out from her grasping fingers. I watched as Sarah cracked it and then chugged the whole thing without stopping or choking once. She then threw the empty beer can on the ground, stomped on it with her foot, crushing it into a flat piece of aluminum, and spitting on the ground right in front of Vikki's feet.

"Uh, what a freak!" Vikki exclaimed. Her mouth gaped open, showing how appalled she was.

"You know, you're not as cool as you think you are... nor will you ever be," Sarah replied, turning on her heels back to me and her open beer.

I sat there, shocked by what had just happened. I'd never seen anything like it. Girls could do weird things to each other, I

Sly Darkness by Kya Aliana

tell you what. If only I could understand them better. Why exactly had Sarah done that? What did she need to prove to Vikki? Sarah was already incredibly better than Vikki in each and every way imaginable, and I knew Sarah knew that... so what pushed her to go to that extent to prove it? It made no sense to me. Either way, it was hot, and cool, and sexy. I had no idea why it turned me on as much as it did.

"You sure showed her," I stated under my breath as Sarah walked past me.

"Shut up, Cowboy," she replied, flopping down next to me and taking a swig of her beer. What did that mean? I didn't read into it that much. I finished my beer, crushed the can and tossed it into the fire.

By my third or fifth beer (I couldn't remember exactly how many I'd had) everything was starting to get hazy. I couldn't see straight and the fire was doing things that normally fires don't do. The ground around me moved every time I started to walk and I laughed at everything, even if it wasn't funny. I could still think straight, though nothing I said came out right. I watched as Sarah cracked open her sixth can for the night.

"Okayokay, so everybody gather around," Chad said, stoking the fire, causing orange ashes to fly up in the air. He rested his elbows on his knees, slightly bouncing his wrist, waving the stick up and down... up and down. I focused my eyes in on him.

"So, there's something about these woods you should know," he said very seriously. "Something about what my Great-Granddaddy witnessed out here." He paused to look all of us dead in the eyes for a very long minute.

"So," he eventually continued. "My Great-Granddaddy came out here with his buddies on a camping trip... it was all fun and games at first. They even brought their girls along for shits and giggles." Vikki gasped, for all I could assume it was only for dramatic effect.

"But, you see, those girls wouldn't put out... they absolutely refused to sleep with any of the guys. So, the guys got

Sly Darkness by Kya Aliana

bored and decided to go out exploring... they came across this old cabin with a crazy guy in it... well, he wasn't crazy yet, I guess. He was an old hermit, who liked his privacy. So, when my Great-Granddaddy and his friends cut across his property, he got right mad at them, cursed 'em out and threatened to kill 'em.

"Well, they got out of there pretty quick... but they came back that next night to play a prank on him. But, when they looked in the cabin he wasn't there... he came out of nowhere, screaming and shouting like a berserker! He waved a flail above his head and carried an ax in the other. They all got out of there alive... but then, some crazy shit started to happen." Chad paused, and there was a dead silence around the campfire. I had to break the silence. I scoffed, smiling and shaking my head. This was way too cliché... even for a campfire story.

"You think this is funny?" Chad asked. "I'm serious! This happened!" he said strongly. Not allotting me a chance to speak my mind, he continued with his story.

"But the next night, some crazy shit started to happen. Teens started disappearing one-by-one...by-one...by-one...by one... by-"

"Get on with it, Chad, you're drunk," I said, rolling my eyes.

"Geesh, chill out." Chad snapped. "The girls died first! There was blood trailing everywhere... body parts scattered all over the woods... This continued until my Great-Granddaddy was the last one left. He followed the trails back to the crazy man's house, where he saw the heads of all his friends, staring him dead in the face! They were all lined up along the crazy old hermit's deck! He was the only one to get alive... lucky. Now, word's got it that the crazy old hermit still lives... and that's what's happened to our good ol' boy who we're after... and that's what'll happen to us if them girls don't put out!" Chad said with a chuckle.

"Well, if it'll save us, then of course I'll be happy to comply!" Vikki said, pawing at Chad. I rolled my eyes, shook my head, and guzzled another beer just to numb how disgusted I was.

Sarah's fingers fumbled over a new beer can, trying

Sly Darkness by Kya Aliana

desperately to crack it open.

"I think you've had enough, young lady," I said, reaching out to grab the beer and ended up toppling over and lying on the ground for a second.

"Looks like you've had a little more than enough," Sarah said, plopping down next to me. I laid there looking at her for a moment. I loved her eyes. I loved seeing me in her eyes. I looked different than I did when I looked at myself through my eyes. I wondered if that was the way she saw me. My eyes lingered at her lips and I suddenly felt the urge to kiss them. All of the sudden, I didn't care if Chad was right there to see it. I didn't care if she was Chad's crush. All I cared about was her. I knew Sarah wouldn't be happy with Chad. I knew Chad wouldn't treat her right. I also knew I couldn't treat her like she deserved, but at least I knew I could treat her better than Chad could. I knew I would at least talk to her more than Chad would. I knew it'd be a lot better if she were with me as opposed to Chad.

I leaned in toward her face a little more. Her eyes glistened like the dancing fire behind her. Her cheeks were flush and looked so soft to touch. My hand reached out toward her and brushed against her cheek. I felt her quiver and then relax as she looked at me. I inched toward her head and pressed my lips against hers. The feeling was electrifying and sent a shockwave through my entire body. I slowly parted my lips as my face stood, inches away from hers.

"Oh shit!" Chad exclaimed, followed by a loud thud. My head shot back and I sat up quickly. I couldn't even look at Sarah anymore. What had I done? What would this do to the rest of the trip? How badly was Chad going to beat me up? What if Sarah didn't want me to kiss her?

I couldn't see Chad anywhere, but I could hear something. A short moaning noise... I looked around and I saw Vikki lying on top of Chad, holding down his hands as she rubbed her body all over him. Oh. The exclamation was only because Vikki knocked Chad over... Chad hadn't seen me kiss Sarah after all.

Chad pushed Vikki off of him and tripped over everything

Sly Darkness by Kya Aliana

as he headed toward me. Uh-oh, I thought, he did see me after all. Oh, what am I going to do now? I didn't think I was sober enough to fight him... I'd probably get my ass kicked. Then again, Chad seemed pretty drunk as well.

"Hey, Zander, man, you mind if Vikki and I borrow the tent for tonight? You can sleep outside again, right? Like, you don't mind do you?" I breathed out slowly. He didn't see. He didn't see! He didn't let me answer; he just walked back to Vikki and grabbed her ass as they both flopped inside the tent.

The glimmering firelight against the tent allowed me to see the not-so-vague silhouettes of Chad and Victoria. I turned the other way, I wasn't too keen on the idea of watching two drunken teens get it on inside the tent I'd be sleeping in the next night... on second thought, maybe I'd just sleep outside again.

I thought about Chad and Sarah as a couple. It would be tragic. I knew exactly what kind of guy Chad was, and it wasn't the good kind. He would trap her; he would manipulate her, and suck all her independence out of her. He would treat her like no woman should be treated... he was and always would be a terrible man. Something had to be done. I had to eliminate Chad's chances at getting with Sarah... or any other girl like her. I knew what I had to do, and I turned back to Sarah, hoping to kiss her again.

She was still on the ground, running her hands up and down against the rotten leaves and dirt clods.

"You okay?" I asked. I felt like I was sobering up a little bit, and then I stumbled. I caught myself on the nearby ground. Luckily, I managed to miss Sarah by a few inches.

"I think I'm gonna be sick," she said, her eyes were closed and I could tell she was fighting to open them.

"Yeah, I know, Chad and Vikki really make me sick too," I replied, thinking that at least I now had the green light with Chad. It was beyond obvious that they were back together.

"No, I mean, I think I'm really gonna hurl," Sarah said. Her eyes opened abruptly and she stood up and ran to the side of the woods.

I sat up and followed her. She looked like she could have

Sly Darkness by Kya Aliana

fallen over if I didn't put my arm around her tummy and my other hand on her forehead, so that's what I did. She turned to face me and rested her head on my shoulder.

"This part," she said in a barely detectable voice, "is a little less fun." I nodded in agreement. The first time was always the worst. She really drank a lot too. Not to mention she was a total lightweight. I didn't think she could weigh a pound over one-hundred-and-ten.

"I need to lie down," she said after a moment.

"Okay," I replied. I helped her walk back over to the fire, and we sat down and watched it for a while. Sarah rested her head on my shoulder and she let me put my arm around her.

"You know something crazy, Cowboy?" she asked after a long time of watching the glow of the fire.

"Hmm?" I asked.

"I'm kinda scared," she said with a heavy sigh.

"Scared of what?" I asked quietly.

"About seeing a dead body," Sarah replied. Without looking at her, I could tell she was biting her lip. "And then having to look at it and move it back to town. We set out with the idea of being heroes, but did anybody actually think about the reality of what we're doing?"

"I guess not," I said. I had, but I had to admit that seeing a dead body, and then carrying it back to town, wasn't exactly my idea of a picnic.

"I just can't stand the thought of seeing another dead body. I'm only sixteen for Christ's sake," Sarah said. I looked over and saw she was crying.

"*Another* dead body?" I asked. "You mean to say you've seen one before?" Sarah took in a deep breath and looked at me with wide eyes.

"No! I mean, of course not. Just in movies, you know. But, listen just forget I said anything, okay?" she said all too fast.

"Okay, okay, if you don't want to talk about it, you don't have to," I said, running my hand up and down her arm.

"My head hurts," she said, lying down beside me. I laid

Sly Darkness by Kya Aliana

down next to her and remembered earlier when I kissed her.

"You should sleep. Morning's gonna be hell," I warned. She nodded her head. "You want some water? It will help, I promise," I said.

"I don't feel like drinking anything else," she replied, her eyes closing slowly.

"You sure?" I asked.

"Yeah, I'm sure," she said softly. Her voice was fading with the night. The fire danced behind us, but barely gave off any heat.

"Cowboy?" she asked after a minute.

"Yeah?"

"Keep me warm tonight? Just like you did last night?"

"Of course," I replied, cuddling up next to her.

Sly Darkness by Kya Aliana

Chapter Nine

The morning sun slowly rose over the mountain range; a short moan escaped my lips... morning already. My head pounded and my stomach was making odd gurgling noises. It'd been far too long since I'd last drank something. The entire night was a blur. Everything was jumbled up and hardly made any sense. I needed water, water would help. I didn't feel like drinking it, but I knew I had to. The golden glow of the rising sun was just bright enough for me to make out the gallon jug sitting a few feet away from the dying fire.

I took a few swallows of water, and sat there watching the sunrise for a little while. The more I focused on the sunrise, the more my head stopped pounding so hard.

I watched as they, my followers, circled the rising sun, like they did every morning, trying to fly higher and higher into it, but unable to do so. I wondered why Sarah and the others hadn't noticed them yet. I wondered why she hadn't said anything about them. Surely she had noticed them... I knew she was smart enough to make the connection between them and me.

They swooped down, flying just inches above my head. I watched as they played in the morning sun, chasing each other in circles, flying higher and higher into the sky and then swooping back down the ground. They were happy this morning, which was rather unusual. Normally they sulked every morning; they sat about and rarely even flew. If they did fly, it was only because I was already moving on, in search of something I figured I'd never find.

The sunlight flickered in and out through their holey wings. Getting too far from their bond to me, they would spiral back down toward the ground like that old child's toy, whirlybirds. I chuckled to myself as I watched them eagerly go back toward the light... hoping for something more... something better. They would never escape... never. They were bound to me,

Sly Darkness by Kya Aliana

never to be free. This was their fate... their terrible fate... but they deserved every bit of it.

Their hope this morning was unlike anything I'd ever seen before... normally they drooped in the morning, wings barely fluttering. They loathed me, got in my way, doing anything to keep me from going on with life. It never worked though, I always pushed through it. I had too... for my mom... my destiny.

"What are you doing?" Sarah asked, sitting down next to me. I'd been so entranced in watching them, I hadn't noticed Sarah wake up or walk toward me.

"Watching them play," I said absentmindedly.

"Watching who play?" she asked, her voice was soft and smooth. I thought she sounded just like an angel would.

"The wraith moths... the ones who follow me wherever I go. They have ever since--" I trailed off, not wanting to finish the story. I didn't know why I'd even started.

"You know, sometimes you surprise me, you know that, Cowboy?" she asked with a giggle.

"What do mean?" I asked.

"You've been through a lot, Cowboy. Anyone with common sense would know that."

"So? What does that have to do with anything?" I asked with a shrug.

"So, it means that you don't know whether to talk about it or forget it. You don't know who to trust or why you do half the things you do. You don't want to talk to people, but you end up doing so anyways."

"How very astute of you," I said sarcastically. "It's like you've known me for a couple days or somethin'," I said with an eye roll.

"I wasn't finished," Sarah said with a half-smile. "I figured out why you do all that stuff. I figured out what it means."

"Do enlighten me," I encouraged, my head was starting to hurt more. I wondered why Sarah wasn't having trouble with a hangover. Maybe she was just better at hiding it than I was.

"You're caught between who you are, and who you want

Sly Darkness by Kya Aliana

to be." I didn't really want to admit it, but it made sense. It felt weird to know that someone understood me and understood that idea. I wondered why Sarah even cared enough to try and figure that out for me.

"So?" I asked, wondering what her point was.

"So, nothing, I just thought you might want to know what I thought." I nodded. I did want to know what she thought. I didn't know what to say, so I said nothing. The wraith moths flew in circles, fluttering above my head. One landed on my knee and I stared at it. Its ink black wings were old and decrepit, patchy with tiny holes. The faint facial design on his wings was fading. They all had faces on their wings... light trappings of what they used to be... who they--

"I'm glad we're doing this together." Sarah interrupted my thoughts, resting her head on my shoulder again. "You have no idea how much it means to me to have someone to trust." I thought about kissing her again, but I wasn't sure if I should. I wondered if we should tell Chad that we kissed. He probably wouldn't care. He and Vikki were still sound asleep in the tent, probably cuddled up naked together, keeping each other warm.

"I'm happy too," I said, nuzzling my face toward her. I wanted to kiss her again so much. I felt my cheek brush up against hers and the jolt of electricity zapped through me, just as it had the night before when our lips touched.

"I mean, I've never met a guy I could trust before. Someone who's okay with being a friend. Someone who's not looking to just get in my pants or something. Someone I can get totally drunk with and he doesn't even try to take advantage of me or be sexual with me in any way." Oh, Christ! she didn't remember. She didn't remember anything about me kissing her, or even Chad and Vikki getting it on. She didn't remember. I pulled my head away from hers and resumed watching the wraith months in the morning sun.

"Cowboy?" she asked. "Are you listening to me?"

"Of course, I'm really happy I can be all that too. It's just a lot to take in, that's all," I lied. I wanted to go curl up and go back

Sly Darkness by Kya Aliana

to sleep. My head was hurting more than I ever remember it hurting before. There was a giant rock caught in my throat and no matter how hard I tried, I couldn't get my breath to steady.

"You okay?" she asked.

"Yeah, I'm feelin' pretty rough. I drank a lot last night."

"I know what you mean, my head is killing me. You wouldn't mind if we were just quiet for a little while, would you?" she asked.

"Of course not," I replied. I tried to make my voice sound steady, but it wavered anyways.

"Wow, you sound how I feel," she said. *No,* I thought, *I sound better than how I feel, and you have no idea how that is.*

It was around noon when I started to feel better. It was also around noon when Chad and Vikki stumbled out of the tent. I don't know why it surprised me when Vikki came out of there shirtless.

"Hey, have you guys seen my shirt? Or at least my bra?" she asked. I sighed and looked away.

"No, Vikki, I haven't. Maybe you should have thought about that before you decided to take it off," I suggested. Why did she have to act like such a slut? It really bothered me.

"Oh, come on, you can't blame me. I don't even remember taking it off. Shoot, you're the one who brought the beer," she said. "So technically, it's your fault."

"Bullshit! It's not my fault. You're the one who drank it, and a lot of it for that matter."

"Okay, you know what, whatever. I'll find my clothes without your help," she said, sticking her nose in the air.

"Damn right you will," I retorted with another heavy sigh. Chad walked over to me.

"What's wrong, Zander? You seem wound up too tight," Chad said, resting a hand on my shoulder.

"Nothing is wrong, Chad," I reassured. He sat down next to me.

"You know, that was the first time in six months... feels

good." I rolled my eyes. I'd rather not think about Chad's sex life. Why was he even trying to talk to me about it? Oh yeah, I'd almost forgot he used to be a football star. He was used to the guy's locker room talk. I was so not into that. And why did everything weird happen six months ago? There was something more.

"About that six months ago thing. What really happened?" I asked, hoping to change the subject.

"I already told you, big party, big fire, town freak-out, it's nothing really," Chad said, but walked away before I could question him again. I wished I could get some solid answers out of him.

I stood up and walked over to Sarah, who was sitting by the fire, sipping some water.

"You look rough," I said, deciding that even I wasn't going to get down about her not remembering me kissing her. After all, at least I could talk to her, keep building trust, and then maybe she'd kiss me. Besides, it's not like it would be an issue with Chad anymore because he was back with Vikki.

"It's starting to get better. I don't think I'm ever gonna drink again, though," Sarah replied with a bitter look on her face.

"Yeah, we all say that after the first time," I said with a cocky smile.

"Well, I mean it," she said. I nodded my head, knowing it would only last so long. After all, never was a long time.

"So what's with this kid, Hector?" I asked. I'd seen lots of visions of him that morning, marking trees, walking along, stopping for breaks, I swear he even smiled at me, but I knew that wasn't possible. They were visions, not reality, so therefore he couldn't see me.

"What do you mean? I didn't even know him," Sarah replied.

"Oh, well why would he go camping this time of year?"
"It's April," Sarah replied.
"Yeah, I know."
"It was a gorgeous spring weekend when he left."

Sly Darkness by Kya Aliana

"Oh, so I guess no one saw this coming at all?" I asked.

"Yeah, no one," Sarah replied. We were both silent for a long time after that. Neither of us wanted to admit it, but we were both thinking about the dead body.

"Do you think he decided to commit suicide and that's why he marked his path? So someone could find him?" Vikki's voice was sharp and piercing. I honestly didn't want to envision Hector's body hung from a tree in the forest somewhere.

"Vikki, I think most of us are freaking out a little bit about seeing a dead body. I believe we'd all like it if you'd stop talking about Hector," I said, thinking of Sarah as well as myself.

"I don't know why I have to. We're most likely going to find him today, just because some people are touchy about dead bodies doesn't mean we shouldn't face reality."

"Victoria, have you ever *seen* a dead body?" I asked, raising my eyebrows.

"Well, no, but-"

"But nothing, Vikki, just think about what that dead body is going to look like, pale, cold, eyes wide open, flies buzzing in and out of the nose, ears and eye sockets. Think of the smell that must be omitting, the rotting corpse smell. Sure you've probably read about it in some of those books of yours, but let me tell you, it's real different when you're actually faced with it."

"God, you're so morbid, Zander! Who would even ever like you? Why don't you do us all a favor and leave?" she said as she threw herself in the other direction to walk away.

As soon as she was out of sight, Sarah approached me.

"Look, she's just a bitch, that's all," Sarah said as she put her hand on my shoulder.

"Do I look hurt?" I snapped. Sarah removed her hand and looked at the ground.

"No, it's just, well,"

"What?" I demanded to know. "You pity me? Well you shouldn't!"

"It wasn't that, I was only trying to help," Sarah said and started to walk away. I bit my tongue and went to my backpack to start packing. I watched Sarah struggle with rolling up her sleeping bag and I didn't even care. I wasn't going to help her. I didn't see why I should. After all, she was the one who pitied me.

We started to move on around two in the afternoon. We followed the marked trees, the apprehension getting thicker with every step we took. We knew it wouldn't be long now, I didn't know how, but we all knew.

Sarah walked up to me and grabbed my hand; I felt the impulse to pull away, but stopped myself. She swung our hands back and forth as she smiled at me.

"Yes?" I asked.

"We're getting close," she said, her eyes dancing with the slight breeze.

"And that makes you giddy?" I asked, pressing my eyebrows together. I ignored the scowl that escaped from Chad; I wondered what that was for.

"Well, it's like this weird adrenaline rush. I feel excited and nervous and all this other stuff, and I also know that as soon as I see... it... I'll come crashing down." I thought what she was saying was fair enough. I was pretty sure that was how we all felt.

Sarah and I walked hand in hand for the next mile. The leaves crushed under my feet, twigs snapped and branches scraped in the wind. All of the noises made me jump. I knew what to expect, it was just a dead body. Even more, a dead body of someone I didn't even know. So why was I so jumpy? It made no sense.

Sly Darkness by Kya Aliana

Chapter Ten

A thick eeriness consumed the air as we saw the body lying there. No one spoke a word, and yet we all slowly trudged over to it. It was sprawled out on the ground, covered in its own blood. Its neck had been mutilated, and there were small scratches all over its body. I didn't want to breathe... I couldn't breathe. Even when I didn't breathe, I could still smell the stench emitting from the body. The buzzing of the flies drown in my ears as I watched them crawl all over it. I could hardly believe it used to be a human. A raccoon scurried away from the body as we had slowly approached it.

Although the sight was sickening, I couldn't help but be sidetracked. This wasn't the boy I kept seeing in my visions. This wasn't the right boy, was it? Was this the body of Hector? How could that be? This was not the boy from my vision at all. Everything was different about him, his skin color, his eyes, his height, his hair. Everything! But how could it be? If the visions had led me here, and the dead boy wasn't the one from my visions, who was? And why did it lead us here?

"Is this him?" I asked, but there was no reply. I looked around at everyone. Vikki was just staring at it, biting her nails. Chad looked horrified and wide-eyed. And Sarah, well, she looked like she was going to cry.

"I think I need a moment," Sarah said, jolting me back into reality. How long had we been standing there?

I watched Sarah walk away and slide down behind a giant tree. I wished I would see one of my visions. I wanted to know if my theory on how he was killed was correct or not. If it was, we had reason to be worried. A whole bunch of connections clicked in my head. Tonight, I was going to get some answers about what exactly happened six months ago. I finally knew the right questions to ask. I finally knew how to ask them. I was excited because I knew I would finally get some answers. If I asked the

Sly Darkness by Kya Aliana

right questions at the right times, I knew that I could get the answers to everything I wanted to know. I would know who was marking the trees and why, I would know if Hector brought a friend with him.

Maybe this was what the old man at the general store was warning me about. Darkness, of course! Maybe darkness wasn't a feeling, emotion, or something you couldn't see. Maybe the dark was a thing - a living, breathing, thing that dwelt in the woods and moved by the slyness of dark, following people and killing them. We could be in trouble, we could be in a whole heap of trouble, and nobody knew but me.

I walked over to Sarah and sat down beside her. It felt good to have the body out of my eyesight. That didn't change the fact that every time I closed my eyes, I could see it. I could see its eyes staring back at me, bleak and hopeless. I remembered another pair of eyes like that, but I didn't want to think about it. I pushed the pair of eyes from my mind and took Sarah's hand.

"Are you okay?" I asked, squeezing her hand slightly. She nodded, but looked far from okay.

"I'm trying not to be sick." Her eyes were closed, but tears streamed down her face. She looked pale and her hand was cold and sweaty.

"No one will blame you if you need to be," I said, slipping an arm around her. She rested her head on my chest and started to sob quietly. I went to run my fingers through her hair and then stopped myself, making a fist behind her back. I soon opened up my hand again and rested it on the back of her head, hoping that was okay with her.

"I can't take it," she said after a minute. I glanced back at Chad and Vikki. I knew they couldn't hear us; they were having their own moment of freak out together, hugging and crying all over the place. I rolled my eyes and focused on Sarah again.

"What can't you take?" I asked, knowing it generally had something to do with the body. But what exactly couldn't she take anymore?

"Seeing it again, I just can't take it," she sobbed, wrapping

Sly Darkness by Kya Aliana

her arms around me. "It's just, who would do a thing like that?"

"I know, shhh," I said. I knew she had a secret. Where had she seen a dead body before? She sobbed hard for the next few minutes and then slowly, it started to subside.

"We have to get out of here, now," Chad said. His deep voice startled me. I'd never heard him sound so serious before. I knew he knew something that I needed to know.

"Why? In case you can't tell, Sarah's kinda having a rough time right now," I said, pushing him to tell me what I wanted to know.

"I know, but she can have a hard time as we're walking away from here. We need to go... now," Chad demanded, looking around nervously.

"Why?" I demanded to know.

"Okay, listen, I will tell you on our way, let's just go, okay? Please," he begged, bouncing on his knees slightly.

"Okay," I said with a sigh. I helped Sarah up as she continued to sob on my shoulder.

"Come on, sweetheart, it'll be okay," I said, as soon as the words came out of my mouth, I froze. Did I really just call her *sweetheart?* No, I couldn't have. Could I? Oh no, what would she think about it? Why did I say that? What could I say to fix it? I had no idea.

"Thanks, Cowboy," she replied. Maybe she hadn't noticed... what was she thanking me for?

"Umm, guys," Vikki said. Her voice was shaky and when I looked at her, she was gripping her hair with her hands.

"What's wrong?" I asked, rushing over to her. I don't know why, but I knew something was seriously wrong. I could feel it. I could sense it. Chad caught Sarah where I'd left her. She gripped him tightly, as if she would fall down without his support. I felt a sharp twang inside me, but I ignored it. This was more important.

"There's more than one tree marked. Oh God! Oh God! We're lost. We'll never find our way back!" Vikki said, her voice getting sharper with every word.

I looked around me, seeing that it was true. We were in a

Sly Darkness by Kya Aliana

circle of marked trees. Chad and I looked at each other. I knew we were both aware. We were the only ones who were had knowledge of them. I could easily detect that *he* didn't know I understood perfectly well.

I looked around and saw the boy from my vision, marking the last tree. He smiled at me and then stepped behind the tree. I slowly walked so I could see behind it, but he was already gone.

"Chad, can I converse with you for a second, please?" I asked, my heart thudding inside my chest. He nodded and squeaked a *"yes."* He walked over toward me. We kept our voices low; I didn't want the girls to freak out completely. They were already nervous wrecks.

"I know, okay? We're in serious danger here, but at least we're next to the body and we know generally where we are. We need to stay here until we can recognize the threat, demolish it and then we'll worry about how to get back to Riverwolf Pass, okay?"

"Easier said than done. Just how exactly do you plan to demolish it?" Chad asked. His voice was quiet, but high pitched. I could tell he was really scared.

"I know what to do, don't worry," I said. I was realizing that the boy I'd been seeing wasn't actually a vision after all. He was real. He was following us. He was stalking us. He was plotting against us. This was his plan. He led us to the body, but why? He had us here, lost, confused, scared, and near a dead body, so what now? What was his next move? Nobody knew... all I could do, was my best to be prepared.

"I trust you, Zander. I'm trusting against trust. My instinct is to run, you know that?"

"Listen, if you run, he'll catch you; the one who's been following us. The... *thing*... that's been following us. We have to be smart, don't run. That's what it wants. He'll get you if you run. Don't let the darkness get you," I warned.

"The what?" I asked.

"Never mind," I said, secretly loving the adrenalin that came with the fear. I could feel it swarming off the others. I felt

Sly Darkness by Kya Aliana

alive, it was amazing. I felt like I could do anything. I knew I could. I knew I would. I was going to save the day. I knew just what to do. All that was left now was to wait. Everything would be great after that.

"Okay, but you're starting to freak me out. It's almost like you think this is a game. But, Zander, this is real," Chad said. It was like he thought I didn't know what I was talking about.

"Don't worry," I repeated myself. I walked back over to Sarah, who was sitting on the ground, staring at the body. I sat down next to her. She didn't move.

"Sarah, maybe you shouldn't look at it," I suggested. It almost felt weird to say her name. Why did it feel weird to say her name, yet earlier *sweetheart* was so easy to say? She didn't reply or move. "Sarah?" I asked. She sniffled as the tear streams against her face dried up from the harsh bitter cold that had taken over the day. I touched her shoulder, but she didn't even acknowledge it. She just sat there, staring at the body. Her mind and eyes were distant. So distant that she wasn't even conscious of what was going on around her.

"Sarah, please say something," I begged. A giant rock was being pushed up into my chest. I didn't know what to do. What should I do? This was my fault. If it wasn't for me, nobody would have gone out into the woods in search of the lost boy. If it wasn't for me, we wouldn't be lost. If it wasn't for me, some hermit freak wouldn't be stalking us in the woods right now. If it wasn't for me, nobody would be in fear right now. Most of all, if it wasn't for me, Sarah wouldn't have escaped into a different world. If it wasn't for me, Sarah would be totally responsive and conscious right now.

"Sarah, no, please, come on! Snap out of it!" I screamed, shaking her shoulders. She did nothing. Her empty eyes stared right back at me. I stopped shaking her and sat back down next to her. Her eyes adverted back to the body and she took in a small sigh.

"Sarah?" She didn't reply. I felt something hot roll down my cheek and I quickly wiped it away.

"No, Sarah, you can't do this. You have to deal with this,

Sly Darkness by Kya Aliana

you have to!" I said, starting to shake her again.

"Zander, what the hell?" Chad yelled at me, running over to me and pulling me away from Sarah.

"She's-she's-she's in shock," I said, getting a grip on myself.

"Who isn't?" Chad asked, shrugging his shoulders.

"No, I mean, literally. She's not responding," I said, urgency in my voice. Chad looked at me with sympathetic eyes.

"Zander, listen to me, it's going to be okay. She'll be okay, I promise," he said. "Just don't shake her. She's fragile; you wouldn't want to hurt her, would you?" I shook my head slowly, but something inside of me lurched.

We sat there in silence as the sun set and the darkness set in. The moon lit the woods just enough to make out shapes that passed from behind the trees.

"He's here," I stated. Chad nodded his head.

"So you can feel it too?" I nodded slowly. So this was Chad's secret. But how did he know? And why didn't he know that I knew? He probably thought he was special in some way.

There was laughing and a short rustling sound. My eyes frantically searched around me, but I saw nothing. I could hear it all around me. I had no idea which direction it was going to come from.

I picked up a thick branch from the ground beneath my feet, snapped it two and gripped it tightly. Chad eyed me suspiciously. I glanced at Vikki, who seemed completely oblivious to what was about to occur. She was too preoccupied with being lost in the woods. Little did she know, that was the very least of our problems at the moment.

It ran slow enough to where I could barely see it darting behind the trees, running from tree to tree, stopping behind them for a split second. An insane laughter rang out into the woods, echoing in my ears. I was surprised to find that it was my own. The feeling was amazing. The rush of adrenalin was empowering. I knew I could do anything and everything. I was excited for the fight that was to come. The rush I got off it was purely

Sly Darkness by Kya Aliana

indescribable. I could hear everything, every rustle of every leaf, every snap of every twig, every step it took, I could hear everything. Every. Last. Thing. And it was purely fulfilling in every aspect of the human senses. My heartbeat filled my chest, pounding the adrenalin in my veins with every thud.

It finally stepped out from behind a tree. At last, I could finally get a good look at it.

"Kurt," I said smoothly, letting his name roll off my tongue. I smiled slightly and shook my head in almost a discerning manner. "I should have known it was you," I said, closing my eyes for a second, quietly scolding myself for not catching on quicker. Kurt spread his arms wide and took a short bow as he kept eye contact with me. He smiled that famous *I got you* smile of his. I'd seen it before, time and time again.

"So, I'm just curious, how hard *is* it to be a smart vampire, Kurt? How hard is it to fool people you're human? Is it really so hard you have to go dragging a rich boy out into the woods, mark a path to his body, just so you can eat to stay alive? Hmm? Is it really Kurt? Or are you just naturally stupid?" I asked, in a very demeaning tone.

"Oh, Zander, the poor little lost boy. Poor little Zander with all the daddy issues, he's such a loner, he's so depressed, oh if only there was a way to save poor little Zander's lost soul," Kurt retorted in a daunting manner. I felt my blood start to boil in my veins; I expected blood blisters to appear on my skin at any given moment.

"At least I don't hide under people's porches because I'm scared of what I've become," I snapped.

"What the hell? You two know each other?" Chad asked. Kurt and I simultaneously turned our heads to look at him.

"Oh yeah, Kurt and I go back... 'bout six months back," I said with a laugh. "Kinda funny how a lot of things trail back to six months ago, isn't it?" I asked. I should have made that connection long ago. Of course, a fire, a police cover up, a dinner party, a mansion, how could I have been so naive?

"Didn't I turn you into a vampire?" Kurt asked after a

Sly Darkness by Kya Aliana

moment. Chad... of course! Kurt had told me about him.

"I was saved," Chad replied, his fingers nervously twitching at his side, his other hand tightly gripping the cross on his necklace.

"What's going on?" Vikki asked. Kurt, Chad and I all ignored her.

"So what, you two gonna kill us all now?" Chad asked, his voice high and shaky.

"No, of course not," I said coolly. Kurt and I went back, but we didn't go that far back.

"It's a fight!" Kurt exclaimed.

"I thought we just established that," I said, raising my eyebrows. Kurt let out a growl and his fangs appeared.

"Now now," I said. "I still want to know what your master plan is. Tell me, what happened to you that forced you to lure people out into the woods just so you can kill them?" I asked curiously.

"You have no idea how hard it is being a vampire. Having to kill people for food. Killing to live isn't all it's cracked up to be in books. I was terrified after I fed off of poor Chad here, so I hid under a porch for days and nights. Until some guy forced his hand in my mouth. I had no choice but to feed off of it, no choice at all. After that, I had the craving for blood. I was close to emaciation. I hadn't fed for days. With the taste of blood fresh in my mouth, my entire body was screaming for more. I couldn't control myself. I was more monster than human. More zombie than vampire. I couldn't disguise myself well enough on fucking Halloween, man. They recognized me, what I was, after I'd already fed on two little girls and was starting on my third. They drove me out of town. That's when I met up with you," he said, looking me dead in the eye. "After you helped me become healthy again, I came back here."

"You came back?" I nearly screamed. "After all I did for you! After all the help I gave you! After everything I taught you, you came back? You know, I'm starting to think maybe they should have put *you* in the mental hospital as opposed to that guy

Sly Darkness by Kya Aliana

who figured out what the vampires who changed you were," I said, remembering Kurt telling me his blood was heavy with meds.

"I couldn't help it. This is where I'm from; this is where I'm supposed to be. I have to live here. Riverwolf Pass is mine, all mine," Kurt said, his voice wild and over protective.

"Needless to say, they caught me again and ran me out of town, this time into the woods."

"So here you are, feeding off of boys with rich daddies, making trails to the body so you can get your next meal. Tell me, Kurt, when was the last time you fed? A week ago? You're going to turn into more of a zombie than a vampire again, you know... or have you been keeping yourself vampire by feeding off of the little helpless bunnies?"

"They're harder to catch than you might think," Kurt said with a laugh.

"Well, let me tell ya, Kurt. You're not feeding off of anybody in this group. Why don't you do yourself a favor and let me put you out of your misery and bunny chasing?" I said, clutching the wooden stake in my hand.

"Like hell I will!" Kurt said, fire dancing in his eyes. "Tell you what," he said. "I'll let you walk, with the body so you can get your reward, that way you'll have money to keep on being a loner and depressed and you can find yourself another town to drift in and out of, leaving your mark of course. And you leave these others for me to feed off of, what do say buddy?"

"First off, I'm no vampire's buddy. You're extremely lucky I helped you out. I only did it because I felt sorry for you. And second off, I'm not going to let you hurt these people."

"Oh, I suppose they're all part of your master plan, you're technique, your mark. After all, everybody's gotta mark their territory in some way," Kurt said. I could feel my blood get white hot under my skin. I was itching to drive that stake through his heart. I wanted to see his face twist up; I wanted to see his veins bulge from under his skin. I wanted to see him turn to dust as the sun hit his dead, decapitated, body in the morning.

Sly Darkness by Kya Aliana

"You know nothing about what I do, how I work, or my plans," I said, my voice was on the verge of yelling and breaking into a complete monster tone.

"What are you talking about?" Chad asked.

"Nothing," I replied, not even bothering to look at him anymore.

"Of course, you want to surprise them. What would be the fun in it if they saw it coming?" Kurt asked, smiling wide. I was about ready to kill him, literally.

"You know Kurt, I really thought that you and I were friends," I said sadly. "I'm so sorry I'm going to have to kill you now. It's just, when you lure me and my friends into the woods to feed off of us, that's where I draw the line," I said. My lips turned into a small smirk. It was no accident that I used the word friend.

"Will someone please explain to me what's going on?" Vikki demanded. Chad walked over to her and started whispering things into her ear.

"Oh don't try to comfort her, she's not worth the trouble, trust me. I've been with her type before," Kurt offered his whole-hearted advice to Chad. He, of course, ignored it.

"You about ready?" I asked, swinging the stake around in my hand.

"Come on, Zander, let's avoid this whole scene. They're not really your friends and you know that. That girl over there, she's in shock, she won't even feel anything. Vikki, there, I recognize her, slept with her a couple times. She's just a stupid sloppy second; she reads so many girly vampire books she'll probably think it's romantic that I'm gonna drink her blood. Who knows, maybe she'll even climax off of me biting her. I've always wanted to make a girl do that, you know." He wore a wry smile on his face as he talked about it. I took in a deep breath. How sick was he? I almost regretted helping him out.

"And what about Chad?" I asked, curiously.

"Easy, I'll snap his neck before I suck his blood... either that or I'll get off on the struggle and adrenalin rush he'll give us both," Kurt said with an evil smile. After that, there was no doubt

Sly Darkness by Kya Aliana

in my mind; he was already more monster than human or even vampire. This was too far, even for a creature of the night. Something had to be done about it, and I was going to put an end to it. I had to finish what I started. I had to kill what I helped to create. That was the last time I showed a vampire how to turn off all emotion... well, most emotion. Obviously he was still emotionally attached to the town of Riverwolf Pass. What was with that town? There was some sort of weird captivating draw to it... something that attracted a certain type of people aside from the normal old-timey people who lived there.

"Fuck you, they're mine!" I said strongly without thinking.

"Have it your way," Kurt said with a smile. I could tell we were both going to enjoy the fight. I loved the way the adrenaline built up inside right before I threw the first punch. Kurt's head violently whipped to the side as exhilaration exploded inside of me as I listened to the crack of his neck and the deep breath he took in. He turned to face me, a wry smile escaping the otherwise emotionally indecipherable face.

I lurched toward him, baring the stake in my hand. Kurt dodged and I fell hard on the ground. I stood up quickly and brushed off my hands on my pants. I looked around, but Kurt was nowhere to be seen.

"Come on, little Kurt. I'm not scared of a vampire like you. Just come out and fight," I demanded. He obliged and stood in front of me. His nails scraped against my chest, tearing my only shirt. Now I was pissed. Not only had he tore it, but there was also blood soaking into it. I tore off my shirt and strutted toward him. I thrust the stake at him once more, and again he dodged it. I looked around for him, he was fast, but I knew I would get him sooner rather than later. I saw him, standing in front of Sarah.

"Sarah!" I screamed just as he was going to sink his fangs into her neck. She didn't even blink. I lunged toward Kurt, knocking him over just in time. I pinned him on the ground.

"Nobody messes with her, do you hear me?" I screamed, and stabbed the stake right into his heart. He froze up, sputtered

Sly Darkness by Kya Aliana

blood and then slowly, his veins started to swell up to the point where I thought they would burst. I quickly moved away from him. Sure enough, he was one of those vampires that exploded. Fleshy pieces of vampire filled the air and came crashing down. Blood exploded and splattered all over the trees around us. Chad hunched over Vikki, saving her from getting sprayed. Afterward, Chad's hoodie was covered in vampire blood. He quickly took in off and tossed it in the fire we'd started just before dark.

    I looked over at Sarah, who was covered in vampire blood, but she remained unresponsive. What was I going to do about that? I wondered if she had even taken in what had just happened... I doubted it. I'd seen movies where people had been in shock before, and they didn't remember anything. As hard as I tried, I couldn't remember how they ever got anybody out of shock in the movies. But that didn't matter anyways, most of the times the movies weren't right.

    "I think I need to sit down," Vikki said, standing there looking very pale. I glanced over at Chad just in time to see him collapse to the ground. He fainted. Seriously? What was I going to do with these people?

    I rolled my eyes as I walked off into the woods to grab some fresh leaves to cover the vampire blood. I would clean Sarah up later with an old t-shirt and some water. I was just grateful that the sleeping bags were in the tent, safe and clean. The tent would need to be wiped down, but cleaning a tent was a lot easier than cleaning sleeping bags.

*　　*　　*

    "Okay, fill me in," I said to Chad once I was back and had everything all cleaned up.

    "On what?"

    "Six months ago," I demanded, though I doubted it had any relevance to our future.

    "The Dyebukos moved in from nowhere... it seemed to happen overnight. They watched the town from the mansion,"

Sly Darkness by Kya Aliana

Chad said dramatically.

"Yeah, but what happened?"

"I'm getting to it," he promised, drawing images in the dirt with a stick. "My best friend at the time, Ivan, he was big time into horror... he was always telling me that he had my back if vampires, werewolves, or zombies came. I guess he kept that word... but he just up and left afterward... some friend," he said, bitterness attacking his voice. "He became smitten with Latianna, the Dyebukos' daughter."

"Vampire too?" I asked.

"No, only half. On the way back from seeing her, he warned me about the vampires... I should've listened. Kurt came to me that night... he basically compelled me to let him in."

"He shouldn't have been able to do that," I stated.

"He just kept asking... how could I say no? I mean, he wasn't a close friend, but I knew him from school."

"Oh, I see," I stated.

"Yeah, I didn't remember him coming though, and I started freaking out when I felt different... My hunger consumed me, but nothing would satisfy. I called Ivan, who helped by locking me in his fucking closet for days!" Chad threw the stick across the campsite.

"At least it saved you," I said.

"Yeah, sure, with my help. He dragged me along to the fight, but I wasn't very good at it. He ended up killing the Mr. and Mrs. But his parents, they didn't make it. He was bruised up pretty bad, so I took him to the hospital and lied about how he got so bad off... and what does he do to thank me? Huh? He takes off with that good-for-nothing girl, Latianna. She wasn't even *that* pretty. I'm not sure if I'd even bang her or not," Chad scoffed, shaking his head. "He didn't even say goodbye. Just left me there, half-terrified, unsure how to explain anything to *my* parents. I couldn't just fit back in with my friends... so I started hanging out on my own.

"That's all pretty crazy," I sympathized.

"Yeah, I wouldn't put it past him to have taken off with

Sly Darkness by Kya Aliana

that crazy Mr. White! Fuck, I hope he really is crazy. Ivan was always talking bullshit about him. How he was so fucking cool, you know? All because he used to help Ivan smuggle horror books past his goddamn parents,"

"Well, any idea on where they headed?"

"Ivan always felt a weird attraction to Oklahoma... like something was there for him," Chad replied.

I smiled to myself, thinking of my home state. I wondered what was there for Ivan... if our paths would ever cross.

"But," Chad continued. "Mr. White hated that place for some reason... so I doubt they all went there if Ivan went with him."

"Hmm. Well what else did he say about Mr. White? Has he always been crazy?"

"I don't know, I never really listened," Chad said with a shrug. "Well, now you know, that's my story."

"It's not that bad... I mean, sure, it's a lot, but a couple deep breaths and Band-Aids and you'll be fine," I said with a smile.

"Huh, yeah, sure," Chad said as if his drama was bigger than anyone else's. What bullshit. He was a drama-king, that's for sure.

"Zander?" Chad asked.

"Yeah, what?"

"How was Kurt out in the sunlight? I know vampires can't be out in the sunlight."

"He wasn't... he tracked us by night, using his super senses and smells, just like I taught him to track people."

"You taught him to track people?" Chad screamed.

"Yeah, well, it's a good thing for a vampire to know," I explained with a shrug.

I couldn't believe how Kurt had fooled me like that... I saw visions of him during the day of what he'd done the night before... He knew me, he could read me... he knew what I would pick up on and what I wouldn't. He was smarter than I gave him credit for.

Kurt's words about my daddy issues rang in my ears... I

Sly Darkness by Kya Aliana

couldn't afford for my secrets to all be revealed so soon in this trip. I was finally building trust with all these people, even if it was only a little. Sharing issues too soon only caused more issues... only raised eyebrows and gave unjust suspicions.

I was so angry at Kurt for saying anything about what I did in my towns... my mark. How dare he bring up my mark! I told him all that in confidence... I trusted him too soon. I told him too much.

I hoped that Chad and Vikki wouldn't read into it too much... I supposed they wouldn't. Vikki was too stupid to, and Chad didn't exactly think Kurt was the most trustworthy sort. Maybe, just maybe, I'd lucked out.

Sly Darkness by Kya Aliana

Chapter Eleven

The fire danced in the night. Vikki and Chad had retired to the tent for the evening. No one ate anything that night; the pure shock of the day's events was enough to wipe out four teenagers' appetites. Sarah hadn't recovered from shock yet, and I was getting worried. I wished I knew what to do when someone was in shock. She wouldn't let me move her. Whenever I tried, she would always walk back, staring at the body or the fire. At least I'd gotten her to stare at the fire, but I still wasn't sure if she even registered what she was looking at. I hoped she could. The image of the body was haunting enough without being completely stuck on it.

I was getting tired as I watched the moon reach its apex and start to sink back into the sky again. The cold night wind whipped its way through my bones and I shivered. I glanced over at Sarah; she looked cold. I picked up an extra blanket and walked over to her. I draped the blanket over her shoulders and to my surprise; she gripped it tightly and pulled it around her body.

"Sarah?" I asked, sitting down next to her. She didn't say a word, but she laid her head down on my shoulder and took in a deep sigh.

"My father used to own a restaurant," she said after a minute. Her faint voice chimed through the air, as if she wasn't even talking to me... I was alarmed at how distant she sounded. I wondered if she even knew she was talking.

"Really?" I asked, hoping to get some kind of response from her. She was really starting to scare me.

"Yes, it was an Italian restaurant. He had it before we moved here," she said. Her eyes didn't move from the fire. I wished she would look at me. It felt as though she was in another dimension. The whole conversation felt surreal already.

"Where was the restaurant?" I asked. I wondered if she had to go through some familiar memories before she could come

Sly Darkness by Kya Aliana

out of shock. At least I could ask questions to help with that.

"New York City. That's where I grew up. That's where I lived all my life... until..." she trailed off. No, I couldn't lose her again, not now! Not when I was so close to breaking through.

"Until your family decided to move here?" I asked. She shook her head no.

"Until we *had* to move here," she corrected. At least she was talking, but for some reason, I felt like this was going to be a heavy conversation. This wasn't a memory; this was an issue... something that she needed to work through. This was the thing related to the dead body; this was the thing that had sent her into shock. This was the reason the body pushed her over the edge.

"You didn't want to move here?" I asked slowly, quietly. I didn't want to push her, but I also didn't want for her to slip away again. If she slipped back into shock, I didn't know how, or when, or even if she would come back out again.

"No, I didn't even know this place existed before..." she paused, a frown plagued her face, "before I had to move here," she changed her words after *before*. I knew that much. Whatever she was originally going to say after *before* was what she needed to talk about.

"Why did you have to move here?" I asked. I bit my tongue as soon as I did. I hoped I wasn't pushing her too hard.

"I started to tell you," she said, finally looking at me.

"You did?" I asked. "Could you start to tell me again?" I asked.

"My father, he owned a restaurant. We didn't know it, but the strip he opened it in was owned by the gangsters... no, the mobsters, there is a difference you know," she said, nodding her head.

"What happened between your father and the mob?" I asked. I knew it was a forward question, maybe too forward. But I didn't care, I almost felt as if I was running out of time with her.

"It's a long story," she sighed. I knew she didn't want to talk about it, but I also knew that if she was going to be okay, she didn't have a choice.

Sly Darkness by Kya Aliana

"I have time," I said. I put my arm around her shoulder and ran my hand up and down her arm. Her skin was cold, sweaty and covered in gooseflesh. I pulled her closer in hopes to warm her up and set her nerves at ease.

"I'm not supposto talk about it," she said. Ahh, one last attempt to avoid the subject.

"That's okay, I won't tell anybody," I said comfortingly. I knew anyone in that situation would probably say that, but I actually meant it. She could trust me.

"Do you promise?" she asked. I smiled to myself.

"I swear a most sacred swear," I replied earnestly. Her goosebumps were slowly vanishing, but as soon as she started to talk, they resurfaced.

"Well, at first, they just wanted a percentage of my father's profit. It seemed like a big deal at the time, but after a couple months, it just became normal. Once a week, they would come to collect, we would give them the money and everything would be happy. There were no issues..."

"Until?" I asked, knowing this was going to take some gentle cajoling.

"Until," she continued, "a few more months passed. They came back and they wanted a higher percentage now that we were on our feet. My father was reluctant, but agreed in the end. It happened three more times after that. My father became outraged. He was stressed out about everything. Money became tight. We no longer had the funds to buy the extra things. They came one more time and my father refused to give them more than they were already receiving." She paused and took in a heavy sigh.

"It's okay; it's good to talk about this. What happened when your father refused?" I asked, gently urging her to go on.

"They beat him up, and really badly too. He came home, cuts and scrapes all over, covered in blood. It wasn't a pretty scene. He scared me. I didn't know what to do. I screamed for my mother and then she started screaming too. We took him to the hospital, saying he'd been mugged. They fixed him up. There was no permanent damage... only a couple of scars from where he

Sly Darkness by Kya Aliana

required stitches." She started to cry. As much as I hated to see her cry, I knew this was good. She was coming back; she was talking about something she really needed to talk about. This was better than good, it was great. And at the same time, I felt horrible for pushing her to talk about this.

"What happened after he got out? Did the mob come back after him?" I asked. I hated to push her, but I was also ready to find out what happened next... and ultimately, it was working to jolt her back to reality.

"Of course, they're the mob. When they came back, my father agreed to higher their percentage once more. After that, life got really hard. We barely had enough money to keep food on the table. The quality in the restaurant food went down significantly as well. So that meant, we lost a lot of business. Repeat customers stopped coming as often, some at all. A few weeks in, the mob came, and my father couldn't pay them. This time, they didn't beat him up, which was scarier than if they had. We lived in constant fear for the next month. They didn't come to the restaurant, they didn't call, and we saw nothing of them. We had no clue as to what they were going to do," Sarah said. She had stopped crying and now her eyes were wide, staring at the fire... or back off into space; it was hard to say which one it really was.

"What did they end up doing?" I gently cajoled.

"They broke into the house one night. I woke up to the crash of the window breaking. I heard yelling and screaming from upstairs. I knew what was about to happen. I couldn't breathe; my heart was beating a-hundred times as fast as it should have been. I tip-toed out of my room and into my father's study where I knew he kept a handgun. I grabbed the key to the drawer from under the coffee mug he always kept in his office. I unlocked the draw and I took the gun in my hand." She stopped and took another deep breath and released it slowly. I didn't say anything. I knew she would continue when she was ready. This was the part that was hard to talk about. This was the part she had regretted coming to; I could tell by the look in her eye.

"It was the same gun that I'd been told not to touch when I

Sly Darkness by Kya Aliana

was younger than thirteen. It was the same gun that my father taught me how to shoot on my thirteenth birthday. It was the same gun that my father showed me where the key was when I was fourteen. It was the same gun that my father signed me up for a shooting class with when I was fifteen. And there I was, barely sixteen and holding it in my hands. I knew I would have to shoot it. I knew if I didn't shoot it, my father was going to die.

"It didn't take a whole lot to figure out that the mob had hired a hit-man to kill my father. I walked upstairs, light on my feet. I knew exactly where the floor creaked and where it didn't. I knew how to walk so no one could hear me coming. So that's what I did. I walked into my parents' bedroom, where the screaming was coming from. The sight I saw was..." She stopped and started crying again. I couldn't imagine how hard this had to be for her. I drew her closer and held her tight.

"It's okay, shhh, it's all okay," I whispered in her ear.

"There-there were two of them." She paused another moment to stop sobbing so hard. After a moment, she continued. "One was holding a knife to my father's throat. Another was... was... he was-" she choked down the words. I didn't even want to ask. I was scared of what the answer could be.

"He was in the bed," she said slowly. "With my mother," she finished. She couldn't stifle her sobs any longer. "Her screams," she hiccupped. "They were like no other I'd ever heard." She took another moment to get a hold on herself. My heart thudded, the liquid in my ears was hot and I could feel it spread through my entire body.

"Oh God, I am so sorry," I said, holding her tightly. "No one should ever, ever have to go through that." She nodded her head and took a few deep breaths. When she could speak without erratic pauses, she continued.

"I stood there, for a long time, unable to move. No one even noticed me. I was still and silent. I couldn't even breathe. My heart had stopped beating. I was scared. More scared than I'd ever been. I snapped out of it, though. After a couple minutes, I wasn't scared anymore. I was just mad. Everything I was feeling was

Sly Darkness by Kya Aliana

pure anger. I aimed the gun at the guy on my parents' bed. I was a really good shot; missing never occurred to me, it never happened. I shot the man dead. Blood spurted all over my mother and she screamed more.

"The man who had the knife to my father's throat and was slowly pushing it into him, released his grip on my father and frantically searched around for me. I stood against the wall. I could see in the room, but he couldn't see me. As soon as he stepped away from my father, I shot him. He saw me, his eyes flared and he reached for his gun. But he was too late; he dropped to the floor before he could grab the gun. I stepped in the doorway.

"My mother looked at me and fainted; my father ran over and hugged me. I couldn't think; all I could do was stand there. I could finally breathe, but I couldn't feel my heartbeat. I started crying and I wasn't sure why. I wasn't scared. I wasn't angry. I was something else... something in-between happy and grateful and sad all at the same time."

She looked at me for the first time. I smiled at her, sympathetic like, and brushed her hair from her eyes. She gave me a funny looking half-smile and then started to cry again. I pulled her in for a hug right before my shoulder became soaked with her tears. It was silent for a long time after that.

"You have no idea what it was like," she said. Her voice was muffled through my shirt. "Killing someone... I know they were... hurting... my mom. I know they were going to kill my dad. But seeing a dead body, knowing you killed it, knowing you took a human life, even if it was in a self-defense or family-defense or whatever it actually qualified as... it's still a horrible feeling. Since then, I've always dreamt about them. I see their dead bodies... come back to get me. Sometimes, I just remember killing them.

"My mother's screams still echo in my ears. I can't forget what it sounded like. I'll never forget how scared she was. How much they hurt her. How terrified my dad was. I'll never forget us hugging and crying together for the next two weeks as we waited for the trial. That night at the police station - We even talked to

Sly Darkness by Kya Aliana

the F.B.I. I'll never forget any of it, I can't... sometimes, it haunts me," she said.

Her eyes pleaded for help. I could tell she wanted to forget it. I could tell it was something she wanted to stop talking about it. But I could also tell that it had helped to talk to someone about it.

"Oh Sarah!" I exclaimed. I felt so horrible for her. No one should ever have to go through that.

"Don't call me that, okay? That's not my name," she said, looking at me with her big eyes.

"What do you mean?" I asked. Was she okay?

"After all that, we had to go into witness protection. That's why we moved here. They changed our look, our personalities, our names, everything. The only thing I could keep was my writing. That's why I go to the old mansion to write. It's an escape from all the memories I have. It's an escape to write about those memories in a fiction environment, with different characters, different traumas, some is exaggerated and some isn't, and some I just make up on my own. Anyway, it's my escape and my way to cope with reality and deal with things. Everyone needs one, no matter how easy their life is. They could have the life you and I dream of, and still have issues and need an escape. No matter what, you don't get out without baggage," Sarah said, looking down at the ground.

"I understand. I write too, that's my escape. I keep a journal," I said. "And I sketch." She smiled at me and I knew everything would be okay between us. "So, what's your real name?" I asked.

"Azalea," she replied, smiling at me.

"Azalea," I repeated. I loved how that sounded. It was so much better than *Sarah*. It fit her more. How could the witness protection give such an extraordinary girl such a mundane name? It seemed almost cruel.

"Only, you can't call me that in front of anybody else," she said. I nodded.

"I know. You can trust me," I promised. She smiled at me

Sly Darkness by Kya Aliana

and trailed her hand along my cheek.

"I've never been able to trust anybody before," she said. She nudged her face closer to mine. I wanted to kiss her. Every bit of me wanted to kiss her. She wanted to be kissed. This was the perfect moment. I wondered why I didn't take it.

"You should get some sleep," I said, standing up. "I'll grab a sleeping bag and a few extra blankets." I walked over to the side of the tent and grabbed two sleeping bags and the blankets. I set it up so we were right next to each other, right near the fire. I couldn't sleep in the same sleeping bag as her tonight. I just couldn't. If I tried, something would happen and I knew that.

"Oh, okay," she said, looking down. I knew she wanted to. But, I could only let her trust me as much as I trusted me... and I didn't trust myself enough to sleep so close to her again tonight.

We cuddled into our own, separate, sleeping bags. It took me a while to fall asleep. I watched Sarah breathe and listened to it slow and lighten as she slept. Her face was in the other direction, but I could still picture it, bright and full of life. It didn't seem fair that she had to go through so much... especially when she didn't do anything to deserve it.

Chapter Twelve

"What happened to my clothes?" Azalea asked when she woke up. The sun had already risen, a beautiful sunrise with lots of pink. I wondered what that meant. They were beautiful, but for as long as I could remember, that was a warning. *Pink in the morning; a loner's warning.* The line repeated in my head all morning. What did the day hold?

"Good morning, Azalea," I said, loving saying her real name. It felt better than calling her Sarah.

"Good morning to you too, Cowboy, but seriously, what's with these new clothes?"

"We had to burn them," I said, rolling over to face her. I didn't want to get out of my sleeping bag. It was warm and comfortable in there. I wondered if that was how caterpillars felt right before they turned into butterflies.

"Uh, why?" she asked. "And where did these come from?"

"They're Victoria's, leave it to her to have a whole wardrobe in her pack," I said. Azalea nodded slowly. "I picked the ones that I thought looked most like you and the least slutty." I smiled wide.

"Thanks..." she said slowly, as if she was unsure if she should thank me. "But, what happened to my clothes?"

"I told you, we had to burn them," I replied.

"Why?" she asked. She sounded like she was becoming frustrated.

"How much do you remember about yesterday?" I asked, raising my eyebrows.

"Not much. I think I kinda blanked out," she said.

"I'd say," I said, almost a little too strongly.

"I remember seeing the body, going and crying behind the tree, and then I don't remember anything until you and I were talking by the fire last night."

"Yeah, you missed a lot. It's pretty heavy, I'm not sure if I

Sly Darkness by Kya Aliana

should tell you or not. Seems like you're dealing with a lot right now." She smiled at me and thanked me.

"I guess I'd rather not know anyways," she said. I smiled.

"I thought that could be the case," I said with a wry smile.

I loved how well I knew her. I felt like we would make a great team. I almost wished that it had only been her and I who had gone out into the woods together. If that had been the case, we would be so much closer. Chad wouldn't have been a factor in the beginning. At least he wasn't now that he was back together with Vikki.

If it had been just her and I, it would have been a true vacation for me. I wouldn't be so plagued with these horrors following me. I wouldn't have to help the world, or do my rightful job. I wouldn't have to... *No,* I thought to myself, *just let it all play out. Don't plan it. You know what you have to do. It's just a matter of doing it now. You know these people now; you can trust what their future would be like.*

Azalea and I talked a while before Chad and Vikki made it out of the tent for the day. Vikki came out first and started to complain about there not being breakfast. I climbed out of my sleeping bag and went over to the pack with the food in it. I started to cook some hot dogs while Azalea rolled up the sleeping bags and folded the blankets.

I listened to Vikki complain about how hot dogs were not a breakfast food.

"Well," I said to her after I was really sick and tired of listening to her obnoxious voice. "If you slice them up into little rounds, maybe you can pretend that it's sausage... that's a breakfast food, isn't it?"

"Why do you have to be so mean, Zander?" she asked after a moment of taking that in.

"Why do you have to complain about every little thing, Vikki?" I asked with a smile. Vikki rolled her eyes and stomped her foot.

"That," I said with a smirk, "was real mature." I laughed as she stuck her nose up in the air and went back into the tent

Sly Darkness by Kya Aliana

where Chad was.

Azalea approached me slowly. She crouched down so she was sitting next to me as I bent over the fire, frying the hot dogs in the pan that we had.

"I want to thank you," she said, resting her hand on my shoulder. I felt the jolt of electricity flow through me again. I wondered if this was what it was like with every girl who meant something to you. Sure, I'd kissed girls before, but I'd never cared about them as much as I cared about Azalea.

"For?" I asked, standing up and pulling her up with me.

"For letting me talk to you last night. I really needed to talk to someone about that. My parents won't even talk to me about it," she said, looking really sad.

"Why not?" I asked.

"They like to act like it didn't happen. They pretend that we've always lived here. They pretend like it's always been like this. It's maddening sometimes."

"Oh, Azalea, that's so not fair! You're going through so much. You're working through everything you have to deal with because of what happened. You should at least be able to talk to your *parents* about it," I said, grabbing her shoulders firmly.

"At least I can talk to you now," she said. "You have no idea how much that means to me."

"You have no idea how much it means to me that you're willing to talk about it," I said, pulling her in for a hug. I felt her chest press against mine and a cool shiver ran through my body.

"Careful, you wouldn't want to burn those hot dogs. We all know how short on food we are." Chad's voice startled me and I jumped away from Azalea - or Sarah as he knew her. I had to remember that nobody else knew she was Azalea. I had to remember not to call her that in front of Chad and Victoria. It would take a lot. I loved the name Azalea so much. And it fit her so well. I just wanted to sing it from the rooftops, but of course, I couldn't do that. First off, there weren't any rooftops around here, and secondly, no one could know her real name.

"Right, hot dogs, yes," I said, pulling them off the fire.

Sly Darkness by Kya Aliana

Lucky for me, they weren't burnt.

We ate in silence. Nobody was sure what to say. Finally, Azalea spoke up.

"So what's the plan for today?" she asked.

"Oh yeah, that's right. You don't remember," Vikki said, almost in a cruel tone. "We're lost."

"What do you mean we're lost?"

"Zander, why don't you explain it to her? You two seem so close," Chad said, glaring at me.

"Uhh, okay," I said slowly. What was he hinting at? "Anyways, Sarah, we were being followed. Hector wasn't actually the one who marked the trees. It was the guy who killed him,"

"Hector was murdered?" Azalea asked. She sounded more alarmed than I expected her to. I nodded my head slowly. Hoping this wouldn't set her off again. She nodded slowly, taking a deep breath. "Anyways," I continued. "I took care of it. He's not following us anymore. But the thing is, he was the one to mark the trees... and he marked more than just the path back home. So now, we're in the circle of a whole bunch of marked trees and we have no idea where we are," I finished. Azalea looked at me with nervous eyes.

"So... we're lost... in the woods... with a dead body... and we have no communication with the outside world... what the hell are we gonna do?" she asked. I almost swore that I could hear her heart beating faster than ever.

"I've been trying my cell phone, but there's no reception in these woods!" Victoria complained.

"Well, duh, it's the woods," I said. I almost felt bad for her. Had she even known what she was getting into when she came out here?

"So, I think we should start walking in some general direction. We should at least pick a path to follow and try and figure out some familiar sights or something," Azalea suggested. It was the best suggestion I'd heard so far.

"I say we should stay here. We're four missing teens. They're going to send out a search party for us. If we wait here, they'll probably find us," Chad said.

"No, they won't. They didn't find Hector, did they?" I said.

"So? That doesn't mean they won't find us. Besides, if we move, we'll just get more lost."

"We're already lost, so what's the biggie?" Vikki asked, rubbing Chad's shoulders. He pushed her off.

"Knock it off," he demanded.

"Geesh, I just don't see the big deal about trying to find our way back. Besides, if we're trying to find our way back, and they're trying to find us, we'll probably find each other along the way." I know it was crazy, but that sounded like the smartest thing Vikki had said since I'd known her.

"Okay," Chad sighed.

"Great, now let's start packing so we can get a good long day of walking in," Azalea said. I nodded in agreement and started to pack my stuff in my backpack.

"Listen," Chad said once Azalea and Vikki were out of ear shot.

"Yeah?" I asked, looking him in the eye. He looked mad.

"I know yesterday was hard on Sarah, seeing that dead body and all. And I appreciate all you did to help her and comfort her. But listen, you have to back off. She's still mine. I called her. You're not allowed to have her."

"What?" I replied. "You can't *call* a girl! She's not a goddamned seat in a car, Chad!"

"You heard me," Chad said, stuffing his oversized sweater into his backpack. "Don't get all bullshitty feminist whatever on me. It won't do any good."

But something must be done about it... if you can't change him... do your job. My thoughts spiraled in a downward rant, going off on Chad and how I wished I could make him see things my way.

"But I thought you and Vikki were back together," I said after a moment spent getting a grip on myself.

"Ha!" Chad said, getting closer to my face. "This is a stupid camping trip. The fact that we're back together is just for

Sly Darkness by Kya Aliana

shits and giggles. It doesn't mean anything. It's a total meaningless fuck. I know you understand," Chad said with a wink.

"What I understand," I said slowly. "Is that you are nothing but a stupid, ex-quarterback, meat-head jock who's anything but trustworthy and serious. You're just a dumb high school teenager who doesn't think things all the way through and uses girls for his own pleasure without even thinking about anything else. You know, it may come to your surprise, but girls have feelings too. Even girls like Victoria. They *all* have feelings, and *none* of them deserve to be used like you're using them. You wanna hate their attitude, fine. You don't wanna be with them, fine. But if you wanna pretend like you're with them just so you can get a meaningless fuck out of it, that's not fine. That's not okay. It's not even acceptable. And I will be damned if I let Sarah be with you or any other guy like you," I said.

I never raised my voice, but my tone was serious enough that he cowered in front of me... it only lasted a second, but he cowered none the less. After that second, his face rose back, his eyes locking with mine. His face was a hard grimace.

"Fine, you wanna play that way, it takes two," he said, giving me the death stare. I smiled. It was on.

I walked over to Azalea and took her hand.

"You ready?" I asked, sweetly staring into her eyes. She nodded slowly.

"Um," she started as Chad and Vikki walked over toward us.

"What is it?" Chad asked, smiling at her and giving her an intimate look with his puppy-dog brown eyes. I cast him a glare. Azalea wouldn't fall for that. She couldn't fall for that. She was so much deeper than that. He would have to talk to her if he wanted her to fall for him... right?

"I was just wondering how we were going to uhh..." she stuttered over her words. I wished I knew what she was going to say, that way I could help her.

"Carry the body with us?" Chad asked, finishing her

Sly Darkness by Kya Aliana

sentence. She nodded, smiling at him and looking at him from under her long eyelashes. I felt like screaming at myself. Azalea and I had made such a strong connection. She trusted me. She talked to me. I was good and didn't do anything she didn't want me to do... I know I kissed her that night when we were both pretty wasted, but that didn't count, right? Besides, she didn't even remember that. I couldn't lose her to Chad's silver tongue. He'd obviously had a lot of experience with making girls fall for him. He knew the right things to say. He knew how and when to say them. He knew just the right looks to give. He was even in that coming out of being depressed state that girls ate up.

Why didn't I kiss her last night? I felt stupid for not doing so. What had stopped me? Why hadn't I just planted one on her?

"Exactly," Azalea said with a brilliant smile. I'd missed what Chad had said to make her agree with him. I wanted to punch Chad in the face right then. How dare he! He knew that Azalea and I had something unspoken. If he didn't know that, he wouldn't have approached me earlier that morning. Why did he have to be so mean? Why did he even care so much?

"Okay, we need an old blanket to wrap the body in, and then Chad and I will take turns carrying it," I said. Azalea giggled.

"Weren't you listening?" she asked. "That's what Chad just said." She giggled and covered her mouth while looking at Chad with sly eyes.

"Okayokay, whatever," I said, bustling past everybody to get to get an extra blanket. I listened to Chad and Azalea talk, laugh, and giggle as I maneuvered the body on the blanket and smartly wrapped it around.

"Anybody know where a little extra rope or something is?" I asked. I saw Chad holding a rope already. He then made some sexist joke relating to bondage. I sighed and rolled my eyes. A twang of pain shot through me as I saw Azalea blush. That wasn't fair. I wanted to be the one to make her blush. I wanted to be the one to make her smile, giggle, laugh, cover her mouth, and bite her lip. I wanted to be the one who got all the flirty looks from her... the one that she sighed over. The only thing I had on Chad was that she'd cuddled with me in the night. But, that didn't mean a whole lot when nothing happened. Oh, how I regretted not kissing her. What had come over me? Why hadn't I?

Nobody answered my question, so I walked over to Chad and took the rope from his hands.

"In case anybody forgot, we're tying up a dead body here. We're lost in the woods. Not to mention, we're officially out of water and we're in desperate need of food," I said, looking from Azalea, to Chad, to Vikki, and then turning around to go tie the blanket on the dead body.

"Gawd, excuse us for trying to make light of it," Vikki called after me. I turned to face her.

"It's nothing to make light of, Victoria. In fact, it's incredibly serious and I think we should all get a grip on that."

"I think you need to get a grip, Zander, we're only laughing," Vikki said. I sighed and continued to tie the rope around the body.

I heard footsteps from behind me and felt a hand on my shoulder.

"Are you okay, Cowboy?" I turned to see Azalea there. I nodded my head.

"Don't worry, just go on having fun with your friends," I said, brushing her hand off my shoulder.

I turned around and lifted up the dead body. I felt bones crack as they hit my hard shoulder. The body was strangely light. I knew that it'd decayed some, but it didn't seem like it should be *that* light. Then I remembered he'd been killed by a vampire. That meant he'd been drained of blood. That explained a lot. I hoped Chad wouldn't say anything to Azalea about Kurt. It didn't seem fair to burden her with things she didn't need to know. If she thought about vampires and knew they were real, it couldn't help her life or her stress level.

"Hey, listen, I wasn't trying to make you mad. And if you're upset because we're laughing and trying to make ourselves feel better, you need to get over yourself, because that's not being

Sly Darkness by Kya Aliana

a good friend," she said, waving her finger in my face. I pushed it aside and walked to the head of the pack.

"You guys ready?" I asked.

"I guess," Chad said. I didn't care if they were or weren't. I started walking, following a trail of marked trees.

* * *

"This all looks familiar!" Azalea complained after a couple hours.

"It is hard to tell if we're on the right path," Chad said, sympathizing with her.

"I think we're going in circles," Vikki whined, bringing up the back.

"Whatever. We're going to follow this trail until it stops," I said, switching the shoulder I had the body on.

"I'm tired. Can't we take a break? We've been walking for hours," Azalea said, looking at me with hopeful eyes.

"Okay, one five minute break," I said, dropping the body and sitting down to take a breather.

"Geesh, Zander, you could be a little more respectful," Azalea said, looking at the sheet that covered the body of Hector.

"You wanna carry it for two hours?" I asked, raising my head from my chest. She shook her head and I tucked my head back down, resting my arms on my knees.

"I'll carry it, Zander," Chad's voice came from behind me. I bit my cheek and tried not to scream out in frustration.

"Thanks," I muttered.

"I'm gonna try and find a river or something," Azalea said and started to walk away.

"Don't go too far. We don't need to be separating and getting even more lost, especially from each other," I said. Azalea nodded and then walked off.

"Be careful!" Chad called after her. I heard Azalea's cheerful laugh ring through the woods.

"What are you doing?" I asked, turning toward Chad.

Sly Darkness by Kya Aliana

"Telling her to be careful," Chad said innocently. I gritted my teeth. "Just don't forget," Chad said, looking at me. "You started this. The night you let her sleep in your sleeping bag, you started this."

"Nothing happened!" I exclaimed harshly.

"Obviously, or she wouldn't be so willing to fall for my meaningless sweet talk. Just you watch, by tomorrow night I'll have gotten in her pants. Just you wait." His eyes glinted like fire and a smile tore at his lips. I didn't even want to start to imagine what he was thinking.

I breathed hard as I watched Azalea approach Chad and I. She walked right past me and over to Chad.

"I found a river not too far away. We should bring our water bottles and fill them up; the water is delicious!" she exclaimed.

"You drank it?" I gasped. She looked at me with a confused look.

"Aren't *you* thirsty?" she asked.

"Yes, but any river water should be boiled prior to drinking," I said, rolling my eyes. "Didn't they at least teach you that in girl scouts or something?" I scowled.

"I never joined the girl scouts," Azalea replied harshly. "But I do know a thing or two about the woods and drinking water from the river. As long as you get it from a mini waterfall, as long as it falls over a small group of rocks, it's okay to drink. But you're absolutely right, boiling it works well too," Azalea said with a small smirk on her face.

"That doesn't make any sense," I protested.

"The rocks act as a natural filter. You don't want to drink from stagnant water, flowing water is much safer," Azalea said very matter of factual. I wondered where a New York City girl like her learned something like that.

"Wow, that's really cool. I'd love to know where you learned that," Chad said, looking deep into her eyes. I watched her blush and her feet scurry back and forth awkwardly. A tiny giggle escaped her lips.

Sly Darkness by Kya Aliana

"I went on this outward bound thing in Main one time," she said, smiling. "I really didn't want to at first, but I learned a lot of really cool stuff in the end. It was all so helpful, especially during this trip. And it was way more fun than I expected it to be," Azalea said. Her eyes had a dreamy gloss to them and she bit her lip as she listened to Chad go off on how that was so cool. I rolled my eyes. I was starting to get sick of this.

"Okay, how about you show us where this river is," I said, standing, picking up the body with me. Azalea cast a glance at Chad and he looked at me.

"Oh, don't worry about that. Here, it's my turn to carry it," Chad said, dropping his pack and taking the body from me.

"Thanks," I said under my breath. It would hurt my ego too much to say it any louder than I did.

"Sure thing," Chad said, patting me on the back. He hoisted the body like it was nothing. He cast a look of surprise and question at me. I gave him a look that said *think, dummy*. Sure enough, I could see that the answer came to mind pretty quickly, it was written all over his face. I nodded at him and then continued to follow Azalea deeper into the woods.

About three minutes later, we came across the river. It was gorgeous, crystal clear water flowing gently all over rocks and down into a small pool of water.

"I know we haven't gone that far today, but it's so beautiful here, what if we just set up camp early and stayed here today?" Azalea asked hopefully. I wondered why she seemed so eager to stop early.

"It'd be best if we didn't. We're running out of food pretty quickly," I said.

"Okay, so we'll skip lunch, that leaves hot dogs for dinner tonight and lunch and dinner tomorrow, for breakfast we can have trail mix and then end of the beef jerky," Azalea replied with a content smile.

"And what about after that?"

"Hopefully we'll be back in Riverwolf Pass before we have to figure that out," Azalea said optimistically.

Sly Darkness by Kya Aliana

"But what are the chances of that?" I asked.

"Zander, chill out, it's been hard on everybody today and yesterday. I think Sarah's right, we need an early dismissal today," Chad said, looking at me with a wry smile. Was he in on this too? What had he and Azalea concocted together?

"This isn't school, Chad, this is real life and we're in a real life detrimental situation. We can't just get an *early dismissal*," I said, gritting my teeth.

"Please, Cowboy, I really just need a break right now. I think everybody does. Besides, it's not like we're lost anymore," Azalea said.

"I'd like to know how you figure that," I said curiously. Just what made her think that we weren't lost anymore?

"Well, I saw a river just like this one in the backyard of the mansion. If we follow this, it'll lead us right back to Riverwolf Pass," Azalea said with a smile. She looked proud of herself.

"Sarah," I said. It sounded weird to call her Sarah now that I knew it wasn't her name. But, then again, come to think of it, it always felt weird to call her Sarah.

"There are tons of rivers in the woods, and they all look alike. What makes you think this is the one that leads back to the mansion?" I asked.

"Well, it's better than picking randomly marked trees to follow, if you ask me. But I guess that's just my opinion," she almost screamed at me. I could tell she was really frustrated. Maybe we really did need to call it a day... even if it was stupid because we'd only been walking for two hours.

"I agree with Sarah, I think we should give it a chance," Chad chimed in. Of course he agreed with her. If she said pigs could fly he'd agree with her just because she said it.

"Yeah, we should follow this river for sure," Vikki said, sitting down and glancing at her nails. She looked at them pitifully.

"What's wrong, princess, you got dirt under your nails? Whatever will we do?" I asked.

"God, Zander, you don't have to be so mean to her!"

Sly Darkness by Kya Aliana

Azalea snapped at me. She threw her arms up in frustration and walked off into the woods. Chad dropped the dead body, even more disrespectfully than I had, and followed her into the woods.

Sly Darkness by Kya Aliana

Chapter Thirteen

"Well, that went well," Vikki said, smiling at me.

Azalea and Chad had been gone for a long ten silent minutes. I wondered what they were doing. I wondered when they would be back.

"You know," Vikki said, after I didn't acknowledge her last comment. "It really wouldn't hurt if you learned some tact."

"Tact is for people who care," I said.

"You mean to tell me you don't care about Sarah?" Vikki asked. The smile she wore was sly and her eyes said she knew something I didn't want her to know.

"Well, I mean, sure I care about her. I care about all of you. That's why I didn't let Kurt kill you guys yesterday... even if I could have walked off on my own with the body, collect the reward, and say I never even knew you guys," I said. Maybe everything I did would finally sink into her thick skull.

"Yeah, yeah, we all know you're human, Zander," Vikki said. "You stay out in the woods long enough with anyone and you start to care about them at least a little bit. But what I mean is don't you care *care* about Sarah?" What was it with teenagers repeating a word twice? It was like they thought saying it twice intensified the meaning of the word. That made no sense to me. Just what were teenage girls thinking half the time? I wasn't sure I really wanted to know the answer to that question.

"Whatever," I said.

"Oh come on, that's why you've been all pouty all day long. Any girl will tell you that you're just jealous. You and Sarah have been talking to each other. Sleeping next to each other whether anything happened between you two or not, like sex you know, it still builds a connection. Not to mention, she actually trusts you. And you wanna know something else? I think you trust her too. And now that Chad is showing an interest in her, you're

Sly Darkness by Kya Aliana

jealous, and mad, and angry, and don't know what to do. Besides, it's not like you can be debonair like Chad, it's just not in your nature," Vikki said. I thought about what she was saying and it was all true. I wondered how she knew all that. I was quiet for a moment.

"I mean, let me know if I'm wrong on anything here," she said, looking at me. She expected me to respond.

"How did you know all that?" I asked.

"Please, it's written all over your face. Besides, it's not like I'm actually as shallow as I let on to be. Sure I throw it around sometimes, but that doesn't mean I can't be deep and have insight. I just like to have fun and be rebellious too," Vikki said.

"So why do you do that? Why did you sleep with Chad when you know that he doesn't actually care about you?" I asked.

"Because I have nothing better to do. Besides, it feels good and it lets me know that at least someone notices that I'm here. I mean, sometimes, it's like no one even notices me, at home I mean. Sometimes I can be sitting in the same room as my dad, and it's like he doesn't even know I'm sitting there. Sometimes, I even wonder if he knows I exist. It used to be like that at school too.

"But then as soon as I grew boobs, the boys started to notice me. It was the first time since I could remember that I'd received some good attention. Everything I do at home for attention only got me grounded or yelled at or even..." she paused and blinked back a few tears.

"Sometimes he even hit me. I told myself for so long that it was only because he loved me. It was only because he wanted what was best for me. He was only trying to teach me right from wrong. That's all..." she said, pausing again. "But now I watch it happen to my little sister, and it's like I'm going through it all over again. I see that he's wrong. I see that he can't possible understand us. I see that he never will. And it makes me so sad," she said, unable to hold back the tears anymore.

For the first time since I'd met her, I saw Victoria for the person she was. I saw why she did the things she did. I saw her

Sly Darkness by Kya Aliana

reasoning and I saw that she too was a real person. She had issues just like we all did. She had secrets, just like we all did. And she needed someone to talk to... just like we all did.

"Whoa," I said, a little taken aback that she was talking to me about this.

"Yeah, but anyways. I grew boobs and the boys looked at me. They talked to me and asked me out. It was the first good attention I'd gotten that I could remember. Even when I was little, and I mean real little, I'd get yelled at for getting into things I wasn't supposto. And the more provocatively I dressed, the more good attention I got from the boys at school. When I hit high school, I started dating, and kissing, and it got a little out of control one night. That's when I got my bad rep, but it didn't matter to me because even more boys came to me to ask me out. I guess it's just a whole big circle cycle from there on," Vikki said, drying her eyes.

"You know, you don't have to do that for good attention," I said.

"But I do," she disagreed.

"Why?"

"Because I've tried to stop, but it doesn't work. I just end up getting depressed and becoming emo. Eventually I end up cutting myself just to make sure that I still have feelings. To make sure I'm still here. To make sure that someone will notice me. Let me tell you, if there's one things parents notice and recognize, it's blood. Then I think about killing myself, and that's where it all goes bad and I end up scaring myself back into being like this. Trust me, it's my best option."

I didn't know what to say. I didn't know what to do. I didn't know anything at that moment. I didn't know what she should do either.

"But I'll be damned if I don't get out of Riverwolf Pass the moment I turn eighteen. I'm gonna go someplace where nobody knows my name, some place where nobody knows about my rep or my family or anything and I'm gonna start fresh. I'm gonna open an art gallery. I'm a pretty good painter, you know. People

Sly Darkness by Kya Aliana

are gonna love my art and one day I'm going to be a respected artist whose work is sought after and sells for hundreds, maybe thousands of dollars," she said in a dreamy tone of voice.

I smiled at her. I hoped that everything would work out for her. I stood up; I was going to start setting up the tent and get a fire started. Azalea was right. Today, we needed to call it quits early.

"Oh, wait, I almost forgot to tell you what I meant to when I started this conversation," Vikki said. I turned back around and sat down next to her.

"Yes?" I asked.

"Don't let Sarah get together with Chad. You have to do everything you can to make that not happen. Don't worry about me getting hurt by Chad, I know he's a jerk-off, but Sarah doesn't. She's sweet and innocent. If they get together, she's going to get hurt. But I know you're a good guy. If I didn't think you and Sarah were meant to be, I might consider changing the way I act so I could make you my boyfriend," she said with a smile.

"Thanks," I said. "No pressure then."

"Don't worry, she feels a connection with you... all she feels with Chad is a case of the butterflies. He has a silver tongue... but silver tongues are no match for real chemistry," she said with a smile. She rested her hand on mine. "I mean that," she said, looking into my eyes.

"Am I interrupting something?" Azalea's smooth voice cracked behind me. I turned to see her walking up behind me with Chad.

"No, not at all," I said, jumping up. "Look, if you want to rest here for today, then I guess we can afford it," I said, it took everything I had inside me to allow that to occur.

"Thanks, Cowboy," she said with a grin.

"Just don't go whining to me when we run out of food," I said sharply. I had to remain right about something.

"Don't worry, Cowboy, we'll find our way back before we completely run out," she assured, resting her hand on my shoulder. I nodded and bit my tongue. I hoped she was right. I

Sly Darkness by Kya Aliana

didn't want to have to deal with three whiny teenagers all because they didn't want to keep going today. I knew I could handle it; I'd gone days without food before. I doubted that they ever went one day in their entire lives without dinner.

"Hey Zander, what do you say we head out and start collecting some firewood? I think it'd be good to keep it going all night tonight. I have this feeling it's going to be super cold," Chad noted, pulling Azalea closer to him and rubbing his hand up and down her arm. I took in a deep breath and tried not to let it bother me so much.

"That sounds great," I said as I walked past him, trying to shake the image of Azalea and Chad together as a couple.

"You girls stay here and start getting things all set up. Zander and I will be back soon," he said, slowly dragging his fingers through Azalea's hair. He looked into her eyes with a look that I think was supposed to pass as meaningful. He walked over to me and we started to go off into the woods together.

"So, I guess you and Sarah aren't as close as you thought, huh?" he said once we were far enough away from the girls. I gritted my teeth, unsure of what to say. My alpha-male dominating instinct was to hit him. Just who did he think he was, trying to pick up Azalea like that? She was *obviously* mine. No matter who actually liked her *first*. That was such horse shit. She *connected* with *me*. Chad should be able to understand that. He just should.

"Okay, maybe we shouldn't talk about Sarah anymore," Chad suggested, eying me suspiciously.

"That would be very smart," I said, tilting my head to the side as I looked at him.

"Are you threatening me?" he asked, his stance didn't back down. I wasn't scared of him.

"Should I be?" I asked, crossing my arms. Chad shook his head slowly. I smiled smugly to myself. "That's good, Chad, that's real good," I said. It was silent for a few minutes, excusing the snapping of twigs and branches as we collected firewood for later that night.

Sly Darkness by Kya Aliana

"So, how did you find out about vampires anyways?" Chad asked. "It doesn't seem likely that Kurt was the first, seeing as you helped him learn how to become one." I nodded my head. It was a fair question. That didn't mean I wanted to tell Chad the answer.

"I've been on my own since I was fourteen. With the heightened interest in supernatural creatures with teenagers these days, do you really think it to be unlikely that I wouldn't run into one eventually?" I asked.

"Guess that seems fair. I still don't understand why you would teach a vampire how to be a vampire. Why not just kill it?"

"What reason would I have for that?" I asked. "He was already dead."

"But he kills people. You could have saved Hector's life if you'd just killed Kurt. Do you always help out vampires?"

"Listen Chad, some things remain a mystery even to me. I have no problem with vampires. They're just part of life, they're creatures too. They're animals, just like you and me, cats and dogs. Some are just better than others. To be honest, I took pity on Kurt. I thought he'd be one of the smarter ones... I guess I was wrong. But if you're asking me if I regret not killing him earlier, I'd have to say no. It's just the circle of life, bud. I'd get used to it if I were you. Spend your time focusing on the more important things... you never know when your time could be up. I mean, one false move and, pow--" I turned with the machete in my hand and whacked it against the tree that Chad stood against. His eyes were wide with fear and he couldn't control his breathing. I smiled.

"And you're dead," I finished, slipping the machete back into the case that hung on my belt.

"You," Chad said after a moment. "Could have killed me!"

"But I didn't. That's the important thing," I said. Chad gritted his teeth.

"So, I guess I should stop flirting with Sarah?" he asked.

"I didn't say that," I said with a smile. I was happy that he picked up on my vibe.

"But you implied it," he insisted.

Sly Darkness by Kya Aliana

"Did I?" I asked turning to face him.

"You threatened me! You basically just said if I moved farther with her I'd be dead." Chad exclaimed, I knew he was trying to get me to admit that I was threatening him.

"I did?" I asked. "How very interesting that you jumped to that conclusion," I said with a smirk on my face.

"You knew I would!" he snapped at me. Dropping the firewood in his arms and marching toward me.

"So, you're saying I know what you're going to think?" I asked, raising my eyebrows high on my forehead. "Sorry to disappoint you Chad, but not even vampires can read minds, you know. Your thoughts are your own, you choose them, you have them, and you can share them, or keep them private. The choice is yours Chad; I can't control what you think, or how you think, or even what you do. All I can do is look out for my friends, my potential girlfriend, people I care about... I can't control how you think or act."

"You've never been so right before in your life. I'll do whatever I want, Zander, and you can't stop me. You can't even stop me and Sarah from being together," Chad insisted. I smiled.

"Just be careful, Chad, natural consequences do exist. Not to mention, accidents happen. We wouldn't want any accidents on this escapade into the woods, now would we, Chad?" I asked.

His eyes were big, and scared. I felt adrenaline rush over my entire body. I could feel his adrenaline soaring through his veins. I could feel it so much, it was almost like it was becoming mine; I was feeding off of it, sucking it dry.

"Accidents? What kind of accidents? What are you talking about, Zander?" Chad asked.

"One wrong move, Chad," I said, turning back around and picking up some heavy logs that would burn for a long time. I could hear Chad gulp. I could almost hear his heart beat faster than a bunny rabbit's. I could feel his panicked energy. I could feel everything. The woods were alive and so was I. In fact, I'd never felt so alive in my entire life. It felt like I was finally waking up. I couldn't wait to see where that feeling brought me.

Sly Darkness by Kya Aliana

What would happen because of that feeling? Something was going to happen that night, I just knew it.

"I think we have enough firewood now," Chad said, or more like squeaked.

"If you say so," I said with a shrug, grabbing a few more small logs and hoisting them into my arms. I stood there for a moment looking at Chad. "Well, after you," I said with a smile.

"Oh, I don't think so," Chad said strongly. "I'll be following, thank you very much."

"Have it your way," I said and started to walk back to camp with a very wry smile. Wes Determan Jr. was right; the sly darkness was out here. I just never thought it would be so fun, so sly, so filling, and fulfilling. It was absolutely incredible. It made me feel alive. The woods were full of mystery and so was I.

Sly Darkness by Kya Aliana

Chapter Fourteen

Back at camp, Azalea and Vikki had set up the tent nicely. They had also dug a pit for the fire and even drug a few rocks and large logs over for sitting purposes.

"This looks absolutely amazing, Sarah," Chad said, walking over to her and cupping her face in his hands. He looked over at me. Malicious intent gleamed in his eyes.

"Vikki helped," Azalea said, her eyes searching around for Vikki. I looked around too, but I didn't see Victoria anywhere.

"Where is she?" I asked.

"I... don't know," Azalea replied, looking around in a very confused manner. I wasn't happy that Vikki was suddenly missing, but I was happy that Azalea seemed to be so perturbed about her disappearance, that she had thrown Chad's hands off her face.

"Don't worry, I'll find her," Chad said, sounding like it took more bravery than it actually did.

"Find who?" Vikki's voice came from the edge of the woods.

"You!" Chad exclaimed, running over to her. "Are you okay? What happened? Where did you go? Who took you? Is there more than one? Who's following us this time? Did you see his face? Or maybe it's a girl?"

"Chad, chill, you're starting to act crazy and you sound like it too."

"Sorry, it's just you had us so worried," Chad said, glancing at Azalea, who was rolling her eyes and shaking her head at him.

"I was gone for like two minutes. I just went to brush my teeth, that's all," she said with a shrug.

"Oh," Chad said, his cheeks turning redder by the second. "I see."

"Gawd, you're started to sound as crazy as Wes Determan

Sly Darkness by Kya Aliana

Junior," she said, walking past him.

"What did Wes Determan Jr. say to you?" I asked, curiosity rising up in me.

"Well, he's constantly talking about these woods to kids. Telling us not to go out here, to stay away from the mansion, the graveyard, and the railroad tracks. Says something about the dark, I don't know," Vikki said, flopping down on one of the blanket mats that were spread out on the ground.

"Huh," I said, thinking to myself. I wondered what Wes Determan Jr. had been through... I wondered what he'd seen, experienced, witnessed. It had to be interesting. I hoped I would one day get a chance to talk to him about some things. Who knew, maybe I could actually learn something from him... or at least gather a few ghost stories to tell around a campfire.

"So, anyways, what are we planning on doing until tomorrow?" Vikki asked, glancing at me.

"I don't know! Why is everybody looking at me?" I asked.

"Well, you're the one who had the beer last time," she said with a shrug.

"Yeah, and you're the one who helped me take it out, so you should know there's none left," I said, sitting down on a log. I looked over at Azalea. I wanted her to sit next to me. Instead, she smiled and walked over to Chad.

"Well, I wasn't expecting you to have more beer... but maybe something else that's just as fun... maybe more?" she asked, giving me a wry smile and biting her lip.

"Sorry, I don't do drugs," I said. I was serious too. Drinking was one thing, drugs were another. I knew how much I could drink. I knew when to stop. Not once had I ever drank so much that I couldn't remember what the night had entailed. I'd stopped other people from driving home drunk. I was a responsible drinker. But I wasn't about to put my life in jeopardy by doing something that could kill you – or even worse, addict you. 'Sides that, I just didn't see any point in doing it. Were teenagers so hard pressed for a good time that they had to turn to getting high to do so? It seemed absolutely ludicrous.

Sly Darkness by Kya Aliana

I wasn't judging this as a naïve kid either; I'd tried some weed a while back. Some of the older kids had called it shwap... I wasn't sure what that meant, but from what I could deduct it meant it was bad. At first, I didn't feel anything... then when I did, I started to crash... and fast. It sucked worse than a hangover... that was when I decided to never do any type of drugs again.

Vikki sighed and laid a pillow over her head.

"Well fine," she said. "If you guys are going to be a bore, I'm going to get some extra beauty sleep."

I chuckled to myself. I could think of a rude remark to make, but I restrained myself. Something about Vikki had changed since our talk. Or maybe it wasn't Vikki, maybe it was my perception of Vikki. Besides, I didn't want to feed into her insecurities, even if I was only being sarcastic.

"Sweet dreams," I said, putting my feet up on the rocks that surrounded the fire pit. I knew a fire needed to be started, but it was hardly cold yet. In fact, it was a beautifully warm day compared to what I'd gotten used to out here on the trip.

Vikki sat up and looked at me. Her eyebrows scrunched together for a moment of surprise, and then the tension on her face relaxed. She smiled at me.

"Thanks," she replied. She laid back down, put the pillow back over her head and slowly drifted off to sleep.

I sat there for a moment, watching the clouds slowly move in the bright blue sky overheard. I'd lost track of the time. When I came to, I saw Chad and Azalea talking by the corner of the woods. I looked back up at the sky and pretended like I wasn't paying attention. There was a momentary pause in their conversation, but it soon picked back up again. I focused hard on listening to them. It took a minute, but eventually I could make out what they were saying.

"You mean he literally threatened you?" Azalea was asking.

"Yeah, but it was more like a real threat on my life, not just one of those stupid, teenage, male-ego things," Chad replied.

"Well, I never took Zander to be the stupid, teenage, male-

Sly Darkness by Kya Aliana

egotistical kind of guy." I chuckled to myself for a moment. This was going to get good. I wondered how Azalea would lay into him first as he started to explain how I threatened him. I knew he wouldn't be able to prove it; of the many things I was, stupid wasn't one of them.

"So what did he say?" Azalea asked. Her weariness to believe Chad was strongly suggested in her tone of voice.

"Well, it wasn't exactly *what* he said, but *how* he said it," Chad replied slowly.

"Oh come on. Maybe you're blowing this out of proportion, Chad. I mean, we're talking about Zander here... *Zander.* You know, he's not exactly the best at talking and phrasing things the right way. He's had a hard run," Azalea said. I smiled to myself. This was going just how I'd planned.

"No, I know that, but Sarah, this was different," Chad assured her.

"Chad, what did he say? Different how?"

"Well, I don't remember exactly, but he was talking about how accidents happen, and one wrong move and you're dead, and other stuff like that."

"That's just Zander, that's how he is. I think you're taking this a little personally," Azalea said. Though I couldn't see her, I knew she was resting a hand on Chad's shoulder, and that made me mad.

"No, Sarah, you don't understand. He almost hit me with a machete!"

"Chad, I'm sure it was an accident, or maybe he was just showing off, you know, like *normal guys* do," Azalea said in an odd tone. If I didn't know any better, I would say she sounded agitated. But, then again, what reason would she have for being agitated?

"Okay, listen, I can't explain it, but there's something going on with him right now. I think he could be dangerous, I mean, how much do we really know about this guy? He just walked into Riverwolf Pass out of nowhere... that doesn't just happen. There's no such thing as coincidence,"

Sly Darkness by Kya Aliana

"Okay, we are *not* bringing a stupid opinion belief into this! Coincidence or fate, and I really don't care which route you want to take, I don't see any reason why Zander would be dangerous. He's Zander for Christ's Sake. And maybe, if you would actually talk to him, you would get that he's just like that, it's how he is, Chad!" Azalea exclaimed. I heard a twig snap where her foot must have stomped.

"Sarah, I'm not trying to make you mad, I'm just telling you what happened when I was out in the woods with him. I just think you should stay away from him, that's all!" Chad exclaimed, his voice was getting louder and I heard Azalea hush him.

"Oh," Azalea breathed out softly. "I get it."

"You do?" Chad asked.

"Yeah, I do. I really do. This is a jealousy thing, isn't it?" she asked. *Way to go, Azalea!* I thought to myself with a stifled chuckle.

"What?"

"Yeah, you're jealous of Zander. God, Chad, *you're* the one with the stupid, teenage, alpha-male dominating ego! Seriously! I can't believe you," Azalea snapped, she was now talking loud enough that I no longer had to strain to hear.

"So, you're telling me that I have *no* reason to be jealous of Zander?" Chad asked, raising his voice slightly. I could tell he was looking my direction. Azalea didn't reply, I glanced over for a quick second and saw she was looking down at the ground, kicking at the leaves beneath her feet.

"See?" Chad retorted. I took in a deep breath. What did that mean? *Did* Chad have reason to be jealous of me?

"Listen, just back off of him, okay?"

"No, not okay! Listen, if I have a reason to be jealous of him, I'm going to stop at nothing until I have you and don't have to worry about it," Chad said. I could almost see the cute puppy-dog look in his eyes.

"Chad, that's really sweet, but you don't need to be worried about Zander, or him threatening you, or anything. You just don't know him like I do," Azalea said. I went back to

Sly Darkness by Kya Aliana

watching the clouds move slowly in the sky, thinking to myself about Azalea.

"Listen, Sarah, I know you haven't been here long, but Riverwolf Pass attracts a... certain type of people," Chad said, drumming his fingers together.

"What are you talking about, Chad?" Azalea asked, taking in a deep breath.

"Look, it's hard to explain, but there's a reason that the people who live in Riverwolf Pass aren't too keen on visitors or passersby. It's just; Riverwolf Pass is an extraordinary town that a lot of crazy stuff happens in or around. Zander showing up here can mean a lot of different things, and frankly, I don't think it's all that good."

"Chad, you sound crazy. Just like you sounded crazy earlier with the whole Vikki thing, I mean what is it with you two anyways? First you're back together, having sex may I add, and now you're chasing after me like I'm the last girl on the face of the earth. Chad, something weird is happening and I don't think it has anything to do with Zander. The sooner you realize that, the better off we'll all be," Azalea said. I could hear the twigs snapping as she walked away. I smiled smugly to myself and wondered what was going to happen next between them.

"Sarah!" he called after her. His footsteps were fast and then suddenly stopped. Out of my peripheral vision, I could see him standing close to her, his hands on her shoulders.

"What?" she asked exasperatedly.

"You're right," Chad breathed out slowly and quietly. What? What was he doing?

"Excuse me?" Azalea said, tilting her head. As soon as I realized I was looking at them again, I stopped myself.

"You're right. I shouldn't have accused Zander of threatening me in the woods. You're right, it was just my perception. I guess I am kinda jealous of him. I mean, I like you, Sarah, I really like you. And seeing you get close to someone else makes me feel... well, I don't know how to explain it because I've never felt it before. Please, Sarah, forgive me for being such an

Sly Darkness by Kya Aliana

ass?" He'd planned this! I just knew it. He knew this was just a way to make the girls swoon over him. This was just one of his tricks to get girls into bed. Of course! It made perfect sense; pick a fight with them, and then tell her that he was wrong and they only got in the argument because he cared so much about her. God, he really was a player. A true blue player.

"Oh, Chad," Azalea gasped. "Of course I forgive you. It's completely understandable what you're going through, and I should apologize for yelling at you, it was completely uncalled for." This was making me sick.

"I'm going for a walk," I said, standing up to face Chad and Azalea.

"Fine with us," Chad said with his wry smile. I took in a deep breath of air as I looked at Azalea with pleading eyes. She looked from me to Chad very quickly. I was worried about leaving them alone, but I knew I had to.

I walked off slowly, leaving them alone in the woods. Victoria's warning hung in my mind, echoing in my ears. I wished that I could make Azalea see that Chad was full of it. I'd give anything to open her eyes to that. I could hardly believe that she was falling for his sweet talk. She seemed smarter than that. She seemed deeper... at least deep enough to realize when someone was bullshitting you just to get in your pants. But what could I possibly say to her that wouldn't just make her mad and get with Chad out of pure spite? I knew girls sometimes did that when they got mad. I was caught between a rock and a hard place, and there was nothing I could do about it.

I walked down river, hoping to find a secluded spot where I could wash up. I probably smelled like a dead skunk. It was no wonder Azalea didn't want to hang around me all day. The river became wider as I traveled downstream. I wondered which way Riverwolf Pass was... upriver or down... I'd have to ask Azalea if she remembered. I hoped she would, otherwise we were either going to find our way back, or get even more lost in the woods.

Finally, I reached a spot in the river that was surrounded by enough trees that I felt comfortable. I squatted on the edge of

Sly Darkness by Kya Aliana

the riverbank and cupped my hands underneath the cold water. I felt my face tense as the water splashed against it, the cold temperature stinging every pore.

  I felt alive. I took in a deep breath as I tear streamed down my face. I thought about Azalea, how Chad was slyly deceiving her. I felt different. I never knew I could feel that way. I never knew I could care about someone like I cared about Azalea. I never knew someone could trust me the way Azalea trusted me. I never knew I could talk to someone like I talked to Azalea. I never knew a lot of things before I met Azalea... and now I knew them all and what I didn't know was what to do with it. How to express them, what to say, how to act, I didn't even know what I thought anymore.

  I thought it was funny how I could know so much after not knowing and still not know what to do.

Sly Darkness by Kya Aliana

Chapter Fifteen

The sun was just starting to set as I returned back to camp.

"Boy, you've been gone all day, haven't you Cowboy? Where did you get yourself off to?" Azalea asked as I sat down next to her and Chad. They were holding hands and smiling at each other when I walked up. I wondered if I was too late. Suddenly my gut wrenched inside of me and my heart tugged from inside my chest. I ignored the feeling and stared at the fire.

"Not much to go to. We're in the middle of the woods, remember?" I asked with a shrug.

"Kinda my point. Where were you?" Azalea asked. I shrugged again.

"I followed the river a little I guess. You wouldn't happen to know if town is upriver or down, would you?" Azalea slowly shook her head. Great. This was just great.

"Guys, chill out! We'll just follow it one way for a while and if that doesn't work, we'll go the other way," Vikki said. She was sitting cross-legged, on the other side of the fire, looking up at the three of us sitting on a log.

"Yeah and how long will that work for? We only have so much food, Vikki. What happens when we run out?" I asked. Vikki sighed and threw her head back. Reality was finally sinking in.

The hot dogs tasted pithy and on the verge of rotten... this would be the last them; everybody picked at them as opposed to eating them. We were all too worried to eat. Nobody knew what to do. Nobody knew what to say. Nobody knew which direction to go. Nobody knew how long the food would last. Nobody knew if we would even find our way back. Nobody knew anything and there was nothing that could be done about it.

Dinner was filled with silence that drifted into the night. I don't remember how long it was before somebody talked. All I

Sly Darkness by Kya Aliana

remember was just sitting there, in silence, for a very long time, watching the fire pop every now and then.

"Well, I don't know about you, Sarah, but I'm gonna have some girly fun tonight... one way or another," Vikki said, standing up.

"Fun?" I repeated. "What are you talking about fun? We're lost in the middle of the woods!" I exclaimed.

"Exactly, and Lord knows if we'll ever make it out, so we might as well have fun while we're out here," Vikki said. I sighed once more, shrugged and went back to watching the fire.

"What's there to do for fun?" I heard Azalea ask. She looked up at Vikki with hopeful eyes.

"Well, I feel absolutely disgusted with myself!" she answered.

"With that face," Chad chimed in. "I would too."

"That was mean," Azalea snapped, smacking Chad on the arm. He looked at her and shook his head.

"It was sarcastic, that's what it was," he corrected, rubbing his arm.

"Seriously?" Vikki asked while rolling her eyes. "Well, anyways, Sarah, I'm going to wash up in the river, you coming?" she asked. Azalea looked at Victoria like she had three heads.

"What?" she asked.

"Come on, it'll be fun, plus you'll smell better," Vikki said with a smile. I don't think she meant it to come out the way it did. I chuckled to myself.

"It's freezing! Who knows how cold that water could be?" Azalea exclaimed, inching toward the fire.

"Yeah, it's perfect for skinny dipping. Come on, just us girls, it'll be fun, I promise."

"What about towels?"

"Don't worry, I brought some," Vikki replied, jumping over to her bag and digging around in it.

"You brought towels?" I asked.

"Of course, I figured I'd need to dry off at some point during this trip," she replied with a wink at me. I wondered what

Sly Darkness by Kya Aliana

the wink was for.

"Alright, I'll go," Azalea said finally, standing up and walking over toward Vikki. She handed Azalea a towel. I watched as Azalea looked back toward me with a worried look on her face.

"Don't worry, it's not cold enough that you'll catch pneumonia," I replied with a smile. Vikki smiled at me again, grabbed Azalea's hand and started bouncing up and down. Taken aback by her strange behavior, I blinked twice and resumed watching the fire.

"I was more worried about hypothermia," Azalea said, biting the side of her lip.

"Don't worry, I'll defrost you," Chad replied with a devilish grin and a wink.

"I-I've never been skinny dipping," Azalea said timidly.

"Well, there's a shocker," Vikki said with a snort. "Listen, it doesn't even really count because the guys aren't going... unless you want them to come... or would that be cum?" Vikki asked, laughing hysterically. I didn't think it was really that funny or good of a pun, but Azalea laughed along too. She also turned a few shades of red, which made me chuckle to myself. She was so young, innocent, and very naïve when it came to the nature of guys. I couldn't bear to watch Chad corrupt her, I just couldn't. Something had to be done.

"No, I-I don't really want..." Azalea trailed off, not knowing what to say.

"Don't worry, hon, it was only a joke, the guys are most definitely staying here," Vikki said, eying both Chad and I very carefully. I didn't respond, but Chad jumped up and put two fingers to the side of his head.

"Scouts honor," he promised.

"Chad, I've known you since the first grade. You were never a boy scout," Vikki said, looking at him with tired eyes.

"I know," Chad replied with a very perverted smile upon his face.

"Be good, Chad," Vikki warned, pointing her index finger at him.

Sly Darkness by Kya Aliana

"No promises," Chad said with a laugh, sitting back down. Vikki and Azalea both glared at him as they slunk slowly into the woods.

After about two minutes, Chad stood up.

"You're not actually going to spy on them are you?" I asked.

"Aren't you coming along too?" Chad asked, scrunching his eyebrows and tilting his head at me.

"No. Why would I? If I want to see a girl naked, I'm going to make sure it is one-hundred percent consensual," I replied, ready to stop him.

"Fine, suit yourself," Chad said as he started to walk away.

"Chad, seriously!" I said, standing up.

"Seriously what?"

"What are you, fourteen with a perpetual erection?" I asked.

"Guess you can say I'm really *hard up,* if you catch my drift," he said with a wink. I wasn't amused and I gave him a look that told him so.

"Relax, I'm not really going to spy on them," Chad said, raising his hands in a defensive manner.

"Oh really? In that case, enlighten me, where are you off to at such a late hour in the night right after the girls left? Hmm?" I asked, crossing my arms and giving him a death stare.

"Dude, I gotta take a major dump, that's all," Chad replied, throwing his arms out to the side. I looked him up and down. I couldn't tell if he was lying or not.

"Fine," I sighed, knowing that even if he was lying, there wasn't much I could do to stop him.

"Oh yeah, and one more thing," Chad said, turning around.

"What's that?"

"You *will* pay for threatening me out in the woods and making me look like a dick in front of Sarah. *You* know you threatened me and *I* know you threatened me, and once we get back to Riverwolf Pass, I'm pressing charges! Trust me when I

Sly Darkness by Kya Aliana

say, 'my daddy's rich.' I *will* have a good lawyer," Chad said, pointing a finger at me.

"I have no idea what you're talking about Chad, what reason would I have to threaten you?" I asked with a smile on my face. Oh, how I loved where my words took me.

Chad stood in front of me, his face expressionless. He then raised his hand slowly and continued to make a rude gesture with a certain finger before sulking off into the woods. Somehow, I doubted he was going to stay away from those girls. But I sure as hell wasn't going after him. He'd probably pin the whole idea on me once he got caught. What would Azalea think of me then?

The fire roared, popped, and cracked before I heard anything else. I was enjoying the silence, planning the night out, dreaming about the rest of the night and how I would love for it to go.

I heard screaming in the distance. At first, I didn't think anything about it. But then, it started to get louder, and closer. *Maybe it's just the panthers,* I told myself, even though I knew it was a lie. It was so close to the camp; I didn't know what to do. I reached over and grabbed the machete from beside me. Not a second later I saw Vikki and Azalea run into the camp, wrapped in towels, hair soaking wet, and flop down on a cushion of blankets.

"Well..." I said, raising my eyebrows at the two girls. "That was shorter than expected." They talked so fast, I could barely understand them.

"Whoa, whoa, whoa! Slow down. I can't understand you guys when you talk in the same high-pitched, fast voice simultaneously saying different things," I said, scooting closer to them. Something about seeing Azalea wrapped in a towel with beautifully wet hair made me want to be closer to her. Seeing her like that made me go crazy inside. I just wanted to kiss her. I just wanted to hold her close. I just wanted her to be mine, all mine. I just wanted her. She needed to be mine, not Chad's. How could she even consider that meat-head jock? It made no sense to me.

After a few minutes, the girls calmed down enough that I

could understand what they were talking about. Someone had been watching them in the river. I took in a deep breath; I knew it'd been Chad. Who else could it have been? The girls were in denial though.

"Who would do that? It's invading my privacy!" Azalea said. She shivered in the cold and scooted closer to me. She pressed up against my side, and I slipped my arm around her and rested it on her arm. Her cold skin was electrifying.

"Glory, Sarah!" I exclaimed. "You're colder than a witch's titty in a brass bra!" She suppressed a laugh and Vikki rolled her eyes.

"I bet it was Chad... how long ago did he leave, Zander?" Vikki asked.

"About ten minutes before you two came rushing back," I said with a shrug.

"Yeah, it was him alright. God, he was so creepy... standing there... leaning against a tree... watching us... probably jerking off or some shit..." Victoria's voice trailed off.

I didn't know why they were so surprised. I mean, girls can't just go announcing that they're going skinny dipping, to just any guy, and expect him not to follow them. Seriously, how thick were these girls? Azalea I could understand. She was inexperienced when it came to guys... but Vikki? No, she was a girl with experience. She should have known better. I was mad at her for putting Azalea through this... she seemed to be taking it pretty hard.

"No one's ever seen me... you know... naked before," Azalea said in a hushed tone just as Chad walked back up to us.

"Hey girls, back already?" he asked, sitting down next to the fire and warming his hands.

"Where did you go, Chad?" I asked sternly.

"I told you, Zander. God! You're so weird," Chad exclaimed, standing up. "Well, anyways, I'm tired. Wanna join me in the tent, Sarah?"

I felt like punching him. I didn't know what stopped me. How could he be such a jerk?

Sly Darkness by Kya Aliana

"No, I think I'll stay out by the fire tonight," she said, cuddling up to me. I smiled a very cocky smile to Chad as I watched him walk by me and crawl into the tent.

"Well, uh, I'm just gonna," Vikki stuttered over her words after a few minutes had passed. "I'll just leave you two... you know, I'm gonna go in the tent for the night," she said, and walked past us.

"So, did you leave in such a hurry that you forgot your clothes?" I asked, wondering why Azalea was still wrapped up in her towel.

"Yeah, actually," she replied. "I'm really cold."

"Well, your hair is dry now, so hopefully you'll start to warm up soon," I replied, running my fingers through her slightly tangled hair. It looked so hot on her, how it was all roughed up from being in the water.

"Yeah, well, I still don't want to spend all night in a towel... I'm kinda scared to go back out there by myself," she said, twisting a strand of her hair with her finger. "Could I get you to come with me?" she asked, biting her lip.

"Sure," I replied with a shrug. I helped her to her feet and she started to walk off toward the woods. I followed, but then she stopped suddenly and turned toward me.

"Could you grab a couple of blankets for me to wrap up in?" she asked. I nodded and mumbled a "sure" as I picked up a few blankets. I loved draping them over her small and fragile body. She pulled the blankets tighter around her shoulders and kept on walking.

We walked for around five minutes before we were down by the part of the river where they'd gone skinny dipping. Their clothes were lying by the bank, in a petite pile. I couldn't help but stare at Azalea's pretty pastel pink bra that laid on the top of the pile of clothes.

"Turn around?" Azalea asked.

"Huh? Oh, sure," I said, complying.

"Is something bugging you?" I heard her ask as the leaves rustled behind her. I heard her towel drop to the ground;

Sly Darkness by Kya Aliana

something inside pulled at me to turn around, but I didn't.

"What would be bugging me?" I asked curiously.

"Oh, I don't know, it just seems like all day today you've been different," Azalea replied. I wondered if I could turn around yet... I didn't though.

"Can I ask you something?" I asked her.

"Sure, Cowboy," she replied.

"When I left you and Chad alone at the campsite today..." I couldn't finish my question. Part of me didn't want to know the answer.

"Oh," Azalea said with a laugh. "Don't worry, Cowboy, nothing happened between us if that's what you're getting at," she said. I could almost see her lovely smile across her face... I wanted to turn around, but I didn't.

"He was coming on to you," I stated dryly.

"I know," Azalea replied.

"You flirted back," I said. It was meant as a question, but it came out as a hurt statement. How could she? After all the connections her and I had made... after all the times we'd talked... after all the trust that had formed... how could she just throw it all away in a day? For Chad of all people!

"I'm aware of that," she said. I felt heat takeover my eyes and suddenly my lungs were lodged in my throat. I couldn't breathe. I couldn't speak. All I could think of was one word... *why*.

"Why?" I choked out after a moment I took to get myself together.

"Oh, Cowboy, you really don't know, do you?" she asked, pity formed in her voice.

"Know what?" I asked, pursing my lips together. For the first time since we'd been down by the river, I didn't want to turn around. I didn't want to look at her. I didn't want to face her. I couldn't. I knew I wouldn't be able to bear looking at her.

"Cowboy," she said with a laugh. "I did it to make you jealous. It wasn't real at all. I thought you knew..." she trailed off. I said nothing. Was she telling the truth? Why would she lie?

"It's just, after you didn't kiss me last night when I so

Sly Darkness by Kya Aliana

clearly wanted you to... after you didn't invite me to sleep in your sleeping bag... after knowing that you didn't jump at the opportunity to be with me, it hurt. I didn't know what to do, so when Chad started flirting with me, I thought it was the perfect situation to make you jealous." I knew she was telling the truth now. I just didn't know what to say.

"Looks like it worked," I replied after a moment. I heard her footsteps nearing me. I wanted to turn around once more, but before I could, I felt her hands on my shoulder. They trailed down on my arms, sending waves of electrifying feelings throughout my entire self. I took in a deep breath as I felt her lips brush against my shoulder. I hadn't put on a shirt before walking out here with her. The feel of her smooth lips against my bare skin was greater than I'd imagined. I felt her body press up against my back. That was when I realized she hadn't put any clothes on.

My brain was going crazy with ideas. I wanted to turn around, to face her and pull her close to me. I wanted to kiss her. I wanted to see her pale body shining in the moonlight. The moon was just bright enough that I'd be able to see her, to make out her features. My heart leaped and started to pound on the barrier known as my chest. I felt her boobs press hard against my back and instantly my shoulders straightened. I felt my whole body stiffen and my heart froze.

As soon as I turned around, my heart started to beat faster again. I couldn't think, I couldn't move, all I could do was look at her. She was magnificent, standing there in the moonlight, ever so tenderly biting her lip.

"Aren't you going to kiss me?" she whispered softly into the night. I was happy to oblige. I pulled her close to me and started to kiss her with a passion that I never thought I was capable of holding. Yet, here it was, burning inside me. I pulled her closer and felt her warm skin press against mine. My lips explored her long and outstretched neck; they gently grazed her collarbone as my hands wandered up her smooth and slightly arched back. I felt her shoulder blades move closer together as she pressed her chest out towards my body. Without a second thought,

Sly Darkness by Kya Aliana

I brought my hands around to the front of her body, slowly cupping her breasts. I squeezed gently as I rubbed them in a circular motion, enjoying every minute of it. I couldn't believe how amazing it felt. I couldn't believe how warm they were, especially in the cold of the night.

Azalea was amazing in every aspect, physically as well as mentally. She was perfect for me. I could hardly believe I was lucky enough to have her. She was mine now. I was kissing her, feeling her boobs. I'd never felt boobs before, which made hers even more astounding. I couldn't believe how much I was enjoying this. It was everything I'd imagined it would be and more. She wasn't stopping me... that must have meant she was enjoying it.

Her hands slid down my side and grabbed my hand as her lips kissed their way up to my ear. She nibbled on it for just a mere second and it made my knees go weak. She stopped and smiled at me as she led me to the spot by the river where she had laid the blankets out. She lowered herself to her knees and pulled me down with her.

I started to kiss her again as she gently laid herself back, pulling me on top of her. I could feel my whole body press against her warm and amazing figure. No words could describe the feeling I had inside. No words could describe the trust I felt for her. No words could describe the connection that was so strong between us. No words could possibly dream of describing how I felt about her. No, nothing could possibly describe what I was feeling; no one could possibly know or understand how I felt. This was different than anything anyone had ever experienced before.

My hands wandered up her body, loving every inch of the way, and up to her face, which I cupped gently before kissing her. I wondered if anybody could possibly know how much I cared for her at that moment. I wondered if love had ever felt like that before. It had to be love; there was no other word for it.

Her hands drifted along my back, up and down until it gave me the most amazing goosebumps ever. I couldn't breathe as

Sly Darkness by Kya Aliana

she slid her hands around and unbuttoned my pants. I lifted my body up slightly so she could slowly pull them down and off. I let out a soft moan as she slowly moved her hands inside my underwear.

"I love you," I whispered into her ear. "I love you so much, Azalea," I wanted to tell her a million times over, however I couldn't manage any more words at that moment. All I could do was smile and slowly close my eyes and kiss her again as she returned the sweet, meaningful three words to me.

And that was the best night of my life.

Chapter Sixteen

He stood over her, a knife in his hand. He smiled a devilish smile as I walked through the bedroom door. Panic attacked my heart and I frantically started searching my mind for something to do. I screeched when I saw the scene. I didn't know what to do. Images raced through my mind faster than a train off its rails. I knew what was about to happen, it'd happened in my mind a million times before.

I awoke with a start, covered in cold sweat. My breathing was heavy, deep and erratic.

"Good morning, Cowboy," Azalea whispered in my ear. I looked around the woods; we were still down by the river. I guess we'd fallen asleep there after we'd...

"Morning," I muttered, rolling over to face her. I noticed that I'd missed the sunrise. That was a first in a while.

"Were you dreaming?" she asked.

"I guess," I said, scrunching my eyebrows together. "I don't really remember what was happening though... I think it was something bad," I stated. Azalea ran her hands through my sweaty hair and smiled at me.

"I had the most amazing night last night," she announced. I thought about last night and became imbued with this electric feeling of being alive. For the first time since I was fourteen years old, I didn't question whether or not I wanted to be alive, whether or not I should have been born. I was finally happy to be alive. I finally loved my life. And nothing was going to screw that up this time.

"I had the most amazing night too," I said with a smile. My hand traipsed along the nape of her neck. My fingers lingered on the edge of her collarbone, hesitating to go any farther. I pulled my hand back.

"We should probably be heading back to camp," I said. I looked around, suddenly searching for the bright colors of the

Sly Darkness by Kya Aliana

sunrise. They were gone. I'd missed it. For the first time since I was little, I'd missed it.

"Where is it?" I asked.

"Where's what?"

"The sunrise, the pretty colors, it's gone! I missed it," I said, looking down at the ground.

"It's okay, Cowboy, they'll always be another sunrise," Azalea comforted.

"I missed it," I repeated the only thing I could think.

"We should probably head back to camp now." Azalea's suggestion seemed absentminded and distant. I wondered what she was thinking, though I didn't know how to ask.

"I wonder what time it is," I said aloud, sitting up and searching around for my pants.

"Ten-thirty," Azalea replied. There was something about her tone that was different.

"Whoa, we slept late!" I exclaimed.

"This is actually normal for teenagers," Azalea replied with a short giggle as she pulled on her shirt. I was sad to see it go on, but I also knew that we needed to get back to camp. There was no time to start fooling around again. We needed to start heading back to Riverwolf Pass. I wondered what would happen once we were back in town, between me and Azalea, I mean.

"I guess I don't have a shirt with me," I said with a shrug.

"Yeah, that one you borrowed from Chad, since that thing happened when I was in shock, doesn't look that good on you," she said with a teasing demeanor.

"Well Vikki's clothes don't exactly look that flattering on you either," I replied truthfully. I couldn't wait to be home and see her in her normal attire. Wait, home? That was an odd thought.

Azalea and I finished dressing, gathered up the blankets, and started to walk back toward camp, slowly and silently.

"Cowboy?" she asked. I smiled and thought about how much I loved it that she called me *Cowboy* all the time.

"Yeah?" I asked, watching my feet carry me away from the riverside.

Sly Darkness by Kya Aliana

"I was just-" Azalea was cut short of her words.

"There you two are!" Chad exclaimed, nearing Azalea. "Glory, you two had us worried. We thought some wild animal carried you off and had you over for supper. What were you two doing anyways, off in the middle of nowhere, stumbling back late in the morning?" Chad inquired. I stuttered over my words. I had no idea what to say. Should I lie? Should I tell? What did Azalea want me to do?

"We're just happy you're back," Victoria said, leaning against a tree. I smiled at her gratefully.

"We're happy to be back," Azalea said with a smile, walking toward the campsite. She started packing things up for both of us.

"We'd better start to walk again, the sooner we get back to Riverwolf Pass, the better," I stated, glancing around for anything that that needed to be packed.

We all agreed and packed up our stuff. I wondered when and if Chad was going to confront me about Azalea. He kept casting me these looks, like he wanted to beat my head in. I rolled my eyes; I could take him in a fight any day. Besides, I wouldn't have to put up with him and his stupid, football quarterback egotistical attitude for much longer.

"I thought about it really hard," Azalea was saying. "And I believe that if we follow the river upstream, we should reach Riverwolf Pass. I'm almost absolutely sure about it," she said definitively. There was no arguing with her. We all hoisted our packs on our backs. I picked up the dead body. Somehow, it seemed to weigh less today.

There was something about today. The sun shown brighter, the air smelled fresher, the woods felt more alive, the body stunk a little more, the only thing dampening my mood, was the dream. It haunted me, whether I liked to admit it or not. I got this weird feeling in my stomach, like something big was going to happen today... something big and something bad.

We stopped for lunch after a few hours of solid and silent

Sly Darkness by Kya Aliana

walking. The woods weren't getting any more familiar. And although I knew we all felt like we were just getting more lost, Azalea, Vikki, and Chad's spirits remained high. *They're in denial,* I thought to myself as I slowly stirred the last of the hotdogs in a pan. That running out of food thing was no joke. All we had after that was trail mix... and not that much of it either.

All throughout our walk today Chad eyeballed me. I know he suspects me of something of which I am guilty. I knew that he knew that I slept with Azalea the prior night. He wasn't stupid, annoying and egotistical but not stupid.

Vikki seemed to be the only one who was keeping everybody from exploding. Whenever things got intense, she would say something that helped calm it down. I wondered where she learned to do that. Her family life seemed like it was pretty explosive, maybe her balance was with her friends.

Azalea had been weird all day long. She hadn't spoken to me since we'd got back at camp. She kept casting me these glances that I had no idea what they meant. I wished I knew what to tell her. I wish I knew something to say. But most of all, I wished I knew what she wanted me to say. I wanted to know what she was feeling and thinking. I wanted to know if she regretted anything that had happened the prior night. I wanted to crawl inside her mind and snoop around for a few moments. I wished I could.

I walked over to her and she cast me a forced smile as I slipped some hot dog bits on her plate.

"Thanks," she muttered. Her voice was barely detectable, so much so that I had to wonder if she'd even said a thank you or if I'd just imagined it. I mumbled a response and walked past her, continuing to delegate the food on everybody's plate.

Breakfast was full of an awkward and intense silence. Though no words were spoken, much was said. Chad knew. I knew that he knew. I also knew that Vikki knew. I could read Chad and Vikki like open books, but whenever I tried to figure out Azalea, I got mixed feelings and senses. I didn't know what to make of her. I felt like I was being judged by all of them. At least

Sly Darkness by Kya Aliana

I knew how Vikki and Chad were judging me. I could only guess how Azalea was judging me, and what for at that.

"Well, I'll go clean the dishes down by the river," Azalea said, breaking the silence. She walked around, gathered our plates in silence, and then walked toward the woods.

"I think I'll start packing," Vikki said, standing up and heading toward the other side of the camp... leaving Chad and I alone, staring at each other. Chad broke the tension with a sigh and stood up.

"I think we need to talk," he said.

"Agreed," I replied, standing up to face him.

"You wanna go in the woods?" he asked. "It might be best if we didn't cause a scene here, Vikki might get the notion that she's supposto help us to work it out." I nodded in agreement and walked out into the woods with him leading the way.

Sly Darkness by Kya Aliana

Chapter Seventeen

I came back alone. My feet stomped as I came through the woods, breaking every stick I could along the way. I grumbled to myself, I didn't even know what I was saying. My hands were balled into fists, and heat filled my body. My adrenaline was pumping and flowing through my veins at a record speed.

"What's wrong, Cowboy?" Azalea asked as soon as she saw me.

"Where's Chad?" Vikki asked, curiosity rising in her voice.

"Fuck Chad!" I said, throwing my arms up. I spun around to face Azalea. "And you!" I exclaimed. "You need to get on top of your game. If you have something to say to me, you damn well need to say it! I can't read your little girly mind game glances!" I wheeled around so I was no longer looking at her. I couldn't believe what had just come out of my mouth. I couldn't believe I'd just blown up at her. I couldn't believe a lot of stuff.

"Zander? Are you alright?" Vikki asked, placing a hand on my shoulder.

"Just leave me alone!" I snapped. I bit my lip to keep myself from bursting out in tears. What the hell was wrong with me? I hadn't cried in years, what made me want to now?

"Fine, Zander, if you're going to be like that!" Vikki snapped. I turned just in time to see her chasing after Azalea, who was actually crying and running off into the woods.

I took in a deep breath. What had I just done?

It took a long time before Vikki and Azalea came back to camp. I'd had time to calm down, think about what to say, how to apologize to Azalea. I couldn't believe I'd yelled at her like that.

"Well," Azalea said, sitting down next to me. She grabbed my hand in hers and I looked into her eyes. They were red and slightly puffy. This horrible gut-wrenching feeling overcame me when I realized that I was the one who had made her cry.

Sly Darkness by Kya Aliana

"I'm sorry," she said slowly, taking in a deep breath. I was confused, why was she sorry.

"Why?" I asked. "I was the one who yelled at you... it wasn't anything about you either, which only makes it more unfair of me. I was just mad because of Chad, okay?" I said. It was the best apology I could come up with. After all, I couldn't ever remember apologizing to anybody. I never had any reason to, and even if they thought I did, I just didn't care enough. It almost scared me that I cared about Azalea so much that I would apologize to her.

"Yeah, well it wasn't exactly fair of me to keep casting those glances at you, expecting you to say something when I didn't even know what I wanted you to say," Azalea said, running her hand up and down my arm.

"I think this is new to both of us," I said, "being in a relationship and all." Azalea nodded her head in a reassuring manner.

"We just need a little more communication... as in the verbal kind," Azalea said with a smile. I nodded my head. We hugged for a long time and it felt good. I'd never felt so accepted before.

"So, I don't mean to interrupt this seemingly sentimental moment, but I can't help but to notice that Chad is still missing... and that you, Zander, were the last one with him... what happened?" Vikki asked. She sounded worried, like more worried than she should have been. I wondered if she really cared about Chad... and if she did, Chad sure didn't really care about her.

"Chad took off on his own. Said he was sick of putting up with me and all the drama," I said with a shrug. "He said he was gonna find his way back to town by taking a different path than us."

"And you let him go?"

"Hey, he's his own person, Vikki, he can make his own decisions about who he does and doesn't want to hang with, and which way home he does and doesn't want to take," I said. There was a long pause and a lot of worried looks.

Sly Darkness by Kya Aliana

"Okay, so at which point did you get blood on your shirt?" Azalea asked, biting her lip in a nervous way. I looked down at my shirt to see blood smeared across my chest. I sighed and was quiet for a second.

"Look, we kinda got in a fight... I knocked some blood outta his nose and it smeared on me, that's all," I said, taking my shirt off and standing up.

"Where are you going?" Azalea asked me.

"To wash my shirt in the river... you two finish packing up here and we need to start heading back toward Riverwolf Pass."

I washed my shirt off and headed back to camp. I knew I couldn't put the wet shirt on if I wanted to avoid hypothermia. But the cool wind and light rain that was starting to come down stung my chest. I hoped that I could find another shirt of mine back at camp. I couldn't remember how many I had... I never thought I'd go through so many in so little time.

I walked back to camp to find Vikki and Azalea talking quietly under their breath. As soon as I approached them, they stopped talking.

"Okay, remember that whole verbal communication thing that was mentioned earlier?" I asked. They nodded. "Well, now might be a good time to initiate that," I suggested, sitting down with my arms crossed... partially to look intimidating and partially because I was cold.

"Okay, here's the thing," Azalea started. "We find it a little weird that Chad would just take off, without even coming back to get his stuff."

"We think that he's just mad... he'll probably come back... you know, and if we leave... and take his stuff... well, don't you see what we're getting at? Besides, I know Chad wants that reward money just as much as the rest of us... it just doesn't seem like him to take off like that," Vikki said, looking at me with hopeful eyes.

"Well, like him or not, that's what he did. We can't afford to stay here another day. Don't you get it, Vikki? Don't you understand, Sarah? We are running out of food. Do you know

Sly Darkness by Kya Aliana

what happens when you don't eat? Well, let me clear it up for you, you die. Die! You starve to death. Chad hasn't come back yet, and he probably won't. We'll see him in town, happily playing with his quarterback friends, dating girls, and being happy for the first time in God knows how long. We cannot jeopardize *our* lives just because some stupid punk teenager decided to take off because he can't handle it!" I exclaimed, my voice getting louder with each word.

"But how is he supposto survive without his stuff?"

"And what about his share of the money?" Azalea asked.

"Okay okay, listen, we'll leave his stuff here in case he comes back," I said, taking a deep breath. "He knows what direction we're heading in, so it shouldn't be that hard for him to catch up if he really wants to. If he catches up before we hit town and cash in the body, we'll give him his cut; if not, we'll divide it up between us. Sound good?" They were silent for a moment, but then slowly nodded their heads.

"Good, now I know we only have so much daylight left, but we have to keep moving. We're running out of food and it feels like it's going to rain again later... so we better hurry," I said, picking up my backpack. I hoisted the wrapped up dead body over my shoulder and started to walk away from camp. The girls scurried around for a moment, gathering things, and then started to follow me.

We walked along the riverside until dusk rapidly approached upon us. We'd only been walking for around an hour. At this rate, we would never get back to Riverwolf Pass. The wind had picked up and was thrashing itself around harder than ever. Luckily, the light drizzle of rain had vanished... but with a promise to return later that night.

"We have to keep going," I said as the girls dropped their stuff at a clearing in the woods.

"What?" they both shouted in unison. I watched Vikki stomp her foot and Azalea cross her arms in protest.

"Look, it's really not that hard to keep on trekking at nighttime. We have flashlights. If we don't get a good start, we're

Sly Darkness by Kya Aliana

never going to get to town before we run out of food," I said strongly. I knew that it wasn't going to be anybody's favorite thing to do, but I also knew that it had to get done.

"But Zander!" Vikki whined while picking up her pack again.

"Yeah, Cowboy, totally uncool, it's like dinner time now," Azalea said, her eyes were low and sad. I had to ignore them. I knew this was the best and right thing to do.

"Well, you don't want dinner time to come tomorrow and there to be no food, do you?" I asked. They both shook their heads.

"Well then, we'd better keep moving, wouldn't you two agree?" I asked with a slight smile.

"Yeah, yeah, whatever, Zander," Victoria said. I'm sure if she had any gum in her mouth, she'd be smacking it.

"You're right," Azalea admitted with a sigh.

"Yeah, I wish I wasn't, you've no idea how much I'd love to sit down and relax with you by the fireside," I said in a lovey-dovey tone of voice. I slowed my pace so she could catch up with me and I slipped an arm around her.

"We will get to sleep tonight, right Cowboy?" she asked. I nodded my head, then realizing it was too dark for her to see me out of her peripheral vision, I squeezed her tight and said, "Of course."

"So, you two are really together," Vikki said with a giggle and a slight sigh. "You make a good 'n' cute couple, you know that?" she asked. We turned around to see the smirk on her face. "Chad and I were never a cute couple, we were just cliché," Vikki said drolly. Clearly she was wishing it was something different.

"Don't worry, Vikki," I said smoothly. "You'll find your Prince Charming, don't worry," I said. She smiled again and muttered thanks.

We kept up the small chat for a few more miles. It was starting to get really dark. The moon was just peeking out from behind the mountainside, causing the ground to glow slightly. The wind whipped and I felt a few raindrops hit my skin.

Sly Darkness by Kya Aliana

"Ugh!" Vikki exclaimed suddenly. "It's gonna start to rain!" she wailed. I shined the flashlight back to her and Azalea, only to realize what hit her face wasn't drops of rain. Her face was covered in itty-bitty dots of blood.

Azalea let out a sharp scream. My heart froze and adrenaline attacked my veins. Fear rose up inside of me... I could only think of one question: What would this do to Azalea? If one dead body of someone she didn't even know set her off... what would this do?

A deadly silence was upon us. No one knew what to say. No one knew how to speak. Not even the squeamish girls could scream. None of us dared to breath. All we could do was listen... listen to the God awful sound of something wet smacking against something, splatting with every whack. My stomach churned, and my head was starting to hurt. I could feel every particle in my body pulsate. My chest felt tight and the cool air felt amazing against my face.

My eyes slowly searched for any signs of shock in Azalea. My hand shook as I slowly moved the flashlight back and forth. I must have circled our surroundings five separate times before they saw it... before they saw him... hanging there in the tree, covered in blood, obviously mutilated by something. It was no mistake he was dead. It was clear that he had been tortured before he'd died. It was clear that someone had hung him in that tree after he was already dead.

He hung there, swinging back and forth in the wind, slapping against the tree, breaking small branches, and slinging blood every time his limp body collided with the old, tall, round and hard tree.

"Chad!" Vikki screamed, breaking the unbearable silence. Azalea started screaming and fell to her knees. Vikki started sobbing and repeating Chad's name numerous times. And me? I just stood there. Watching. Waiting. I was unable to think. I was unable to comfort. I couldn't remember what it was like to be human. I couldn't remember what I should have done. I couldn't remember anything.

Sly Darkness by Kya Aliana

My body was numb. My emotions were numb. I couldn't remember how to think. I didn't know what I should be thinking. I didn't even remember what I should have been feeling.

Sly Darkness by Kya Aliana

Chapter Eighteen

The sobbing slowly subsided with the sun's morning glow. I'd climbed up the tree and cut Chad down hours ago. The blood on my last shirt was proof enough. The ground was frozen and covered in a light dusting of snow. My hoodie was the only shirt I had left, and I hoped it would last me until we got back.

"We should bury him," Vikki said. They were the first words anyone had said since we'd found him like that.

"The ground is too hard," I replied slowly.

"We have to bring him back to town," Azalea said, the tears were finally drying on her face. I figured she had probably cried so much, that there were no more tears left in her. I wished I knew what to say to help them both.

"So what? So we can be questioned, maybe prosecuted?" I asked.

"Prosecuted for what? We didn't do anything?" Vikki asked suspiciously.

"Yeah, except for me," I stated. "I'm 18, a legal adult, who took minors out into the woods to search for a dead body. I was the last one with Chad. And nobody, I repeat, nobody in town knows who I am. Vikki, Sarah, if we bring him back to town, I'm going to be their number one suspect!" I exclaimed, my heart racing.

"So what, it'll seem less suspicious if we just come back without him? We left as four, come back as three, no questions asked?" Azalea asked me, her eyes wide and fiery. I knew we were all just trying to think of the right thing to do.

"No," I said calmly... not quite believing what I was about to ask them to do. "We lie." After I said that, there was an epic silence.

"Lie?" Azalea repeated quietly.

"Yes, we lie. We say we never saw him. We say that he was never a part of this. As far as I'm concerned, I never knew the

Sly Darkness by Kya Aliana

guy. As far as you're concerned, Vikki, you haven't talk to him since he quit the football team. And as far as you're concerned, Sarah, you saw him around in school... he seemed like a nice guy," I said. "Make sense?" They both nodded their heads slowly and reluctantly.

"So, what do we do with the body?" Victoria asked after another long bout of silence.

"We have two options," I stated, sounding very matter of fact. "We can either leave the body here and keep heading toward Riverwolf Pass," I offered, "or we could stay here longer, burn the body and have our own private and forever secret ceremony," I concluded. There was a heavy moment of consideration.

"What about his parents? Zander, we have to bring him back to town," Vikki demanded.

"I thought we just went through this, we'll be questioned and prosecuted," I said strongly. I was not about to go to jail.

"So what? If you're really innocent you shouldn't be worried. Why should we protect you? What about the welfare of all of us?" Azalea asked. I was surprised how fast she turned on me.

"Trust me, it is in all our best interest if we claim we don't know anything about him," I said calmly with a wry smile on my face. What would these girls do without me to think things through?

"Oh? Enlighten me, because the way I see it is that we'd only be protecting you!" Vikki snapped, crossing her arms, trying not to stare at Chad's dead body.

"Okay, let's just say that they bring us all in for questioning... just bear with me here... so they bring us in, and they decide that I'm guilty. Let's face it, there's not much evidence that I didn't do it. We're built on innocent until proven guilty, but they'll be quicker to prove you guilty before they will to prove you innocent," I said, going off on a rant inside my head on how our justice system was so screwed up. "Anyways, say they said I did it and they take me off to jail. Guess what that makes you two?" I asked. Their faces were as blank as a school blackboard during the summer. "That," I paused for dramatic effect. "Makes you two accomplices... if not that, accessories... do you know what they do to accomplices and accessories?" I asked. "No? Well, let me tell you something. They lock them in jail. So, maybe if you were lucky, you wouldn't be there as long as I would, but you'd still be there. Somehow I get the feeling that jail isn't exactly where you would like to be," I said looking them both square in the eye.

"But," Victoria started, but stopped herself.

"Go ahead and test it if you don't believe me. You'll be in for a rude awakening. Trust me, jail is not a place that you want to be," I said with a gleaming look in my eyes. Vikki frowned for a second and then smiled at me.

"Okay, you're right. We have to just leave him here. We need to get back to town... and fast. The longer we're out here the more they'll suspect us." Vikki had never been more right in her entire life.

"Agreed," Azalea said with a slight nod of her head. With that, we grabbed our bags in silence. I'm not sure, but I think Azalea and Vikki said a short prayer in their head... I know I did. And then, we kept walking, and walking, and walking. We walked for a long time, none of us daring to say a word. We were all too busy, caught up in our own thoughts. We were too busy arguing with our conscience over whether or not we did the right thing. The pain and sorrow on Azalea's face was almost unbearable. Vikki on the other hand, there was something weird about her expression. It wasn't pain, it wasn't hurt, it wasn't guilt, it was something entirely different... I just couldn't figure out what. She kept casting suspicious glances at Azalea, and I wondered what type of signals she was trying to send.

"Zander? Zander!" Vikki snapped. She sounded scared. I wheeled around to face her.

"What's wrong?" I asked.

"It's almost dusk," she replied slowly.

"And?"

"And don't you think we should stop?" she asked.

Sly Darkness by Kya Aliana

"No, we have to keep moving. We're probably really close to town!" I said strongly.

"No, Zander!" she said strongly. "I can't... I mean, God, last night! Please Zander, we have to stop. I-I just can't walk at night again," she said, her voice was getting choppy and I could see the tears forming in her eyes. I hated this. I hated being the one who always had to be the jerk just to keep everybody safe.

"Look, we've all been thinking it. I'm just going to say it... Whatever killed Chad is still out there."

"No! It was just a freak accident, like with an animal or something," Azalea said, panic rising up to high-tide in her voice.

"No, Azalea, you know that's not true," I said calmly.

"Animals don't hang their prey from trees after they mutilate them!" Vikki snapped. I sighed... she didn't have to be so harsh about it.

"It was the crazy old hermit that Chad told us about!" Vikki nearly screamed.

"Don't be ridiculous, Vikki, Chad just told that story to get laid," I stated.

"Well, sure, he told it *that way*. But what if part of it was real?"

"Trust me, it wasn't."

"You have a better theory?"

"Oh my God, Zander, she's right!" Azalea said, getting all worked up. I sighed, giving up on trying to convince them otherwise.

"Listen, *what*ever did this... *who*ever did this... must be following us. It could be extremely dangerous to stop and make camp. It'd be better just to keep going until we reach town," I said.

"So what? So he can stalk us during the day? So he can watch us sleep at night? So he can torture us by always reminding us of how we found Chad?" Vikki asked. "I want sleep and I want it now. I absolutely refuse to walk any farther today," she said, crossing her arms and stomping her foot.

"Goddamnit! Vikki, there's snow on the ground. It's

Sly Darkness by Kya Aliana

freezing. We're out of food now. Completely and utterly out of food! And there's some sort of killer, murderer, sick ass person following us. We *need* to keep going until we hit town."

"No," she said, calm, smooth, collected, and matter of fact like. I clamped my fingers together, making a fist and took in a deep breath.

"Okay," I breathed out into the air. It was cold enough that I could see my own breath. Vikki smiled at me smugly and Azalea just sort of stood there, taking it all in. I couldn't blame her. None of us knew the right thing to do, me included... even if I did act like I knew what to do.

The girls set up the tent and laid out blankets while I started a fire. It wasn't long before dusk was fully upon us and our stomachs were growling.

"Okay, listen, I'm gonna go try and get us something to eat, okay?" I said, going through my bag for my pocket knife. I finally found it and took it along with the machete.

"Good luck," Vikki said with a smile.

"Thanks, Cowboy," Azalea replied, placing a hand on my shoulder and giving me a quick kiss. I smiled at her and Vikki as I headed off into the woods.

It wasn't easy, but I ended up with not one, not two, but three squirrels for dinner. It was fully dark by the time I started trekking back to camp. I wondered how long I'd been gone. It felt like a long time, but most of it I spent being frustrated with my seemingly non-existent squirrel catching skills. Even now, after I'd caught three, I was pretty sure it was only a fluke.

As I approached the camp, I heard hushed voices. My heart leaped, what had happened? Why were they being so secretive? That was when I heard my name. I stopped walking and peered out from behind a tree.

"Look, all I'm saying is at least consider it," Vikki was saying. I saw Azalea shake her head profusely.

"No! No way, Vikki, there's just no way that Zander, of all people, killed Chad." What? What would make Vikki think that?

"Listen, there's evidence... it's not like I just made it up or

Sly Darkness by Kya Aliana

something because I don't particularly like the guy," Vikki was saying with a slight chuckle.

"What? What evidence do you have?" Azalea asked her with wide eyes.

"Just the way he was talking back there... like when we... when we... left Chad," she said. "He talked about jail like he'd been there before."

"What do you mean?"

"You know, like 'trust me, it's not a place you wanna be,' or something like that... you heard him."

"Vikki, it doesn't take a delinquent to know that jail isn't a fun place," Azalea defended me. I was happy to hear her so much on my side.

"Sarah, it wasn't *what* he said... it was *how* he said it!" she claimed. I took in a deep breath. Did she really suspect me of killing Chad? If so, something had to be done about it.

"Is there anything else that makes you think he killed him?" Azalea asked.

"Well, all that innocent until proven guilty not being true rant... that seemed like he was talking from experience," Vikki said, sounding sure of herself.

"Vikki, he's right though... I mean, think about it... if you were going to be the number one suspect of a murder, wouldn't you be thinking about the justice system?"

"Exactly! He's thinking about it... and hard... because he doesn't want to get caught," Vikki exclaimed.

"No, he's thinking hard about it because he doesn't want to go to jail, convicted of murder, for something that he's innocent of," Azalea said calmly, placing her hands on Vikki's shoulders, looking her dead in the eyes.

"That's exactly what he wants us to think! I mean, he even said it himself, there's not that much evidence that he didn't do it... but think about it, there's a ton of evidence that he did."

"Victoria, I think you just need some sleep. It was a shock to everybody to find Chad dead. You just need rest. Stop worrying about who did it, and try and figure out how we're going to get home," Azalea said.

"Yeah, you're right... that is what we should be worried about... especially with a psychopath murderer leading us back to town."

Azalea sighed and stood up.

"No wait!" Vikki called after her. "What about the whole 'go ahead, test it' thing he said? He wanted me to feel like I had the choice to turn him in. Or-or-or, what about the fact that he's the one who cut Chad out of the tree?"

"Vikki, you're making no sense. You're making a mountain out of a mole hill. Please stop and get some rest. Zander will be back soon, hopefully with some food."

"You're certainly right about that," I said, stepping foot into camp.

"Whoa! Zander," Azalea said, wheeling around to give me a hug once she saw the fat squirrels.

"How much did you hear?" Vikki asked worriedly.

"Just the part about me coming back with food," I said with a shrug. "Why were you two plotting something diabolical?"

"Like what? What would you think we were plotting?" Vikki asked. She sounded really paranoid.

"Oh I don't know, like how to spend your mega-cash at the mall all weekend... chill, Vicks, I was just joking... I am capable of doing that, you know, joking thing... I believe your normal reaction would be to laugh... just a guess though," I said with a smile. Vikki forced a laugh. Azalea smiled at me as she took the squirrels.

I sat there and watched as she skinned and gutted the squirrels with such perfection. I was baffled.

"So, have you done this before?" I asked.

"Huh?"

"Prepped animals, have you done it before?"

"Yeah, when I went on that outward bound thing... on my solo day I caught a squirrel, skinned it, and ate it... pretty weird huh?" she asked. I smiled at her.

"Well, did you ever think it'd come in handy?"

Sly Darkness by Kya Aliana

"Not really, but I guess it did."

"So what does it taste like? Any good?" I asked.

"Kinda tastes like a beef cubed steak," she said with a smile.

"Damn, I was hoping it'd taste like chicken," I said with a chuckle. Azalea broke out into a laugh. I knew it wasn't that funny, but sometimes, especially in times of crisis, people just needed to laugh and anything would get them there.

Vikki glared at me. I couldn't help but to feel the words she spoke, the theory she had, echo in my head. I wondered what I could say to her to make her believe I didn't do it. I knew if she didn't believe, it would dangerous for me... Azalea as well... but what I didn't say to the girls earlier that day, is that whoever told the cops, would probably get a break... and a big one... especially if it was one of the girls. I knew that if Vikki told, I'd be convicted of murder, I'd go to jail, life would never be the same for me; and as for Vikki, she'd probably get off scott-free. And I would do my best to keep Azalea out of it, but I highly doubted my word would be worth the same after I tried to *"cover up"* the murder of Chad whatever-his-last-name-was.

"Cowboy?" Azalea said, looking into my eyes.

"Yeah?" I asked.

"Thanks," she said with a smile.

"For what?"

"Everything. None of us could have survived out here without you. And thanks for being my friend, I've never been able to trust anybody the way I trust you."

I smiled and my chest felt hot. I thought about sleeping with her again tonight. I felt my pants get tighter and I looked around, trying to find something else to think about.

Sly Darkness by Kya Aliana

Chapter Nineteen

I approached the door slowly, walking cautiously down the long hallway. I could hear voices of protest and distant sobs. Fear filled my body and my vision became spotted. I held the letter opener from my mother's desk in my hand; it shook more and more as I came closer to the door. I took in a deep breath as the door creaked open.

"Zander!" a shrill voice shouted. Something was wrong. Something was terribly wrong. A bright white light filled my vision and I felt myself go limp and fall to the ground.

"Zander! Zander? Zander? Zander? Cowboy!" *Cowboy?*

I opened my eyes to find Azalea smiling at me. She was propped up on one shoulder and she rested her head in her hand while she smiled at me... had she been watching me sleep?

"Were you?" I started, but was too tired to finish. I couldn't remember which words were supposed to come next.

"Watching you sleep?" she guessed. I nodded my head with my eyes still shut. I heard her scoff. "Not really... you were kinda talking in your sleep," she stated. I opened my eyes suddenly and took in a sharp, quick breath of cold air.

"What did I say?" There was no hiding the alarm in my voice.

"Something about... your mother?" she said as if it was a question.

"Well did I or didn't I?" I asked. I couldn't remember what I'd been dreaming about. I hardly ever dreamt.

"You did... but it didn't make any sense," Azalea said quietly. I glanced over at Victoria, who was sleeping soundly.

"I'm sorry. I didn't mean to scare you," I said.

"It's okay... do you remember what you were dreaming about?" she asked. I shook my head slowly, wishing I could remember. The thought of my mother was starting to take its toll. I sat up and looked around. The moon hung low in the sky and the

Sly Darkness by Kya Aliana

dim light of dawn was formulating behind the mountains and through the trees. I buried my head in my hands and pushed the sweaty hair back. I took a deep breath and ignored the "are you okay?" question from Azalea.

"We're a lot alike, you and me," I said quietly, after a minute.

"What do you mean?" she asked.

"Well, it's just, you're not the only one with secrets," I said, almost not believing that I was even mentioning this.

"Do you want to talk about it?" she asked.

"I don't think I can... not just yet anyways," I replied honestly.

"But sometime?" she asked.

"Yeah," I replied, pausing for a moment. "Sometime," I repeated, lying back down. Azalea rested her head on my chest and after a few short minutes, I felt her breathing become heavier as she drifted back to sleep.

I didn't sleep again that night. I couldn't. I couldn't stop thinking about my mother. About what she had said to me right before she died. I thought about Azalea and how she had saved both her parents. I was jealous and mad. Why couldn't I have been like her? Why couldn't I have saved my mother? It wasn't fair. Her saving both her parents... me only having to save one of them and I couldn't do it. I just couldn't do it. What was wrong with me? How could I have let her go? Why did she have to die?

A wave of guilt filled my entire essence. I could hardly bare it anymore. I watched the sunrise over the mountains as tears filled my eyes. After the colors went away, my tears stopped, my breathing steadied, and my heart stopped aching. It was over. It was done.

I lied there for a very long time, listening to Azalea breath in and out... feeling her heartbeat against mine, enjoying the warmth of her body pressed against mine. It was going to be okay. I knew what I needed to do.

"Good morning, Cowboy!" Azalea said, moving her head

Sly Darkness by Kya Aliana

up to face mine. She gave me a quick kiss before nestling her head on top of my shoulder.

"Good morning, sweetheart," I said. It felt good to call someone sweetheart. I'd have to start calling her that more often.

"I'm gonna heat up some of that leftover squirrel," she said after a minute, standing up.

"Okay... you sure it's still good?" I asked. I hoped she would say yes, I didn't feel like trying to catch another squirrel.

"Yeah, it's at least as cold as a refrigerator out here!" she said, rubbing her arms. I buried my arms inside my hoodie as I stood up and walked over to the fire. I watched as Vikki slept soundly off toward the edge of camp. Azalea started to mix the chunks of squirrel meat around in the pan as it heated up over the fire.

I looked overhead and saw them following me. They circled around in a gloomy manner. There were so many of them... I couldn't count them all. Sometimes, I wished that they would stay still so I could count them all. At one point, they all had names... I wrote them down, but like I said before, I never went back to read what I wrote. Every time there was a new one, I wrote its name down in my journal. I watched them play as I searched my bag for my journal and a pen. I opened to a fresh page and wrote down Chad's name.

"What cha writing about, Cowboy?" Azalea asked, sitting down next to me.

"Nothing," I said, closing the book and slipping it back into my bag.

"What, I can't read?" she asked, making a sad looking puppy dog face. Her lip quivered and it annoyed me because it was so fake.

"It's kinda private," I said with a sigh.

"That's okay... I understand," she said, even though I knew it wasn't true. "You can keep writing in it, I won't read," she promised standing back up and tending to breakfast.

"Thanks," I said as I took it back out again. I did write in it. I wrote in it for a long time. I wrote about coming to Riverwolf

Sly Darkness by Kya Aliana

Pass. I wrote about meeting Chad and Vikki, and Sarah who would later become Azalea. I wrote down everything that happened since I'd gotten to Riverwolf Pass. And when I was done, I slipped it away and promised myself never to revisit it.

    I went back to watching them play, way up there in the sky. I watched them until I lost track of the time.

    "They're in your head, you know," Azalea whispered in my ear. I turned to look at her.

    "What do you mean?" I asked. "You can see them," I said, confusion rising up inside of me.

    "No, I can't, Zander," she said slowly and quietly. I looked at her, my breathing getting faster and my heart rate picking up. I could feel my skin get hot and the hair on my neck stand up.

    "What are you saying?" I asked slowly, trying to control my temper.

    "Look, Cowboy, I just thought you should know... those... *things* that are following you-"

    "They're not *things*! I mean, I know they might be creepy at first... but they *mean* something, Azalea... they used to be som-" I cut my words short, biting my cheek and looking at the ground.

    "Do you even know what a fucking wraith is? You must... you don't just call them that for no reason, Zander! Just what are they ghosts of? Huh? I'd like to know because those wraith moths that are following you... they're not real... they're just in your head. And that's okay, Cowboy, everybody has something... it's just... I see you watching them all the time, and I thought you should know that no one else can see them," she said.

    The tone of her voice was really getting on my nerves. I was about ready to scream at her. She was talking to me like I was some sort of crazy person. What else had Vikki said to her? Did Vikki say something to get Azalea to believe her? I wanted to grab Vikki and shake her. I wanted to grab Azalea and shake her and tell her she was crazy.

    "No, you can see them, you told me you could see them," I said slowly, processing every word that came out of my mouth.

Sly Darkness by Kya Aliana

It took everything I had not to explode. It took everything I had to think before I spoke.

"No, Cowboy, I never said that I could see them, I just didn't tell you that I couldn't," Azalea replied slowly.

"No!" I screamed, unable to control myself any longer. "You can too see them! Everybody can see them! They're there! They really are! Azalea you have to believe me! Just look! Look up there!" I screamed at her. She looked and slowly shook her head. "See!" I exclaimed. "See! I was right! You were wrong! They're right there! Aren't they? Aren't they there?" I asked, gripping her shoulders tightly. She shook her head slowly at me. I could see the fear in her eyes.

"No, Cowboy, I-I can't... I'm sorry," she said, her voice cracking.

"No! You're wrong! You're wrong!" I screamed, shaking her back and forth.

"Cowboy! Stop! Please stop, you're scaring me!" she pleaded.

"What the hell are you doing to her?" Vikki's sharp voice pierced the air. I suddenly realized what I was doing and I stopped.

"I-I... I uh... I-I,"

"You what, Zander?" Vikki said, standing inches away from my face.

"I'm sorry, I'm so sorry," I said, releasing my grip on Azalea and backing away a few steps.

"You know what, Zander?" Vikki asked after a few minutes of a long silence.

"I'm sorry," I repeated.

"Oh, it's okay, Cowboy. I understand," Azalea said. She started to walk toward me but was stopped by Vikki.

"Zander!" Vikki snapped. "This is the last straw! You know what I'm gonna do?" she asked. I knew the question was rhetorical, so I didn't answer. "I'm gonna tell on you! You murdered Chad and I'm gonna tell the cops! Just as soon as we get back to Riverwolf Pass, you're going to be convicted!"

Sly Darkness by Kya Aliana

"Vikki, I didn't do anything!" I screamed at her.

"Not to mention, we'll go to jail too," Azalea said sternly.

"Nah-uh, we're gonna say we were victims! We're going to say that Zander here kidnapped us, took us against our will, and did bad things to us while we were out here!" Vikki said with a wild flame burning in her eyes. "Bad things like *rape!*" she exclaimed, a perfidious passion behind her words.

"Vikki please, you can't just lie like that!" I screamed even louder. I could hear everything echoing in my ears. Everything was louder than it should have been. Vikki's voice was the loudest, but on top of that, I could hear the wind, the leaves, the birds, the squirrels, everything. It was all intensified... infected with Sly Darkness.

"Vikki, I swear to God if you do that I'll claim that you're lying. I'll fight in Zander's defense! He's innocent! You can't just go sending innocent people to jail, Victoria," Azalea snapped.

"I wouldn't be too quick to jump to the conclusion that he's innocent!" Vikki said in a rather snubbing manner.

"Okay, look," I stated, calming myself down. "Go ahead, Vikki, think whatever you want. Go ahead and say that I'm guilty. How about you just forget about the fact that I saved your life, and Sarah's, and Chad's earlier in the woods when Kurt showed up. Just go ahead and forget about that and think that I'm guilty. Because that would make a lot of sense, wouldn't it? For me to save all your asses, while getting mine kicked by the way, just so I can kill Chad myself and risk going to jail for the rest of my life. Do you really think that's what I did Vikki?" I asked, my temper was rising again, but I wasn't about to let it get out of control.

"You know what, how about you just forget that I'm trying to help you get back to Riverwolf Pass too? Why don't you just stay here? Maybe you can forget that we're lost in the woods as well! Shit, maybe you can forget a lot of stuff, and life for you will just be better. So go your own way, stay here and start a fire, which by the way, I'm sure wouldn't attract whoever killed Chad, and have fun by your merry self. But me? Me, I'm going to keep on walking right now because I'm tired of being out here in the

Sly Darkness by Kya Aliana

woods with a girl who thinks I'm a murderer! I don't know about you two, but I'm ready to be back in Riverwolf Pass. I'm walking, you can follow or you can stay, the choice is up to you," I said as I bent over to pack my bag.

It only took a few silent minutes for the camp to be cleaned up, the fire put out, and the girls ready to follow me out of the woods. I hoped I'd said the right things to Vikki. I wished she would stop acting like such a paranoid freak.

"Zander, I'm sorry, okay?" she said around lunch time. "I guess I got a little carried away... Chad's death was just kinda this huge shock to me... I'm still not sure how to handle it... especially because I can't really talk to anybody about it," she said smoothly. I wondered if her words were sincere, or if she was only trying to make things better by giving good lip service.

"It's understandable," I said with a shrug.

"Look, I won't say anything to the cops... I don't *think* you did it." I wondered why she put an emphasis on think. I sighed and once again, saw my breath in the air.

"Good," I said, emotionless. It was quiet for a long time after that. We walked along; listening to every sound the forest had to offer. I heard birds chirping and chipmunks scurrying, twigs snapping, the wind whirling, and the water beside us rushing. It was all rather calming. I wondered why I'd found it unbearable earlier that day. I wondered what made everything seem so loud.

"Can we take a ten minute break?" Azalea asked, sounding hopeful.

"Yeah sure," I said with a shrug. I walked off a little farther, partially to leave the girls alone and partially to give myself a small break. I heard them talking, Vikki in a panicked whisper. I couldn't make out what they were saying and part of me was happy about that.

It wasn't too long before Azalea walked up to me by herself.

"I'm worried about you, Cowboy," she said, lying her head on my shoulder.

Sly Darkness by Kya Aliana

"Oh?" I asked, looking at her with a confuzzled expression.
"Yeah," she replied slowly. "You didn't really take it that well this morning when I said no one else could see those... wraith moths... and Vikki, despite her last apology, still plans on telling the cops everything she can the first chance she gets."
"What a surprise," I said with a hopeless sigh.
"Look, I know all this must be really scary for you, but I'm going to do the best I can to protect you. I believe that you didn't kill Chad. I don't think you're crazy because you see wraith moths. I think there's a reason you see them. I think you're blessed with some sort of special gift or something... look, all I'm trying to say is that I'm here for you," she said with a smile. I looked at her, unsure of what to say.
"Thanks." I finally decided upon.
"Well, who knows how much farther we could have. After all, Riverwolf Pass could be waiting for us just behind that tree!" she exclaimed, standing up as Vikki approached us, slowly and cautiously.
"Yeah, who knows," I said with as much smile as I could muster.
We walked and we walked and then we walked some more. Riverwolf Pass was most definitely *not* just beyond that tree. Now that Vikki had paid me a fake apology, it was easier than ever to keep up the small talk.
Dusk came upon us quickly again. It wasn't an option to keep walking, though I disagreed with it. We needed to keep walking, keep going; we needed to reach Riverwolf Pass. But the girls wouldn't hear of it, so we set up camp and a fire. The ground was still frozen and the sky was a steel gray. The wind was nippy and I knew we were in for a snowstorm. I debated whether or not I should sleep in the tent tonight. It was warmer out by the fire, because you were closer to it. But the tent would protect me from falling snowflakes. It was a hard call to make. Not to mention, I liked sleeping outside by the fire. I got to see the sunrise in the morning as soon as I opened my eyes. Guilt filled my entire head

while I thought about how I'd missed the sunrise the night I'd slept with Azalea.

"Zander?"

"Huh, what?" I asked. I guess I'd gotten lost in my own thoughts.

"We were just wondering if you were going to try and catch dinner again tonight?" Azalea asked, looking at me with her big beautiful eyes. "Please?" she added.

"Yeah, sure. I mean, of course," I said, standing up and grabbing the machete.

"Thanks, Zander," Azalea said with a smile and a quick kiss.

"Yeah, thanks," Vikki said. Sincere was the farthest thing she sounded like. *Maybe tomorrow **you** would like to try and catch squirrels...* I thought inside my head. I let out a small chuckle as I walked out of camp and into the woods.

I was out there for hours. By the time I came back, it was already half-past eleven.

"It's okay, Zander," Azalea said to me, resting her head on my shoulder. "At least you gave it your best shot."

"Yeah," I said, sounding depressed.

"I'm going to bed," Vikki said with a sigh. She stood up and walked into the tent.

"Don't pay any attention to her... she's just a teenage drama queen," Azalea said, cupping my face and directing my vision toward her.

"I know," I said with a half-smile.

"Seriously, Zander, we'll be okay. It's one night. Shoot, we even ate this morning... by tomorrow, we'll all be back in Riverwolf Pass, laughing and eating pizza together," Azalea promised. I wondered why she seemed so optimistic.

"Azalea, we don't even know where we are!" I exclaimed, hoping this wouldn't dampen the mood too much... then again, the mood was already pretty damp.

"Sure we do! We're on our way back," Azalea said with a smile. Snow started to fall from the sky and I pulled her closer to

Sly Darkness by Kya Aliana

me.

"You're right... I'm sorry, it's just been a hard day followed by a hard night," I said, rather enjoying how close she was to me.

"Well," she started. "I have an idea on how to make it better."

"Oh?"

"Mmmhmm," she said smoothly as she brought her lips close to mine.

"Oooh, it's better already," I said with a smile right before I indulged in a very long and thrilling kiss.

She pressed her body tightly against mine as her tongue explored deep in my mouth. My hand gripped her gently and I pulled back slightly, breaking the kiss and revealing her neck. She breathed in deeply as I started to kiss it, using my tongue to apply extra pressure. She thrust her chest up toward me and I started to kiss lower, my lips grazing her collarbone and then the very tops of her breasts, going as far as her shirt would allow.

She pushed herself back far enough to make room for her to slip my shirt off. I took the opportunity to remove hers as well, pressing my bare chest against hers. The feeling was electrifying. She slowly pulled herself up so my face pressed against her breasts. I kissed them, squeezing them gently and barely pinching her nipples.

She slid back down and started to kiss the nape of my neck, slowly moving up to my ear. She bit the lobe gently, sending shivers throughout my entire body.

"I haven't been able to stop thinking about making love to you all day," she whispered softly, kissing down my jawline and back to my lips. I parted them slightly and slid my tongue into her mouth, she started to suck on it slowly, pulling it deep into her mouth; the technique making me think of her sucking on something entirely different.

I moaned softly and my hand glided down her body, grabbing her butt and then slowly, cautiously, and almost nervously moving around to the front. I unzipped her jeans and slowly pulled them down, revealing her undies. The fabric easily

Sly Darkness by Kya Aliana

stretched as I moved my hand inside. She was so wet, I could barely stand it.

Chapter Twenty

"Zander!"

"Hmm?" I opened my eyes slowly. The first thing I saw was Azalea's panic stricken face. "What's wrong?" I asked, as soon as I was conscious.

"Vikki's missing!" she said urgently.

"What do you mean missing? She's probably just sleeping in the tent or went to use the bathroom in the woods or something," I said, rubbing the sleep from my eyes and sitting up.

"No, Zander, she's gone! Her stuff and everything, she's gone. Even the tent is gone, Zander, look," I looked around camp to see that Azalea was right.

"She took off?" I asked slowly.

"No. She couldn't have; it's not like her to take off... just like it wasn't like Chad. God, the same person or thing or whatever probably got her while we were sleeping right here! Zander, I'm terrified!" Azalea said, unable to stop the rush of words that flowed out of her mouth.

"Shh," I calmed, running my fingers through her long and smooth hair. "It's okay," I comforted right before I realized that she was crying. I pulled her closer to me, emerging her in a sweet embrace.

We sat there for a very long time. I watched the sun rise and then start to hang steadily in the sky. I watched the colors fade and the brightness take their place.

"We have to keep walking," I said quietly after a minute. "I don't want to scare you more than you already are, but whatever is out there is still there... and it seems to have taken an interest in us. Azalea, sweetheart, we have to keep moving," I said slowly.

She nodded her head and looked at me, fresh tears streaming down her face.

"It's going to be okay, Azalea, I'm here... and I promise I'll

Sly Darkness by Kya Aliana

do everything within my power to protect you," I promised.

She smiled and nodded.

"I trust you," she said, sweeping my face with her gentle hand.

"Good," I said, standing up and packing our bags.

"Cowboy," she said.

"Yes?" I replied.

"We're the only two left... I'm kinda freaking out."

"It's okay. We'll reach Riverwolf Pass today. I have this great feeling," I said with as much of reassuring smile as I possibly could.

"Okay," Azalea replied with a smile. With that, we started walking. I would've held her hand or put my arm around her while she silently cried, but the weight of the body was too great for me to do anything but walk beside her.

"Glory, that body reeks!" Azalea exclaimed around noon.

"Yeah, I know. We'll be rid of it soon, I promise," I said, looking over at her. She had stopped crying and now her eyes just looked distant and tired.

Neither of us knew what else to say, so we didn't say much of anything. We stopped for short breaks when we got tired and we kept walking after we caught our breath.

* * *

Vikki's body laid in front of us. We stopped walking, the sight making us breathless. I could feel my whole body tingling as the image refused to leave my mind. I drew Azalea closer to me and squeezed her tightly with my arm around her. I felt her whole body shudder and I heard her sniff. I didn't want to look at her. I didn't want to see her cry. I didn't want to see the fear in her eyes. I didn't want to face that... I didn't want to face her. She hurt, and I had no clue how to make her stop hurting. I didn't know what to say or what to do. I couldn't look at her, even when I eventually tried... I did just that, I tried... I couldn't accomplish actually doing it.

Sly Darkness by Kya Aliana

Vikki's arm was completely detached from her body, leaving a bloody trail of ligaments strewn about. Her face had been cut and one of her eyes were black. Her lip was split; her legs spread and her pants were nowhere to be found.

There was blood everywhere... the sight as absolutely unbearable, yet I couldn't look away.

After a long, stifling, fifteen minutes, I grabbed Azalea's hand. I started to walk around the body, pulling Azalea along behind me. The only thing I could think to do was get her away from Vikki's dead body. She followed with great ease, seemingly grateful that I was getting her away from the bloody mess that used to be Victoria.

* * *

As dusk approached, I could feel the heat and frustration seething off Azalea.

"Should we keep walking?" I asked, breaking the long held silence between us.

"How far away do you think we are?" she asked.

"I don't know," I said with a shrug. "But I know that if we start walking at night, it'll probably be harder to stop. It'll be harder to make a fire... harder to stay warm... and obviously harder to settle our minds enough to actually fall asleep."

Azalea nodded in agreement as she set her pack down.

We set up camp in silence. As soon as the fire was roaring and the blankets and tarp was set up so we would stay dry and warm that night, I grabbed my machete.

"Cowboy?" Azalea asked when I started to walk away.

"Yes?" I replied, turning to face her.

"I really don't want to be left alone right now," she said, biting her lip as she looked at me.

"I understand," I said reassuringly, walking over to her and placing my hand on her shoulder. "But we still need food."

"Can't I go with you?" she asked, her eyes wide with anticipation and fear. I looked around the camp.

Sly Darkness by Kya Aliana

"Yeah, just give me a minute to clear everything away from the fire pit," I said with a smile as I walked over to where we had built the fire. We'd neatly put rocks around it and with my foot, I kicked the leaves and twigs away from it, leaving only dirt five feet in each direction.

"Thanks, Cowboy," Azalea said softly. Her voice was low, soft and sad. I hoped that after she got some food in her belly, her spirits would pick up... at least as much as they could given the predicament.

We walked deeper into the woods, so deep that you couldn't hear the rush of the river anymore. It was almost alarming how quiet the woods were. I could hear myself breath, I could hear every thought that I had, I could hear every step I took, I could hear my heartbeat and I could hear Azalea's beat loud, clear and fast as well. I brushed away some leaves and sticks with my foot and sat down.

"What are you doing?" Azalea asked.

"If we keep walking and looking around, the squirrels won't come," I explained. Azalea nodded and sat down next to me. Her face was tired. It was no longer a face of innocence. It was no longer a face that was naive to the world and its cruelty. This trip had shown her what it was like to exist in the real world. She'd had a taste of it before, but now, she'd had a meal... several of them, in my opinion.

She laid her head in my lap and I stroked her long tangled hair until it was smooth and knot free. I listened to her breath, slow and steady. I could feel her heartbeat against my thigh and it made my heart beat slow until our hearts beat in sync. I thought about how young she was when we had first come out into the woods... now the sly darkness had taken her security. It had stolen it from her, thrashed it out of her, beat her down until she seemingly had no secure feelings left inside of her. The sly darkness was as unforgiving as it was unrelenting. I felt badly for a moment that I hadn't warned Azalea of the darkness to come. But I knew even if I had, it wouldn't have changed anything. The sly darkness was out here, it would get to you one way or another.

Sly Darkness by Kya Aliana

I was part of it... Chad and Vikki were victims of it... and Azalea still needed to choose a side. I guess it'd paid off for me to have experienced it before... I guess it'd paid off for me to be chill and copacetic... I guess it'd paid off for me to have a cool head and be able to think under pressure... I wondered what would happen next.

 Azalea and I sat there for five minutes before we saw any wildlife. But soon, a bunny rabbit slowly came into view. I gently and slowly moved Azalea so she slept on the ground instead of on me. I stood up, quietly so as the bunny rabbit as well as Azalea wouldn't hear me. I was thoughtful about where I stepped, watching the ground while I walked and watched the bunny rabbit as I stood still. The bunny looked up and saw me. I stopped and looked it dead in the eye. We stared at each other for what seemed like a long few minutes, and then it went back to eating a little green plant in the woods. I continued forward, back to watching the ground now. After what seemed like a long time, I was only a few feet away from it. It stopped to look at me again, but this time it was quicker to go back to its dinner.

 I watched it very carefully as I started to take the machete out of the loophole on my pants. It barely made any noise and the bunny didn't even seem to notice as I steadied the machete in my hand and hovered it over the rabbits head. The machete came down with a swift swoosh and the bunny was dead in a matter of a micro-second. I bent over to examine my handy work and make sure there weren't any family members hanging around... I didn't see any. The rabbit I'd killed was middle-aged and fat. It would easily supply a dinner and a lunch for Azalea and I.

 "ZANDER!" I heard Azalea's scream and I stood up quickly. My head jerked around so I could see her. She sat there, tears streaming down her face, shaking from the fear pent up inside her. I ran over to her.

 "Are you okay? What happened?" I asked, plopping down next to her.

 "No, nothing happened... I'm okay... Oh God, I just- I thought... I thought the old crazy hermit that got Vikki and Chad

Sly Darkness by Kya Aliana

had gotten you too!" She started to cry harder and I pulled her and held her tightly against my body.

"Shh, it's okay. I'm okay," I promised, whispering it into her ear over and over again. I gently rocked back and forth and slowly her sobs subsided.

"I'm sorry," she said, her voice muffled through my thick hoodie. I relaxed my tight grip on her and pulled back a little to look her in the eyes.

"Azalea, it's okay. You had every reason in the world to freak out and think what you did. There's nothing wrong with that. Something freaky, scary and creepy as all get out is going on here, we should both be alert and thoughtful," I said, bringing her in for another hug. I felt her nod against my shoulder and then I stood up, helping her to her feet as well.

"I caught us dinner," I said proudly, taking her hand and walking over to where I'd killed the bunny. She smiled when she saw it.

"I never thought I'd be so happy to see a dead bunny," she said, squeezing my hand. I chuckled as I picked it up and we walked back to camp.

It was dark by the time we reached the dim glow of the fire. I was happy that we'd already collected wood for the night and I wouldn't have to go back out in the woods again. I placed logs on the fire, building it up higher and brighter, as Azalea skinned the rabbit.

"Don't you think that will attract someone?" Azalea asked, nervously looking at the growing fire.

"Whoever is out there... whoever killed Chad and Vikki is following us... whoever it is, is good at what they're doing... if whoever it is wants to kill us, then they probably already know where we're at... at this point, a fire doesn't even matter." I didn't want to scare her, but she needed the truth. Not to mention, I wasn't about to let us go cold that night because of fear. Azalea nodded slowly, holding back tears.

"Oh, Zander!" she wailed after a couple minutes. "I'm so scared. We're the last ones left! What if... what if they kill us

Sly Darkness by Kya Aliana

tonight... or what if they just kill one of us... or what if-"

"Azalea, shh," I said, walking over to her and taking her hands in mine. "Listen to me, you need to stop thinking what if... something messed up is happening... I don't know why, and I don't know what to do about it. But, what I do know is that I am not going to let anyone else do anything more. I am not going to let them hurt you, do you hear me?" I asked, looking into her eyes with a great intensity. Azalea nodded her head.

"I'm just so scared, Zander," she said, burying her head in my chest.

"Shh, it's okay," I said soothingly. "It's okay to be scared. Anybody in our position would be scared, Azalea. It's okay, it's alright. I've been through some tough shit, and let me tell you something, I know you've been hurt in the past... I know you've gone though some though shit... but I know how to handle myself and I'm not going to let anyone else hurt you," I said. Azalea nodded and we sat there for a moment. I thought a lot in that moment, and I made a decision... a big decision. I decided to talk to her about something that I'd never talked to anyone about before.

"How old were you when all that happened with your parents?" I asked.

"Sixteen," Azalea replied. "I told you that."

"That's what I thought... I just wanted to make sure," I replied.

"Why?"

"Because I want you to think about how much you've grown since then. Has it even been a year?" I asked.

"Yeah... it's a year today... happy birthday to me," she replied solemnly.

"Oh, Azalea!" I exclaimed, gripping her hand tighter. It wasn't fair that all that took place on her birthday... it just made it so much more terrible! I felt a wave of guilt overcome me as I remembered that I'd forgotten to ask when her birthday was, or when any of that happened.

"Yeah," she replied, it sounded like her mind was

Sly Darkness by Kya Aliana

somewhere else.

"I was four," I stated slowly. The words didn't want to come, but I had to make them. "When my mother died," I finished. Azalea looked at me with hurt eyes. They hurt for me. And instantly I felt bad for talking to her about this... but I knew she wanted me to finish. I knew that *I* needed to finish.

"What happened?" she asked after a moment of silence.

"Just," I paused for a second. "Just let me tell the story, okay? Because before you know what happened, you have to know about me," I said. Azalea nodded and I continued the story... my story.

"When I was four, I had this scooter. It was red and metal and the fastest thing in the world in my mind. My mother got it for me for Christmas... the tag had said 'from Santa', but I'd seen my mother buy it one day when I was coming home from school. The look in her eyes when I opened it on Christmas morning is a look I'll never forget," I said, tears filling my eyes. I had to stop for a minute to catch myself... to force myself to go on. "They looked so happy... they almost danced in the light illuminating from the Christmas tree," I said, smiling through the tears as I remembered it.

"I played with it all day, zipping around the house... and when my dad yelled at me to stop because I'd break something I played with it outside... even though it was icy and freezing. All the other kids had sleds... I had this red scooter." I had to stop again, because what I was going to say next wasn't as happy-go-lucky as that Christmas morning was.

"I rode it every day until the summer came... I remember because I was hot and sweaty from riding it and I came inside where my mom offered me a glass of cool water. I took it gratefully and would have gulped it all down if it wasn't for my mother's stern warning that I'd get a belly-ache if I didn't slow myself. I nodded and sipped it slowly, enjoying every last cool sip.

"My mother sat there with me... smiling as she watched me drink. She grabbed my hand after I'd finished and stood up to

Sly Darkness by Kya Aliana

go back outside. She told me that she loved me and that no matter what she always would. It's that moment that makes me think she knew what was coming. It's that moment that makes me think that she didn't care... that she wanted to go, just to get away from it all. She didn't care if I was going to be left alone with *him*... all she wanted was out... out of this world... and to this day, I can't blame her," I said, taking a deep breath as I let all this out. I'd never talked to anybody about it... I never thought I needed to... I never saw why I should... and even as I was doing it, I continued to wonder why I was telling Azalea all this.

"Why would she want to get away from the world?" Azalea slowly prompted. It was when she said this that I realized I'd been quiet for a long time.

"My mother didn't go out a whole lot... not even to the grocery store like most mothers did," I said. "She was never like the other mothers... the other mothers who picked their kids up from school and baked cookies and allowed friends to come over... the other mothers with no bruises or cuts... the other mothers would kiss their husbands before they left for work... the other mothers who thought my dad was the most wonderful man in the world for taking such good care of me. I overheard them talking one time... another mother and my father, that is... they were talking about what a shame it was that my mother was such a drunk... I didn't know what they meant, because I'd never seen my mother drink a drop in her life... it was always my father who drank... every day after work. But the neighbors didn't know that... they saw my father how he wanted them to see him... as a good honest man, who went to church and raised his only son," I couldn't help the tears and I wiped my nose on the sleeve of my shirt as I went on.

"They didn't know... I couldn't tell them. My father said that if I ever told them about the screaming, or the fights, or the bruises on my mother's face that he would hurt her more... and he wasn't lying. One time, I'd said something about my mom having 'a real nice shiner,' and that night I heard her screaming... all night long. My father told me never to say something like that again. I

Sly Darkness by Kya Aliana

promised I never would," I said with a gulp. I took in a breath of air and caught a lung full of smoke from the fire. I coughed for a moment before continuing.

"I was riding my red scooter; waiting for my dad to get home... my mom was humming and cooking dinner in the kitchen... I could smell fried chicken; I heard the sizzle through the kitchen window. My dad sped home with his flashy blue corvette. I thought he was going to hit me, so I jumped off my scooter, landing in the yard and getting a mouthful of dirt. My scooter kept going, and I raised my head just in time to see my scooter become obliterated by my dad's car. He didn't even stop to think twice about it.

"He got out of the car, furious and marched into the house. I heard my parents hushed voices over the fryer and I ran in the house faster than I ever thought I could. 'I'm sorry, it was all my fault, I just let it go... I should have stopped!' I screamed, but neither of them listened to me. My father told me to go to my room, but my mother bustled past him and over to me. She told me that I'd lost my two front teeth when I'd crashed into the ground. She took me into the bathroom and cleaned me up... she was a good mom," I said. I missed her. I wanted her to be here with me right now.

"She sounds like the very best mom," Azalea said. "She really cared about you." I nodded and sighed, remembering later that night.

"I heard them yelling, all night long. My dad told her she'd wasted his money, buying me that scooter and all. She yelled back at him, telling him that she just wanted me to have a good Christmas. I listened to everything they said. I tossed and turned in my bed. I knew I shouldn't get up. I wasn't allowed to be out of my room after eight... but I just had to get them to stop. I thought I could help... after all, it was partially my fault that the scooter had gotten run over," I said. I could remember it like it was yesterday, and I wasn't sure if I could go on. After a moment, I knew I had to.

"After much debate inside my head, I got out of bed. I

Sly Darkness by Kya Aliana

remember the cool air stinging my bare legs as I stood there in my underwear. I stood, staring at the doorway, for a very long time. I was intimidated by it. I was scared for my mom when I heard thumping upstairs, the banging and shutting of my dad's top drawer... and I knew what he kept in his top drawer. I'd stumbled upon it by mistake one day... a long sharp knife that I thought should be illegal... probably was. I raced over to my pillow and grabbed my mother's letter opener. I don't remember why it was under my pillow, but I remember grabbing it. I walked down the long hallway to my parents' bedroom. I was scared and when I opened the door I saw blood... my mother's blood. Her scream echoed in my ears and I fainted. I couldn't do anything. I could just lie there, my vision clouded and her voice echoing in my ears," I couldn't go on... it was too painful... but a gentle prompt from Azalea and I found the strength.

"I came to right before she died... before... before my father killed her. She told me that she loved me... she told me that every morning when the sun rose, she would be there, watching me. She told me that every morning she would make the colors pretty. She said she would think about me every second no matter where she was. She also told me that she was sorry for the life I had... but I didn't know what she meant. She'd always made my life good. She'd made sure I had everything I needed. She even gave me the red scooter that I'd admired every day after Thanksgiving until a few days before Christmas when she bought it." I stopped again. I couldn't believe I'd just told her all that. I took some deep breaths to stop the tears.

"What happened to your father? Did he get blamed for the murder?" Azalea asked after I'd gotten a grip on myself. I shook my head slowly.

"No," I replied. "He said it was a suicide and he'd tried to stop her, but he couldn't. The police asked me a lot of questions, but dad answered most of them for me... including the lie that I'd been in bed while it all happened. He told me what to say before they asked the questions. I obeyed because I didn't know any better. The police investigated the death no farther... They had no

Sly Darkness by Kya Aliana

reason to. The neighbors all said that my father was a good man and would never do anything like that... they also had no good things to say about my mother," I said harshly. I hated those neighbors. How could they believe such lies?

"Oh, Zander, I'm so sorry!" Azalea said, hugging me tightly. I took another deep breath.

"I was fourteen when I realized that my father had abducted my mother when she was thirteen years old. He was much older than her, though he didn't look it. I don't know why I didn't piece it together before then. My mother used to talk to me about her parents, my grandparents. She used to tell me of a better life... a life she had before meeting my father. She told me about her younger brother and how they would play together in the fields after church on Sundays. She told me about her parents and about Christmas in their house. She also told me about how she missed them, and one day we were going to run away together to be with them again. 8673 Chrysanthemum Lane, Riverwolf Pass, North Carolina. That's where she used to live. That's where happiness was, or so she told me. That's why I came here. I guess it was foolish of me to think I would find family... people who loved me and cared for me... people who would be happy to see me... or at least somebody living there," I said.

"Zander, there are records at the courthouse... we could figure out who used to live there," Azalea said, looking at me with almost an excitement in her eyes.

"I already looked it up," I said, though I'd looked it up at the library instead of the courthouse.

"What did it say?" Azalea asked.

"A guy named Mr. White used to live there... but if you ask about him, everyone said he went crazy and took off with his bride-to-be, Gracey. There's no telling where they went."

"Do you think he's any relation to your mother?"

"My mother's last name was White... that is, until my father changed her identity," I said slowly. "All I know is that mom called him Westin, but I couldn't find a first name on him anywhere else... whoever he is, he has secrets... before he left

Sly Darkness by Kya Aliana

town he tried to destroy any records of himself being here... it was really hard for me to find anything about him. I got most of the information from a librarian he used to work with. He was twelve when I was born... which means he would have been eight when my mother was abducted. I found out his parents died about nine months ago." I didn't know why I was telling her all this. I knew there was no hope in finding the guy. He was a drifter and a loner... just like me... he'd gone to find a new life somewhere... with someone else... and he wasn't coming back.

"I'm sorry," Azalea whispered to me after a couple minutes.

"It's okay," I said, sniffling again. "Let's just make some dinner, okay?" I asked. Azalea nodded. I laid there, thinking quietly to myself... watching Azalea prepare the bunny rabbit.

Sly Darkness by Kya Aliana

Chapter Twenty-One

I awoke to the colors of the sun rise. Azalea rolled over and kissed me on my neck, and then wrapped her arms around me.

"You think she's really watching us?" Azalea asked. At first, I couldn't remember what she was talking about. Then I remembered I'd told her about my mother. I nodded slowly as tears filled my eyes. Of course she's watching us.

"I know she is... she has to be," I said. We watched the rest of the sunrise silently, each of us thinking our own thoughts. Afterward, we started to pack up the blankets and tarp. I poured some water from the river on the fire pit to make sure that the fire was completely out.

"Well, we made it through the night," Azalea said, smiling at me.

"We sure did... I'm gonna wash this pan down by the river while you finish packing. Then we'll start heading toward Riverwolf Pass, okay?" I asked. Azalea looked nervous at first... nervous to be left alone at camp.

"Listen, it's okay... if you scream I'll hear you and it will take me a total of thirty seconds to get back here," I promised with a kiss on the forehead. "Trust me, the faster we get out of here, the faster we get back to Riverwolf Pass," I said with a smile. Azalea nodded and I headed off to the river.

It only took me a few minutes to clean the pan. I splashed some water on my face and it felt good. The day was considerably warmer than the ones prior to it. I hoped it would only continue to warm up as we trekked through the woods. We couldn't be that far away from Riverwolf Pass now. We had to be nearing it, I just knew it. I looked around, smiling as the woods and I shared a secret.

As I walked back to camp, I could see Azalea through the trees. She was sitting there looking at something. I scrunched my

Sly Darkness by Kya Aliana

eyebrows together and hunched my head forward, as if that would help me to see better. I saw she was reading a book. I wondered why she hadn't been reading it before. It would've been good to pass the time while we walked. Who knows, maybe I would've liked it if she was the one reading it... or possibly the one who wrote it. I continued to walk toward the camp, snapping a twig on my way. I saw Azalea jump and slip the book into my backpack. I came into view, and she sighed a breath of relief.

"Zander! You scared me," she said.

"Sorry... I didn't mean to. What were you doing?" I asked.

"Oh, just packing," she said.

"Okay," I replied with a shrug and went to take my pack. I peered inside for a quick second to see my journal on top. I zipped the bag up and hoisted it over my shoulder.

"Well, let's get a move on," I said with a wry smile as I picked up Hector and waited on her to grab her two packs.

"Yeah, no time like the present... I'm sure ready to be home," Azalea said, sounding particularly antsy.

We walked for hours, non-stop. Azalea wouldn't allow us to stop. She'd started acting weird. I smiled because I knew why.

Around lunch time, a huge bubble of anger exploded inside of her.

"Why aren't we there yet?" she asked me, her arms thrust outward and she dropped the packs she carried.

"I don't know... it seems like we should have been there hours ago," I said in a comforting tone.

"No!" she exclaimed, placing her hands on her hips. "It doesn't *seem like* we should have been there hours, possibly days, ago, Zander! We *should* have been there a really long time ago. You keep leading me in circles! What's your plan? Are you going to kill me like you did Chad and Vikki?" Azalea shouted. As soon as the words escaped her lips, fear grew inside of her eyes.

"And what would make you think that I killed Chad and Vikki?" I asked with a wry smile, tilting my head and pressing my eyebrows together in a confused manner.

"Nothing... I'm just frustrated, we should keep walking,"

Sly Darkness by Kya Aliana

Azalea said, shaking her head and picking up her packs again.

"In circles?" I asked. "How could I possibly be leading you in circles when we're following a river?" I asked, walking toward her with a slight stagger. I dropped Hector and he fell to the ground with a bone-breaking thud. Azalea stared at the body for a moment and then her focus was back to me.

"I-I don't know... there's really no way possible... I'm just tired and frustrated and ready to be home," Azalea said, brushing by me. I caught her arm and she turned around to face me.

"No," I said with a smile in my eyes. "I really am curious as to where all this came from. I mean, you don't just make an accusation like that without some sort of evidence in your thinking," I said.

"Zander... your voice is so smooth and carefree... when Vikki made this sort of accusation you were furious... why aren't you that way with me?" she asked, backing up against a tree.

"Now, now, Azalea, you are not Vikki. You are far from Vikki. I like you, you know that. We have a lot in common... only you saved your mother when I couldn't," I said, inching toward her.

"Now, Zander, you were four, I was sixteen, that's a big age difference," Azalea said, holding out both her hands. She wanted me to stop nearing her. I could tell I was beginning to scare her.

"It's nothing to beat yourself up about," she added after I didn't stop approaching her.

"Of course not," I said with a smile, stopping to look at her. "You know, if it was only that, I might have been able to look past it," I said with a sigh. "Unfortunately, you had to go sticking your nose where it didn't belong... what were you looking for, exactly? What were you expecting to find? I'm just curious," I said kindly.

"I don't know what you're talking about, Zander. Please, you're scaring me," Azalea pleaded.

"Scaring you? I didn't know you found me scary... whatever could have changed your opinion?" I asked.

Sly Darkness by Kya Aliana

"The way you're acting!"

"Referring to?"

"Right now!" she almost screamed.

"Oh, and it couldn't have anything to do with something, say, you read?" I asked, shrugging as if I were taking a stab in the dark.

"I don't know what you're talking about," Azalea repeated.

"Come, Azalea, think... think hard... you didn't happen to get your hands on something that was very private, now did you? Something that could change a way a person looks at someone... say, a journal... diary... a day to day log, whatever you would like to call it," I said, throwing out suggestions.

"Zander, I'm sorry!" Azalea burst out. "I thought there might be something about me in there... I don't know what I read... I don't know if it's true or not... I don't know what to think or do, or-- Zander, I'm so scared," Azalea said, blabbering out half-sentences.

"Isn't a journal normally true? Not to mention, judging by your outbreak back there, it seems like you trust it," I said with a smile.

"Zander, it said *you* killed Chad and Vikki! It said you weren't lost in the woods at all. It said you'd never been lost... that you'd been leading us in circles! Zander, I don't understand," Azalea said, looking at me for help.

"Well, you caught me. You know how far away the mansion is?" I asked. Azalea shook her head no. "About five minutes that direction," I answered as I pointed north. "Do you know how long it's been that far away?" I asked. Azalea shook her head no once again. "All day long," I replied with a smile.

"Why?" Azalea breathed out.

"I wish it could have been different, Azalea. I liked you... I possibly could have grown to love you one day. We could have been a pair you and me, me and you, you and I, us, together, as a couple... but no, Azalea, no... you had to go and read my journal and now you know. Now you know how crazy I am... now you know all my secrets... you know about the Sly Darkness... you

Sly Darkness by Kya Aliana

know I'm a part of it... you know I live there... you know a lot of stuff that you shouldn't know," I said, shaking my head slowly.

"Zander, please," Azalea said.

"I wish it could be different... but I just can't chance you knowing. If you hadn't known, then I wouldn't have to kill you like I did Chad and Vikki. I saved them, you know. I saved Vikki from being treated just as my mother was... I saved Chad from a life of treating women like my mother was treated. It was all for the better. And the best part," I said with a smile. "Is that I didn't have to save you from anything... because you were mine... I liked you, Azalea... I trusted you, Azalea... but I can't trust you with this... and that's a shame."

"No, Zander, you *can* trust me!" Azalea promised.

"No, Azalea... no I can't. Look at you! You're backed up against the tree, clinging on to it for dear life... thinking about how to steal my journal away so you can bring it to the cops... so I can be locked up for life... but the thing is, Azalea, I'm not doing any bad. I'm saving people from a regrettable future. I'm helping them, Azalea! Can't you see that?" I asked.

"*You* need help, Zander! You can't see the future. You're killing *teenagers* for God's sake!" Azalea said.

"No," I replied slowly. "Not for God's sake... for my mother's sake... for *my* sake, Azalea, *mine*. I have to... I need to help them... it's my job, my *duty*," I said, looking deep into her eyes.

"What about me?" Azalea asked after a moment.

"What about you?" I asked, curious as to what she was implying.

"If you kill me, how does that help?" she asked, her eyes wide with the anticipation of my answer.

"It helps me... it helps me to stay safe... to be able to continue helping people," I said. The answer was simple... I wondered why she'd even questioned it.

"No, Zander, that's not going to help."

"Why do you keep calling me Zander?" I asked.

"That's your name," Azalea replied.

Sly Darkness by Kya Aliana

"You always call me Cowboy... you haven't called me that since you got a hold of my journal." I suddenly pieced together.

"You're not the Cowboy I thought you were," Azalea replied.

"You know, I really hate to do this," I said, taking a step toward her.

"No! Zander! You don't have to do this. Remember me, remember who I am! Cowboy, listen to me, remember when we met at the mansion?" she asked, still gripping the tree for dear life.

"You don't have to tell me to remember," I said bitterly. "Because I never forgot. I never will forget. I don't think I'll ever care for someone the way I care about you," I said, placing a hand on her shoulder. She flinched and I chuckled.

"Don't do this!" Azalea warned. "Don't do this or I swear to God you'll regret it."

"Oh? Will I?" I asked.

"Yes, you'll miss me... you and I have something... something special... something rare... you can't just throw that away," Azalea said. She released her grip on the tree and placed her arms around me, her face inches from mine.

"It doesn't matter," I said, shaking my head slowly. "It doesn't matter because now that you know, things would be different anyways if I let you live," I finished. Her lips were so close to mine it was almost tantalizing. I couldn't believe that I still had feelings for her, even when I knew things could never be the same... even when I knew that she would tell the cops the moment she got the chance... even when I knew that my life would be ruined if I let her live... I still had feelings for her.

"Azalea, I can't," I said.

"You can't what?" she asked slowly, pressing her body up against mine. This was a trick! This was what she was trying to get me to do, to feel. I couldn't buy into it. I couldn't help it. I placed my hand behind her head. I grabbed her hair and gently pulled her head back and I kissed her. I kissed her hard. I kissed her in a way that I'd never even imagined kissing.

Sly Darkness by Kya Aliana

"See, Cowboy, I knew you were good," she said with a smile. I took in a deep breath. She didn't mean it. I could sense the insincerity.

"You manipulative lit-" I couldn't finish the sentence. Anger filled my veins and the adrenaline started to rush inside of me. I pulled her hair so hard that she screamed. I started to walk toward the river silently. I waded in until the water came up to my waist and up to Azalea's chest.

"Zander! Stop! We'll have a family! Please! I'm pregnant with your child!"

"That's bull!" I exclaimed. Even I knew you couldn't tell that fast.

"Zander please! I remember when you kissed me when I was drunk... I acted like I didn't remember, but I do! Please, Zander, I love you! I care about you! I want to be with you! I won't tell any of your secrets! I have secrets too, remember? We trust each other!" she pleaded once more before I emerged her head into the water. She thrashed about. I pulled her out and told her that it would be easier if she didn't fight back. A swift kick to the knee was her reply. I shoved her head under again. This time she kicked and moved so much that she hit her head on a rock. The water around me turned red and I slowly released my grip as she became motionless.

I hoisted her onto my shoulder and lied her down on the riverbank. I moved her bloody hair from her face.

"I will miss you," I said as my hand gently caressed her face. My hand smoothly glided down the nape of her neck. I slowly traced her collarbone before sliding down to her chest. I could feel her heart beat, slow and steady. She wasn't dead, but she wouldn't wake up. I squeezed my hand so hard on her chest that my fingers broke through her fragile skin. I could feel her blood on my hands as I squeezed harder. I could see the blood soaking through her shirt. I watched her placid face and wondered if any part of her could feel what I was doing. I wanted to hold her heat... I wanted to feel it pounding in my hand.

"I'm sorry it had to end like this," I whispered as I reached

Sly Darkness by Kya Aliana

into my pocket for my knife. I opened it and thrust it through her chest, cutting around her heart.

"From the moment I saw you, I knew it would be mine," I said as I held her heart. It beat, just like in the movies. I could hear it. I could feel it. I could see it. I watched it stop and I looked back at Azalea. I squeezed the heart hard and watched the blood drip from it. It ran down my arm and dripped on the ground. I walked over to the river and placed her heart under the water, watching it wash away the seemingly endless flow of blood.

I walked back over to Azalea and picked up her body, cradling it in my arms.

"I wish you could have always been my girl," I said as I walked back over to the river. I tossed her body in half-way across. I watched as it flowed downstream. An animal would probably see it and eat her before the cops would ever find her. It'd be a freak accident. I'd never be suspected.

* * *

I spent a long time washing the blood from my clothes, but eventually I finished. I spent the night at the mansion, listening to the wind wail. I thought about Azalea. I thought about the night we had spent together. I thought about our first kiss. I couldn't believe that she'd remembered and not said anything. I wondered if she really was pregnant with my child. I would never know, but then again, it didn't really matter. What mattered was that I was safe. I did what had to be done and I could continue helping people. Making the world a better place. After all, if there were no bad people, how could the world be a bad place?

That morning, I watched the sunrise and I watched the wraith moths fly above me. I watched as they flew around in circles, bound to follow me wherever I went. I saw Chad and Vikki and all the other people I saved. But Azalea was different, she was majestic... she wasn't a moth at all... she was brilliantly white, brilliantly free... free to fly where she wanted, when she wanted, how she wanted. She wouldn't be bound to follow me...

Sly Darkness by Kya Aliana

she didn't have to. She could fly as high and far as she wanted to. She swooped down next to me and sat there beside me while the sun rose. When the sun had risen and the colors had vanished, so did she. She flew so high that I could no longer see her. She was gone... maybe not forever, but for the moment.

She was the albatross.

My mind rested on Azalea, thinking of all we could have been. She was gone. All gone. I would never see her again... I wouldn't ever see her smile... never hear her laugh. She would never confide in me and I would never trust her. She would never look longingly into my eyes. We would never make love again. She was gone. My heart tore inside my chest, breaking apart into wounds that could never be healed. I would miss her more than anyone... she was my one true love... she was my only chance... and I'd blown it. I would give anything to take it all back.

* * *

I stood up and grabbed the body. I walked into the town of Riverwolf Pass.

"I'd like to collect the reward for the finding of this missing boy," I said, laying the paper on the desk in the town hall. The lady looked at me over her glasses.

"Where's the body?" she asked.

"Outside, I didn't think you'd want me to bring it in," I said. She had me fill out some paperwork. A policeman came in and asked me some questions about how I found him and where and if I'd gone out with anyone. I told him I went out alone. I told him I was just passing through town. I told him a bunch of other lies as well.

"You seen any of these kids?" he showed me couple pictures of Azalea, Chad and Vikki. I scrunched my eyebrows together and pretended to study them hard. After a moment, I pursed my lips and shook my head.

"No, I've never seen any of these kids. Why, are they missing too?" I asked. The officer nodded his head once and put

Sly Darkness by Kya Aliana

the photos away.

"I hope they turn up," I said with a half-smile, standing.

"Thanks," the officer replied, shaking my hand.

"Have a blessed day," I said with a tip of my cowboy hat I had bought at the General Store, offering up a good ol' southern hospitality smile. I was good at lying: good at convincing people I was different. My father had trained me well from a young age. And now, my line of work required me to lie sometimes. After all, making the world a better place was never an easy job.

I talked to the father of Hector too. He wasn't much of a conversationalist... I think it was just because of the condition of his son, though.

After a long and hassling day, I got the reward money and skipped out on Riverwolf Pass. I was on a quest now. A different quest than I'd been on before. I had to find Mr. White and his wife, Gracey. I had to know him. I needed to know him. I had to find him... for me and for my mother. I needed to know.

Sly Darkness by Kya Aliana

Epilogue
Azalea

The first thought I had was of Zander. But that wasn't so unusual. I could feel the cool water rushing over me and I'd known what had happened. I remembered things in phases; the memories came and went... the important ones, the ones I'd wanted to know most, stayed. The others vanished. Zander was one of the important ones. I had to remember every single thing about him. I had to remember every word that he ever spoke. I had to remember every word that I'd read in his journal. I had to remember how he killed me. And I did. I remembered all those things and more.

I emerged from the water, I felt it drip off my smooth skin and I took my first breath of air. The first breath was always the best. I could smell everything, good and bad. I could smell life and death. I looked at my reflection in the water. I'd taken on a new identity, I barely recognized myself. One thing was for sure, before I headed out for Zander, I needed to stop at the mansion and get myself cleaned up.

I smiled as I started to walk back to Riverwolf Pass. I thought about Zander. He wasn't the only one with a dirty little secret. Now he was going to pay. *You'd better watch out, Cowboy,* I thought to myself as I felt the cool breeze against my naked body. *I'm back, and I'm coming after you... and now, I'm heartless.*

The End

Sly Darkness by Kya Aliana

Kya Aliana is a teenage novelist living in the beautiful mountains of North Carolina. She writes fiction novels that she hopes will compel mature teens and adults alike. Writing is her passion and she fully intends to pursue that passion for the rest of her life. Sly Darkness is her second published novel.
Visit her website to follow her blog, read free short stories, enter cool contests to win free stuff, and more!

KyaAliana.Com

Sly Darkness by Kya Aliana

Read exactly what happened six months ago in Kya Aliana's novel, "Impending Doom"

Still thirsty for more? — Read Kya Aliana's standalone novella "Adrenaline" – you can even read the first eight chapters for free on Kya Aliana's website, or Figment.com

Sly Darkness by Kya Aliana

Sly Darkness by Kya Aliana

Acknowledgments

Thank you to my awesome mom and dad! Without their undying support and encouragement, I wouldn't have ever been able to write this book.

Thanks to all the grandparents, who always help me follow my dreams, especially the one to write.

Thank you to my sister, Lexi, who will always give me her best piece of advice and stay up all night with me just so my book will be everything it possibly can be.

Thank you to my brother, Kinden, who always knows just what to do when I'm stuck in the storyline or if one of my characters goes out of character.

Thank you, Grandad, I know I can always call you and you'll make everything all better for me again. Your support in my writing career means a lot to me. I love you with all my heart and am always very thankful for all you do for me.

Sly Darkness by Kya Aliana

Thanks to my Aunt Patty, for her astoundingly amazing help with editing my books! I don't know what I'd do without it! And also for her famous Aunt Patty cookies, the best "brain food" in the world!

Thanks to my true love, Zariel, who always supports me and my dreams, encourages and inspires me always, will hold my hand every step of the way, but most of all, believes in me and who I want to become. And also, who thought up this book's title.

Thanks Isaac, for always boosting my ego about writing... it helps more than you know.

Thank you Owen, for always letting me bounce ideas off of you, talk about my books and short stories, giving me awesome advice on revising my book, and being a great Children's Desk Librarian. My books wouldn't be what they are today if it weren't for you.

    Thanks to Chris Jolly, who will always read my latest writing and give me an awesome, honest critique. I become a better write each time we talk.

Made in the USA
Charleston, SC
01 June 2013